The Outlaw Bride

THE BRIDES OF FATAL BLUFF

KELLY BOYCE

For my family: my parents, Garry and Sharon Boyce, who taught me I could do anything I put my mind to; my brother and sister, Craig and Alyson, for setting the bar so high I had no choice but to reach for the stars; and Cooper, who kept my feet warm on cold mornings. RIP little buddy. You are missed.

And for John—some things are worth waiting for.

Chapter One

September 1873
Katherine Slade's heart drummed in her chest, her breath coming in short, nervous puffs. She slipped into the crowded train depot, slinking along the perimeter of the room to avoid the snarl of people vying for a spot in the ticket lines.

Her husband stood on the other side, his keen eyes searching. Even at this distance, the nasty mark she'd left on the side of his face drew her attention. A small sense of satisfaction fought its way through the fear. It glimmered for only a moment before being squashed by a more troubling question.

How did he find her?

She'd been running for six months, lying low and never staying in one spot for too long. But each time she thought she had eluded him, Rogan tracked her down, more determined than ever to get his revenge. What would he do when he finally caught her? A shudder coursed through her. She needed to get away before her luck ran out for good.

The conductor's booming voice rang throughout the station, announcing the final boarding call for passengers traveling to Fatal Bluff and all stops in between. As the message resonated off the thick walls, panic twisted Katherine's stomach into knots. She had to be on that train to Fatal Bluff.

She had a promise to keep.

With grim determination, she pulled her battered felt hat down low on her head to cover the telltale strawberry-gold curls. The muscles in her legs burned as she cut a path through the crowd. She wanted to hurl herself full speed toward the train, but fear of discovery kept her in check. Rogan would notice any sudden movements that seemed out of place.

She stepped outside the train depot and picked up her pace. Her shoes slipped against the rain-dampened platform. With barely more than two pennies to rub together, she couldn't afford the fare. She would have to find another way. Frantic, she searched for an opening where she could sneak on unnoticed.

The baggage cars bustled with activity. Burly men with rolled-up sleeves tossed crates and trunks into the cavernous vehicles. There was no way she could creep past the men and sneak inside.

The passenger cars were too risky. If caught without a ticket, she would be tossed off at the next stop and probably escorted to the nearest sheriff's office. She couldn't chance it. No doubt the law was just as anxious to get its hands on her as Rogan was. She had to escape, she just had to.

"Miss Stockdale?"

A hand on her arm caused Katherine to jump. She sucked in a gasp and spun on her heel, almost knocking her battered satchel into some poor man who skirted past.

She looked up into the stern features of a tall, reed-thin woman with gray hair topped by a flat, no-nonsense hat.

"Excuse me?"

"Miss Hannah Stockdale? I am Mrs. Blanche Hewitt, your chaperone. I have been looking all over for you. You're late. I find that quite unacceptable. If you had missed the train, I would have been out the fare for your ticket." The woman snapped a slip of paper under Katherine's nose.

"I'm sorry, you—"

A sharp glare cut her protest short. "We have no time for useless apologies."

Long fingers wrapped around Katherine's wrist. The prickly woman dragged her toward the nearest passenger car. "Quickly. We haven't much time before the train pulls out. Have your trunks been loaded?"

"I—" The train loomed closer. Hope flooded Katherine's senses. She could still get on. "Yes."

Katherine's feet worked double time to keep up with Mrs. Hewitt's long, stiff strides. She shot a nervous glance at the porter who helped them up the narrow steps of the passenger car, half expecting him to see through her and demand to see her ticket. Nothing happened.

She was on the train! An intoxicating blend of freedom and relief swept over her. Katherine wanted to whoop with delight, but it wasn't over yet. Not until the train was on its way, with Rogan left behind, would she feel truly safe. At least for the time being.

She allowed herself to be pulled along behind the older woman. The corner of her satchel caught the edge of random seats as they made their way up the narrow corridor of the rail-car. She issued apologies to faces that passed in a blur. Could this really be happening? Her mind dipped and whirled. Blessed freedom! It was so close.

"Sit here." Mrs. Hewitt pointed at a seat next to the window. The polished wood gleamed where a thin strand of sunlight broke past the clouds and struggled through the dingy glass. Directly across from her, two young women stared with curious expressions. Mrs. Hewitt addressed them. "Miss Montgomery, Miss Delaware, it appears Miss Stockdale decided to join us after all."

Katherine slid into the seat and hugged her satchel against her. Mrs. Hewitt sat next to her; hands folded primly in her lap. Angling her head, her sharp eyes flicked over Katherine. The firm set of the woman's mouth told her she had been judged and found lacking.

A few loose strands of hair slipped out of the confines of Katherine's hat at that precise moment, as if to punctuate the other woman's silent condemnation. The damp air made her curls unruly, and her hat did little to help contain the unmanageable mess. She tucked her hair behind one ear and avoided Mrs. Hewitt's cold stare.

"I must say, Miss Stockdale, you are not what I expected. Your letters clearly indicated you were a woman of quality and breeding. But look at you. You are a veritable mess."

Katherine's cheeks burned. She glanced down at her cotton skirt. The color, once a rich slate, had faded to a pale gray long ago and signs of wear and tear and previous patchings showed along the seams and hem. There had been little choice. Rogan hadn't exactly been the generous type. The only thing he'd given her that lasted was eight years of misery she wished she could forget.

"I—I'm sorry. I guess in my rush I didn't pick my best traveling suit." Katherine forced an apologetic smile, knowing full well the calico dress stuffed at the bottom of her bag was in no better condition.

But Mrs. Hewitt didn't need to know that. And Katherine was not about to disabuse the woman of her mistaken assumption she was someone else. No, Katherine decided. For the duration of the journey, she would play the part, slip into someone else's life. She would deal with her conscience in that regard after she arrived in Fatal Bluff.

The train jerked and slowly ebbed away from the station. She imagined leaving the tattered remains of Katherine Slade far behind.

Mrs. Hewitt's caustic tone interrupted her musings. "If it hadn't been for the red hair sticking out from that ludicrous hat, I'm sure I would not have recognized you, Miss Stockdale. Let's hope your groom doesn't have the same reaction."

Katherine's heart sputtered to a complete stop. "Groom?" She gaped across the seat at the other two young women.

The blonde directly across from her smiled, a tight, forced motion that didn't reach her dark blue eyes. "A little frightening, isn't it? Coming all this way to marry a man you've never met?" She patted her pale wheat-colored hair with a dainty, gloved hand, although not a hair was out of place. She was impeccably dressed in blue silk, nary a wrinkle in sight despite what must have been hours of travel.

Katherine nodded, too stunned to form words. Groom. Husband. The words, and what they meant, pounded through her. The train whistle blew. The shrill, deafening sound echoed the scream building inside Katherine's brain. A mail-order bride.

She closed her eyes and tried to breathe.

~

The trip to Fatal Bluff passed in a blur. Katherine waited until most of the travelers made their way off the passenger car before following along behind Mrs. Hewitt and the others. Her pinched nerves unraveled and then entangled themselves anew. How would she get herself out of this fix?

She placed her hand in the porter's loose grip and stepped down onto the boardwalk. The cooler temperature inside the passenger car did not prepare her for the absolute strength of the sun's heat. It was hotter than Hades. Katherine set the satchel down and lifted a hand to her brow, shielding her eyes from the brilliant glare.

A mixture of men, women and children milled about,

flocking near the platform. Voices and footsteps and the bustle of the crowd swirled around her. Katherine skimmed the unknown faces. Unease sizzled in her stomach. Was her intended groom amongst the throng of people gathering?

A trickle of sweat beat a hasty path down her back before the cotton of her shirtwaist absorbed it. Wilted and weary from the long trip, she tried to find a reserve of strength somewhere within her.

"Look on the bright side," she muttered to herself. "At least you made it here alive." And with Grant Langston's envelope still in her possession. She was one step closer to keeping her promise.

And then what?

She pushed the pesky question away. During the endless train ride, she had mulled over the possibility of immersing herself into a new life, of becoming Hannah Stockdale fully and completely. Assuming a new identity would afford her a layer of protection against Rogan tracking her down. She would simply tell Mrs. Hewitt she had changed her mind about the marriage—and pray the real Hannah Stockdale did not show up until she was long gone.

The sound of hammering drew her attention. Katherine squinted against the sun. In a clearing across the street a building was being constructed. She inhaled the sharp tang of new lumber mixed with the less than pleasant stench of manure, sweat, and animal flesh. From what she could see, the town of Fatal Bluff appeared to be thriving. Buildings lined each side of the busy street, some new, others weathered with time, their clapboard fronts having turned a brownish-grey. Further on, near the outskirts of town, homesteads dotted the landscape. Beyond that, thickening copses of trees reached skyward to tickle the horizon. It was a pretty little town. The type of town one would settle into and raise a family.

A pang of sadness shot through Katherine. Given the

choice, she would do just that—stay and make a life for herself somewhere like this. A quiet little existence, where her bad memories would blow away on a gentle afternoon breeze.

Warm air brushed against her face, and her mother's voice drifted into her mind.

"Choices are for them's that can afford them, Katy. We ain't those people."

Tears stung her eyes. Her mother hadn't been right about too many things, but she had been about that.

With a deep, fortifying breath, Katherine turned and walked back to Mrs. Hewitt to deliver the news.

"Mrs. Hewitt, I'm afraid—"

"Not now. The men are here. Try to fix yourself up, for heaven's sake." Mrs. Hewitt turned away from her and waved into the crowd. A group of men approached them, winding their way through the throng of people, side-stepping crates and baggage that littered the platform.

Katherine gave the men a quick once-over. They seemed ordinary, decked out in their Sunday best, with the exception of the one on the end. That one lumbered along like a bear, as if his thickly built frame wasn't quite sure what to do with all of him. And where the other men had obviously put some effort into their appearance, the bear's dirty clothes hung about him in layers of disarray. Why, the man looked like he'd wallowed in the mud before leaving home!

The short, portly man in front approached Katherine and grabbed her hand in his, pumping her arm vigorously. "Ladies, I am so pleased you have arrived. My name is Oliver Hewitt and you've already met my wife, Blanche. My, my, my, but what a lovely sight you are," he continued, thankfully letting go of Katherine's arm before he dislocated it. He retrieved a piece of paper from his waistcoat and flapped it open with a flourish. "Now ladies—"

"Which one is mine?"

The giant bear fixed a beady stare on Katherine and her heart plummeted to her feet with a resounding thud.

Mr. Hewitt's lips pursed into a thin line. He shot the bear an annoyed frown. "If you will wait just one moment, Mr. Figg—"

"Waited long enough. Jus' tell me which one is mine and I'll git over to the church. I ain't got no time to be lollygaggin' around." The bear spat. A stream of dark tobacco juice sliced through the air in an arc and landed with a sickening splat, staining the planked sidewalk.

"Fine." Mrs. Hewitt stepped forward, her no-nonsense manner taking over. Her bony hand gripped Katherine's shoulder and shoved her forward. "Miss Hannah Stockdale, may I introduce you to your groom, Mr. Walter Figg."

He gave her a brief glance, then offered a curt nod. She apparently passed his inspection. One meaty paw reached out for her. "C'mon, wife. Let's git goin'."

Katherine stumbled backward to avoid his grasping hand. "I—I can't."

Mrs. Hewitt's eyes narrowed and her words came slow and measured. "I beg your pardon?"

Katherine jutted her chin in the air and mustered up her last ounce of courage.

"I've changed my mind," she said, turning to face Walter Figg. "I'm sorry. But I can't marry you."

Chapter Two

C onnor Langston rubbed at the ache emanating from the muscles at the back of his neck. He had spent the last hour hunched over the mail packets Dobey Middleton had delivered earlier that morning. Sprigs of hair jutted out at odd angles from his haphazard massage. He patted them down and reminded himself yet again he was long overdue for a stop at Gillis' Barbershop.

Just one more item on his ever-growing list of things to do that remained undone.

Tipping the chair back on its hind legs, Connor dragged his hands over his face and fought off the overwhelming sense that he was in over his head. The feeling threatened to engulf him on a regular basis. Most days he managed to beat it back but it always lurked in the recesses of his mind.

"Whew! It's gonna be another scorcher out there, Con."

Bart Holkum trudged into the sheriff's office, waving his hat in front of his face to create a breeze. He dropped his ageing bones into a straight-back chair opposite Connor.

"Yep." Connor sighed, not moving. He hated the oppressive heat of summer. Give him a cool, crisp autumn any day.

Bart chuckled, his feet landing on the corner of the desk. "You gonna peruse those posters or stare at the ceiling all day?"

Connor groaned and let his chair drop back onto all four legs. Scowling at his deputy, he reached across his desk for the wanted posters. "Yeah, yeah. I'm getting to it."

Eight years ago, Connor had escaped Fatal Bluff, leaving the town and its memories behind. Now here he was, sitting in the sheriff's office with a badge pinned to his chest and more responsibility than he ever wanted resting on his shoulders. He wondered if he was up to the task.

Not that he had much of a choice. He needed this job and the steady pay it provided. Jenny needed food in her belly, a roof over her head, and a sense of security. Connor could provide the food and the roof. As for the security...well, that was still up in the air.

Bart sent him a sidelong glance. "Anything in there worth mentioning?"

Connor's shoulders slumped and the in-over-his-head sensation crept back in. He turned his attention to the posters. "No. Nothing on Slade or any of his known associates."

"Well, maybe next week, huh? Can't lose hope."

Connor ground his back teeth. He had lost hope several months ago. Rogan Slade ran free while his brother lay six feet under, and there wasn't a damn thing he could do about it. He couldn't just take off and hunt the man down. Not now. Not with Jenny. His loyalties tore him in two and bitterness burned at his guts.

"Maybe next week," he said, feeling little optimism.

"Did you hear back from the sheriff in Mercury?"

There had been only one witness to the stagecoach robbery, a woman who had escaped with Grant. Both had managed to make it as far as a remote farm before Grant died from his wounds. The woman then disappeared into thin air. Who was she? And more importantly, *where* was she? Her testimony alone could have Slade swinging from a noose in no time. If she could be convinced to testify. So far no one had been that brave.

Connor waved a dismissive hand at the letter sitting on top of the mess covering his desk. "The man that sold her the ticket barely remembers her. The old codger that owns the farm gave a brief description that was so generic it could have been anyone. He doesn't know where she went or exactly when she left. It's like she turned into a ghost and drifted off into the night."

Bart scratched at his grizzled beard. "Ain't much to go on."

"Sheriff! Sheriff!"

Oliver Hewitt bustled through the door and up to the desk. Connor grimaced. The uppity businessman was one irritation he could do without today. It seemed every second day Oliver had a new problem that required his immediate attention. Most days, Connor managed to take Oliver's complaints with a grain of salt, but not today. The sweltering heat had sapped his energy and his patience, until both were stretched beyond their limits.

"What now," Connor grumbled. Unread mail remained piled on his desk and a stack of wanted posters needed to be tacked around town. He had no time for the likes of Oliver Hewitt.

"Please, Sheriff, your assistance is required most urgently." Oliver pulled a handkerchief from the breast pocket of his well-tailored suit and mopped his brow. "My mail-order brides have arrived."

"Congratulations. Now go away." Connor waved a hand at the door and picked up one of the posters, reading through the description of a man wanted for attempted murder and general mayhem three counties over.

He didn't want anything to do with Oliver's latest venture of securing mail-order brides for Fatal Bluff's bachelors. It was bad enough the townsfolk had been attempting to marry him off since his return. But he'd rather cozy up with a rattler than a bride. The result would be about the same.

Oliver cleared his throat and gripped the lapels of his jacket, pulling himself up to his full height of five feet and a few inches. "Sheriff, one of the brides is refusing to marry Walter Figg."

Connor smirked, but didn't turn his attention from the poster. "You want me to arrest the woman for having good taste?"

Walter Figg had all the personality of a bucking bronco with a burr caught under his saddle. He didn't blame the woman one whit for refusing to marry the man.

"No, but Mr. Figg is quite upset. He is refusing to take no for an answer and Miss Stockdale will not budge an inch."

Connor dropped the poster on the desk. He stood, the chair scraping across the floor behind him. Weariness settled into his bones. He placed both his hands on the small of his back and stretched the muscles. Jenny had not slept well the night before. Connor awoke in the middle of the night to find her standing next to his bed, staring down at him silently with sad, soulful eyes. He'd been at a loss over what to do. In the end, he'd sat up with her until she finally dozed off in the wee hours of the morning.

"If the woman doesn't want to marry Figg, I can't force her, Oliver."

"I understand, Sheriff. I just don't want her to create a scene. I have my business reputation to consider." He patted down the thin ridge of black hair that wound around his shiny head. A sly, hopeful expression blanketed his features. "You know, Sheriff, if she won't marry Figg, perhaps you should marry her. Lord knows you could use a wife, what with your current predicament and all."

Connor's jaw prickled with warmth. He didn't need

anyone musing about his predicament, current or otherwise. It irritated the hell out of him that eight years later the people in this town still looked upon him with pity. He was tired of their sympathy doled out in the tragic clucking of tongues and heartfelt pats on the backs. He didn't need the constant reminder. He just wanted to get on with his life.

"I don't need a wife," he bit out, glaring at the small man.

The sound of raised voices filtered through the half-open door.

"Oh dear..." Oliver's shoulders hunched up to his ears as if he could block the noise out. "Sheriff, please!"

Connor's patience snapped. "Dammit, Oliver! Can't you ever take something on without it turning into a complete disaster?"

The deep baritone of Bart's voice interrupted Connor's outburst before Oliver could respond. "Why don't you run along, Oliver. We'll be right behind you."

"Yes, yes. Perfect. Wonderful. Thank you, Sheriff!" Oliver spun around quickly and hustled out the door, reminding Connor of a waddling duck.

Bart pulled out a cheroot from the front pocket of his shirt and lit the end. "Stop glarin' after the man, son, and let's go break up the brouhaha."

Connor stalked to the door and yanked his hat from the hook, jamming it onto his head. "Why am I getting dragged into this?"

Bart chuckled, a low rumble from deep within his chest. He slapped Connor on the back. "You're getting dragged into this, son, because one day you woke up, rolled outta bed and said, 'Today I think I wanna be sheriff.'"

Connor barely remembered that day. At the time there had been too many other things to think about.

A shriek interrupted his thoughts and he picked up the

pace, running across the street toward the train depot, where a growing crowd waited to greet him.

Though he suspected there wasn't much left in the world to surprise him, Connor had to admit finding a feisty red-headed woman dangling arse end up over Walter Figg's shoulder was a bit startling.

"Put me down! I don't care what you were expecting, I changed my mind. Now let me go this instant and go back under the rock you crawled out from! I will not marry you and you can't make me." Small fists pounded Walter's back with all the fury of a cornered bobcat.

"Shut yer yap, woman."

A string of colorful names rent the air. "Get your filthy hands off me, you flea-bitten warthog!"

Standing in the crowd, Clara Bates gasped and slapped her hands over her son's ears. Several others snickered, the ruckus breaking up the monotonous routine of their day. Walter appeared the only one unmoved by the woman's declaration, or her flailing limbs.

With a frustrated groan, Connor shouldered his way through the growing crowd to stand in front of the jilted groom. This was not how he had planned on spending his day, arguing with the slow-witted mountain man and kicking up a row for all the townsfolk to mull over and discuss for a week of Sundays.

For about the tenth time that day, Connor seriously questioned the new vocation he had acquired. With a weary shake of his head, he pointed to the boardwalk in front of him and addressed the would-be groom. "Walter, put the lady down."

K atherine stopped beating Walter Figg's back when a calm, yet commanding timbre cut through the thick afternoon. Bit by bit the crowd settled, until the murmurs extinguished themselves, leaving silence in their wake.

Beneath her, Walter shifted his weight from one foot to the other, his thick shoulder digging into her empty belly.

"I ain't puttin' her down, Sheriff. I bought her. She's mine."

Katherine smacked him with the flat of her hand. "I am not some sack of grain from the feed store, you mangy cur—"

She froze. Did he say...sheriff?

Her body went limp. Could her luck get any worse?

As if in answer to her unspoken question, a murky cloud of body odor wafted up, filling her nostrils. Her stomach churned. The man smelled worse than a rotting animal carcass.

The sheriff continued, sounding more than a little worn down and a whole lot put out. "I'm sure you and Oliver can reach some kind of agreement."

"Don't need no agreement. Need a wife. Now I got me one."

Katherine gripped two handfuls of Walter's grungy deer-skin jacket and pushed away from him, angling her body to see around the massive mountain man.

Hanging upside down, her vision was skewed and the world turned on its end. The sheriff stood a few paces away. Her gaze traveled up from dusty boots, over faded denims encasing slim hips. Long fingers absently drummed the leather of a low-slung holster. She adjusted her hold on Walter's jacket to allow her to see past his jutting elbow. Katherine took in a trim waist and broad chest before sunlight glinted off the badge pinned near his pocket. Shards of bright light shot into her eyes, momentarily blinding her.

Walter jostled her again and she swung back behind him, losing sight of her reluctant rescuer. The motion jarred her, knocking the old felt hat from her head. It took with it the few hairpins she had left, scattering them on the ground. A cascade of strawberry curls unfurled and blocked her view of the crowd growing behind Walter.

Another wave of stench rose up to choke her. "Damnation! Let me down, you stinking pile of cow dung!"

"I paid money. You're mine. Now quiet down, wife!"

"I am not your wife!"

She kicked her feet. The toe of her boot hit upon something solid. Walter grunted and smacked her soundly on the rump. "I won't be takin' no sass from you, wife."

A pistol cocked followed by a collective gasp from the surrounding crowd of onlookers. Fear leaped up Katherine's throat. She scrambled to peek around Walter Figg, praying she had misinterpreted the sound. She hadn't.

The sheriff's long, lean legs stood braced apart, his Colt aimed at her captor's barrel-like chest.

"You hit her again, I'll shoot. Plain and simple. Now put her down."

"Don't shoot!" There was nothing plain and simple about it. Draped over the man's body, what was to stop him from using her as a shield? "You might hit me!"

A low growl emanated from the sheriff. "Ma'am, my aim isn't that bad." He waved his gun at Walter. "I'm not going to tell you again."

The muscles in Walter's back bunched with tension. Katherine held her breath and silently prayed the sheriff's aim was every bit as good as he claimed. Her body trembled. Her intended husband had all the give of a mule. He was hardly about to just toss her aside and—

"Oh!"

Her feet hit the ground hard and Katherine stumbled

backward, her arms windmilling in a sad attempt to find purchase. Unruly curls whipped around her face, blinding her. She fought to regain her balance but it was no use. Skirts and petticoats entangled about her legs while she spun out of control. Then she was falling.

Hard bands of steel wrapped around her middle and swiftly brought her upright.

"Dammit, Walter," the sheriff cursed, his mouth close enough to her ear that the heat of his breath warmed her skin. A shiver shimmied its way down her spine. His arm tightened pulling her flush against him. "I said set her down, not throw her down."

"She's down either way, ain't she?"

The masculine scent of leather and soap permeated her senses, a wonderful respite from the foul stench of Walter Figg. She wanted to burrow into it, inhale the intoxicating blend until all traces of the mountain man faded away.

"Ma'am?"

Katherine lifted her head. A quick shake tossed her hair away from her face. She ventured a quick glimpse at the man who had saved her.

Dear Lord.

The clear blue of his eyes struck her first. A brilliant cerulean rimmed and flecked with slivers of black. She'd never seen a color quite like it. But more startling than their hue, was the intensity that burned within them. An intensity that was fixed solidly on her. An unfamiliar sensation burned through her body like a brush fire, setting her skin ablaze as if her clothes had fallen away and left her unprotected from the sun's penetrating heat.

Katherine stared at him, mouth slightly agape. "Yes?"

Perfectly proportioned lips twitched with a hint of humor and heat scalded her cheeks. No doubt a man this handsome was well aware of the effect he had on women.

"Are you hurt?"

She blinked and forced the fuzziness that gripped her brain to recede. Reluctantly, it loosened its hold.

"I'm fine," she answered. Gathering her strength, she pushed away from the sheriff, praying her knees wouldn't buckle beneath her. They held, though barely. The hand he rested on the small of her back was nearly her undoing. Lord thunderin', how could a man's touch wreak such havoc? Katherine rustled up a scrap of dignity and straightened her spine. "Thank you."

The sheriff nodded once and his hand fell away, though its effects lingered.

Walter belched and pointed a meaty finger at Katherine. "If I can't have my wife, I want my money back, Sheriff."

The sheriff groaned, pinching the bridge of his nose. Katherine had the distinct impression he wished he were somewhere else. She could sympathize.

"Oliver, perhaps you can work something out with Walter? Refund the man's money?"

Oliver shuffled his feet. "I suppose something can be agreed to, Sheriff. Perhaps Mrs. Hewitt and I could find Mr. Figg another bride in lieu of reimbursement."

He didn't sound very optimistic. Katherine couldn't say she was surprised. What woman in her right mind would marry Walter Figg? Of course, who was she to pass judgment given her own choice of a husband had proven less than stellar.

Walter eyed Oliver, suspicion coloring his expression. "You'll git me another one? Purdy like her?" He jerked his head in Katherine's direction.

Oliver held up his hands in a placating manner. "Yes, yes, of course. Absolutely, Mr. Figg."

Walter spat at the sidewalk and rubbed a grimy finger under his nose. "Alright. Guess that'll do."

The mountain man gave a curt nod then turned and

pushed his way through the crowd, his business with the whole mess concluded. Katherine blinked, stunned at the man's abrupt departure. It was over.

Relief swept through her. She closed her eyes and let out a long breath, tension easing from her shoulders. She was safe. She'd made it to Fatal Bluff. For once, her luck had made a turn for the better.

Mrs. Hewitt cleared her throat. "Speaking of reimbursement, Sheriff, given that Miss Stockdale has broken her agreement with us, I think it only reasonable she repays the cost of her train fare."

Katherine's eyes snapped open. Surely, she had heard wrong. "What?"

Mrs. Hewitt peered down her sharp nose and gave a derisive sniff. "We want our money back, Miss Stockdale. You have gone back on your word. We demand reimbursement. We run a business here, not a charity."

Desperation clawed at Katherine's insides. Her gaze swung back to the sheriff, the only one so far who had shown even the smallest hint of concern over her well-being.

She wondered if she should fess up and tell the truth, admit she wasn't Hannah Stockdale. But who would she be in her stead? She could hardly announce to him her true identity. He was the sheriff, for crying out loud! All her confession would do was land her behind bars and cut short any chance she had at keeping her promise.

"I can't pay them back."

One dark golden eyebrow arched upward, but other than that one small gesture, the sheriff remained silent, unreadable.

"That is unacceptable," Mr. Hewitt cut in with a stamp of his foot. He reminded her of a petulant child who hadn't gotten his way. "You broke the agreement. You owe us the money. We paid for your train fare and a night's lodging. Tell her, Sheriff Langston!"

Langston!

The name struck Katherine with the force of an oncoming locomotive. Air rushed out of her lungs. The landscape tilted and swayed. A sea of strange faces meshed together into one collective blur.

A hand gripped her elbow, steadying her, bringing things right again.

"Ma'am? Are you alright?"

The black dots pinpricking Katherine's vision receded. She blinked and stared helplessly at the hand on her arm. Tanned and weathered, she could feel his strength in that one touch. If she said no, would he sweep her up into those arms and carry her somewhere safe?

The notion held a strong appeal. At least until the name rang in her mind again, causing her to recall just why he had asked the question in the first place.

Katherine searched his handsome face, studying the bold angles of his features, the slight hollowing just beneath his cheekbones, the square chin. Anything that reminded her of the man who had saved her life. She came up empty. Grant Langston had been dark, his complexion paler, his features less defined. Still...

"Your name is Langston?"

His eyes narrowed to slits. "Yes. Connor Langston." Connor angled his head to one side. His gaze raked over her body with such force Katherine could almost feel the physical sensation of it touching her skin beneath the layers of skirt and petticoats. "Do we know each other?"

Grant Langston's final words burned in her memory. *"Tell Con...I'm sorry..."*

Con. Connor. The sheriff.

The world around her began to darken and spin until once again Katherine felt herself falling.

Chapter Three

T he woman's knees buckled. Connor lunged forward and caught her, swooping her into his arms. A bevy of curls tumbled over his arm in a cascade of burnished gold and fiery red.

He glanced down. Her lids remained closed. Pale crescent-shaped lashes brushed against her cheek, shielding him from the sudden fear that had glistened in her sea-green eyes just before she fainted. A smattering of freckles haphazardly dotted the bridge of her narrow nose. Full pink lips parted invitingly. Connor gritted his teeth and glared at Bart.

"Now what?"

Bart grinned. "Now it looks like you got yourself an armful of woman, Con."

Great. "Miss—" He looked around helplessly.

Oliver stepped forward wringing his hands, an eager expression replacing the petulant one of a moment before. "Stockdale, Sheriff. Miss Hannah Stockdale. Quite the story on this one. She comes from a reputable family from Kansas. Owned a small restaurant, they did. Burned down, though.

Miss Stockdale was the only survivor." He clucked his tongue in what Connor could only guess was a show of sympathy.

"Uh-huh." Connor didn't need her biography. He just wanted to know her name in the hopes she'd hear it, wake up, and remove her warm body from his arms. He gave her a small shake. "Miss Stockdale?"

She stirred just enough to roll her head against his chest. Her cheek came to rest near his heart.

Oliver beamed as if she were a small dog who'd just performed a trick. "You know, Sheriff, given your circumstances, I would be more than happy to offer you her hand for a one-time-only deal of half off my commission price."

Connor glared at Oliver and his ridiculous suggestion. "What?"

Oliver's smile disappeared and he took a step back, holding his hands up. "She says the burn scars aren't horribly disfiguring and her cooking abilities will surely make up for it, either way. All around, a nice bargain, wouldn't you say, Sheriff?"

Connor's frustration rose. He wasn't sure which disgusted him more—Oliver bartering the woman off while she was cuddled unconscious against his chest, or the idea of taking a bride.

"I don't want or need a damn wife, Hewitt." He had enough complications in his life.

"You sure you don't want to take her off Hewitt's hands, Con? Seein' as she's already in yours?"

Connor whirled on his boot heel and glowered at his deputy who until now had remained blissfully silent on Oliver's suggestion. Figures his luck would run out on that account. Even Bart was getting caught up in the matchmaking fever.

"Don't start, Bart."

His deputy shrugged and pulled his hat off, looking down

at the piece of baggage Connor held. "Ain't nothin' to be startin', Con. Just thinkin' out loud. She sure is a right pretty thing, ain't she?" Bart smiled and winked, the gesture almost lost in the creases around his eyes.

Connor didn't care if she was Aphrodite herself; there was no way he would even consider getting hitched. He'd been down that road once and nothing short of a shotgun to the head was going to get him there a second time.

"If you're done ruminating about my personal life, you think we can take this woman down to your wife's boarding-house before I lose all feeling in my arms?"

Bart chuckled deep in his chest. "Guess we could do that."

The air in Amelia's boardinghouse proved a smidgen cooler and a lot better smelling than the train depot. Connor's mouth watered at the enticing scent of fresh apple pie wafting through the parlor.

Carefully, he laid Miss Stockdale down on the sofa, pulling his arms out from beneath her. She barely weighed a thing, the loose dress swallowing up the small body hidden beneath it. He wondered when her last good meal had been.

"Land sakes alive, Connor. Now what's all this?" Amelia fisted her hands on her hips and glanced from him to her husband and then back to the Hewitts. "You've brought half the town to my door and this poor bedraggled thing onto my sofa—"

"Seems Oliver's bride venture went a bit awry," Bart said, reaching out a hand to brush a smudge of flour off his wife's nose.

"Hmm."

Connor sat down on the edge of the sofa. Through the window he could see the crowd had followed them. Hell, didn't these people have anything better to do? With a gentle hand, he tapped Miss Stockdale's sun-kissed cheek. The skin was warm and soft beneath his fingertips. She stirred under his touch. His gaze drifted over her small form, searching for the burn scars Oliver had mentioned. But he saw no hint of them.

"Miss Stockdale?"

Her lashes fluttered several times before she opened her eyes. Connor's heart stopped for a moment as they caught him in their gaze. Lost. That was the word that jumped to mind. Lost and afraid. It did something to his insides he couldn't quite name but didn't much like.

"W-what happened?" Her voice whispered like a breeze. Had he not been leaning over her, he might have missed it altogether.

"You fainted."

That seemed to wake her. Her freckled nose crinkled. "Oh no, I'm sure I didn't."

Connor raised one eyebrow. "Then perhaps you can explain how you got here."

Her gaze flitted around the room. "But I never faint," she said, though her conviction slipped somewhat.

"I expect you've had a rough day. Happens to all of us."

He made to get up from the sofa but her words stopped him.

"Did you have a rough day?"

"You might say that." Hell, he'd had a rough six months.

"Did *you* faint?"

"Nope."

She made a face. It would have been comical if it hadn't been so damn cute. And if he weren't trying so hard not to notice.

Blanche Hewitt stepped forward, her brisk tone banishing his wayward thoughts. "Sheriff, if we could conclude our business here. We have two other brides who did not balk at keeping their words." Her eyes cut to Miss Stockdale, who cringed back into the sofa. "We really must finish here and tend to them."

. . .

K atherine eyed the sheriff. He looked nothing like Grant Langston. Tall, golden with impossibly blue eyes that would rival the most brilliant summer sky, he all but vibrated with a masculinity that filled the cramped parlor to capacity. His dust-covered clothes fit him well, accentuating the lean lines of his body. Guns rested low on slim hips, adding to the aura of authority that clung to him like a second skin.

"I—I'm sorry to have caused so much trouble." This wasn't exactly the subtle arrival she had hoped for.

Oliver waddled forward and shook a finger beneath her nose. "You've caused more than trouble, my dear. You've perpetrated fraud, is what you've done."

An older woman with kind eyes appeared with a glass of lemonade. Katherine's mouth, coated with dust and worry, watered at the sight of it. "Don't be so melodramatic, Oliver. Plenty a bride gets a bad case of nerves on her wedding day."

"Especially if she's set to marry Walter Figg," the older man—what had the sheriff called him?—muttered.

The older woman's jaw dropped. "Walter Figg? Lord liftin' Oliver, what were you thinking? You can't marry this itty bitty thing to that lump of mud!"

Katherine liked that someone else shared her opinion, but in truth she would like it even more if the woman would stop holding the glass of lemonade and let her drink some of it.

From outside, a shout was heard. "Hey Sheriff, you agree to marry that girl yet? I's got work to git done this afternoon!"

The sheriff scowled at the window behind her and shouted back. "Then go do it, Williams, and get off Amelia's begonias."

"My begonias!" Amelia shoved the glass at Connor and rushed from the room.

"You might want to give the lil' lady there her drink,

Con," the deputy said with a chuckle. "She's looking a mite parched."

His words snapped Connor to attention and despite the scowl that marred his handsome features, he didn't try to argue. Crouching next to the sofa, he slipped a hand beneath her head before she could attempt to sit up on her own.

His steady palm cupped the back of her head, sliding beneath the mass of unkempt curls. She gripped his wrist. Beneath her fingertips, his pulse beat strong and sure. There was something warm and solid about him. It made her want to turn into him and curl against the strength of his body.

"Our money, Sheriff?"

He sighed. A warm puff of air brushed Katherine's skin. He set her head gently against the pillow and stood, taking with him the brief illusion of safety.

He gazed down at her and a strange, irritating tingle warmed the hollow of her stomach.

"If you're not marrying Walter Figg, it's only reasonable you reimburse the Hewitts for the hotel and train fare."

Reasonable? It hardly sounded reasonable to Katherine. She didn't have the money when Blanche Hewitt had all but dragged her on board the train and it hadn't magically appeared in her reticule since that time.

"And if I can't?"

Blanche smiled. At least Katherine assumed that's what the tight stretching of her lips was meant to represent. "If you can't come up with the money by the time the circuit judge arrives next month, then we will simply let him decide the matter. Judge Malton happens to be a good friend of ours. I'm certain he will make time to hear the matter and rule judiciously."

Oliver gave a curt nod, letting Katherine know that by judiciously, they meant in their favor. "We will, of course, give you ample time to make reparations. One month, Miss Stockdale. Or we take this matter before the judge."

One month! Where in tarnation was she supposed to come up with enough money to repay the Hewitts in that amount of time? Especially if she had to cover her living expenses in the meanwhile. Katherine struggled to sit up but the Hewitts did not wait. Their business concluded, they marched out of the boardinghouse.

Fear balled itself in her throat. She reached up a hand and felt the outline of a gold band hanging from a chain beneath her blouse. All she had wanted to do was keep her promise to the man who had saved her life.

"My satchel." Katherine's gaze skimmed the floor around the sofa. She couldn't lose it. It contained the few possessions she owned, along with the letter Grant had given her before he died.

"Right here. I grabbed it for you, Miss Stockdale." The deputy picked the bag up and pushed it at the sheriff.

Connor grabbed it before it dropped, then bounced it lightly in his hands, giving her a strange look. "Not much in here."

Katherine averted her eyes, avoiding his questioning gaze.

"Guess you lost most of your things in the fire."

She blinked. "Fire?"

One glorious golden eyebrow arched upward. "Your family's restaurant."

She swallowed and reached for her satchel, gathering it against her. "Yes...of course." Katherine didn't have two sweet clues what he was talking about, but it seemed a safe bet to simply agree.

What had she gotten herself into? She knew nothing about Hannah Stockdale's life. How would she ever pull this ruse off? But she couldn't leave. Nor could she go before a judge. With the last name Slade, her fate would be sealed.

Her fears tumbled out before she could stop them. "What am I supposed to do? Where do I go?"

Bart lowered himself into one of the straight-back chairs near the stone fireplace and stretched his legs with a satisfied sigh. "Got room at your place, don't ya, Con? You could use the help."

The question ruffled the sheriff's cool exterior. His eyebrows shot skyward and he rounded on his deputy. "You're not suggesting that she—that I—?"

Bart pulled out a thin cheroot and rolled it between his finger and thumb. "That's exactly what I'm suggestin'. In case you weren't payin' attention, she says she ain't got no money, so she can't afford the hotel. And if you ain't gonna get yourself a wife then you could sure use a housekeeper."

The prospect of a job, money to repay the Hewitts, dangled in front of Katherine like a juicy carrot. "I'm a good worker," she said. "I can cook and clean."

Connor turned to her and gave a firm shake of his head. "Thank you, ma'am, but no. I don't need help."

Bart grunted his disagreement and struck a match, holding it to the cheroot.

Connor ignored him. "Amelia can put you up here until we figure something out."

Katherine protested. "But I can't afford—"

"She can stay at my place if she likes."

Katherine's gaze swung past Bart and Connor. A man dressed in dark trousers and vest lounged against the doorframe, his arms crossed over his chest.

"No one invited you into this conversation, Bentley." Connor's tone edged itself with warning. "Why don't you just get yourself back to The Last Chance and leave this matter alone."

The man shrugged one shoulder but didn't move. "Lady said she needs money and accommodation. I'm only too happy to oblige. What with Luanne having run off and Jane up and gettin' married, I could use a pretty thing like her to serve drinks and whatnot."

Katherine's mouth fell open at the suggestion. She'd grown up in a mining town, and her mother had taken in more than laundry to make ends meet. She knew exactly what Bentley's *whatnot* entailed.

"God dammit," Connor turned suddenly without warning. His angry strides echoed off the walls as he advanced on the interloper.

"Alright, alright, I'm goin'," Bentley said, holding up his hands in surrender. He backed his way to the door. "But if you change your mind—"

"She won't." Connor slammed the door in the man's face. When he turned back around his grim features were set in stone. His gaze caught hers in a hard glare. Katherine pressed her back into the sofa and tried to disappear into the cushions.

"I—I'm sorry. I don't mean to be a burden."

She squeezed the handles of her satchel and thought of the contents layering its bottom. How had the simple task of returning Grant Langston's property to his family become so complicated?

"You're not a burden," Connor told her. "At least not mine."

~

"Why didn't you take her up on her offer?"

Connor hung his head, unable to meet the piercing brown eyes of Amelia Holkum. Despite her small stature, the older woman, with her shocking white hair and forthright manner, was a force to be reckoned with. And after the day he'd had, he didn't have the energy to do battle with her.

Connor pulled out a chair from the kitchen table and dropped wearily into it. "The woman didn't come to Fatal Bluff to be someone's housekeeper. She came to be someone's wife."

"Then you could make her your wife."

"I don't want a wife." The sharp words ricocheted inside the room, trapped by the emptiness.

Amelia wiped her hands on the red checkered dishtowel. She had brought a handful just like it to his brother's kitchen several weeks ago. Pain clenched around his heart. *His* kitchen, now.

"This girl refused Walter Figg. Doesn't sound like she was all that fired up to get married to just anyone." She tossed the towel onto the counter, where it landed in a tumbled heap. "You should hire her while you have the chance, before someone else snatches her up."

The idea of anyone snatching the pretty young bride left his insides unsettled, but he forced his mind away from that. He had enough to deal with. Hannah Stockdale was a grown woman who could take care of herself. She didn't need his protection. Nor was he inclined to give it.

Amelia smacked the palm of her hand down on the counter. "Now you listen to me, Connor—"

Connor held up a hand. "Amelia—"

"Don't you try and shush me. I mean to say my piece and you had better mean to listen, 'cause I'll not be sayin' it more than once."

Well, that was something. He let out a sharp gust of air and resigned himself to his fate. "Fine. Have your say."

Amelia gave a short bob of her head "Come with me."

Connor hesitated a moment, then reluctantly lifted himself out of the chair and trudged along behind through the narrow door that led out to the backyard of the boarding-house. Amelia stopped short on the doorstep and pointed toward the far corner of the small fenced-in yard. A swing hung from the thick branch of an old white oak that shadowed the better half of the vegetable garden beyond it.

Highlighted by the waning sunlight, Jenny sat on the gently swaying swing. Spindly legs peeked out from the hem of her blue dress and bare feet dragged slowly across the small patch of earth just below her.

She looked up as if she could feel their silent perusal. Connor lifted his hand and splayed his fingers in a wave. Jenny returned her attention to the ground without even the slightest acknowledgement. Wheat-colored tresses, reminiscent of his own at that age, fell forward, covering her face.

Connor's jaw tightened. He tried to ignore the stab of rejection that sliced at his heart.

"Do you see what I see?" Amelia asked, her tone demanding an answer.

He swallowed past the hurt. "I see Jenny."

"No," Amelia said, rounding on him with hands firmly planted on hips, a sure sign she meant business. "What you see is a little girl that needs a ma."

Connor opened his mouth to protest, but Amelia's hand cut through the air before he got any words out.

"Don't try and tell me you're doing just fine on your own. You've gotten by these past six months with the help of me and my daughters. But I have my own business and my own household to run, and so do they. I can't be going back and forth between your place and here anymore. And I can't give Jenny the attention she needs. You need to find yourself a permanent solution."

Connor stared down at the smoothly sanded step. Bart and Amelia had been in his life since the time he was Jenny's age. He had always counted on them. When his parents passed away, they had filled the void left in their absence, and when Emily—

Connor bit down on the memory and stared at Jenny. He had taken advantage. "I'm sorry," he said, quietly realizing what Amelia had given up to help him out. At the time, he had been too relieved to consider it. Now, all these months later, it stared him in the face and demanded an accounting.

"You know I love you like a son, Connor. But Jenny needs a real ma. I'll take her for one more day, but beyond that you need to make other arrangements."

Amelia walked around him and back into the kitchen. Connor sputtered in the wake of her announcement. One day? What the hell—!

He swallowed the space between them with desperate strides, chasing Amelia back into the kitchen. "How am I going to find somebody in one day?"

Amelia turned to face him, a sly smile creasing her weathered cheeks. "You almost had yourself a bride today, if I'm not mistaken."

"I almost had a bride eight years ago too," Connor shot back, bitterness twisting each word.

"The past is dead and gone, Connor—and so is Emily. But Jenny's still here and she needs a ma."

Connor threw his arms up in surrender. "And just what do you suggest I do? Go upstairs and offer this woman marriage so she can play mother to a child that doesn't belong to her? Because that's all it would be, Amelia. I've got nothing else left to give."

Amelia poked him hard in the chest, showing more gumption than any man in town. "You have more than you think if you'd knock down that wall you've got built 'round your heart. Besides, you could use a good woman in your bed, Connor Langston. And don't bother throwing me one of those fierce glares you're so famous for. You know I'm right whether you care to admit it or not."

Connor's mouth clamped shut. He tried not to think

about how long it had been since he'd held the warmth and softness of a woman. It did no good to think on things now beyond his control.

"This young woman is stranded with no family and no money and now—thanks to you—the Hewitts are breathing down her neck. I can't have her living in my boardinghouse indefinitely. I run a business, Connor, not a home for wayward brides. Now, she needs your help, and Lord knows you need hers. Help each other." Amelia gave him a pointed look. "Not because you want to, but because Jenny needs you to."

Connor peered through the small window that overlooked the backyard. The sun was quickly fading to shadows. Soon Jenny would be swallowed up by the encroaching dark.

Amelia was right. He knew it. But old hurts died hard, digging their claws into his heart and refusing to budge. He just couldn't bring himself to do it. Yet another failure he could add to the list.

"I can't," he whispered, shaking his head. "I just can't."

Amelia stared at him for a moment then shook her head. "Well, you had better come up with something. I'll stay with Jenny at the house tomorrow and get some chores done. But after that..." She shook her head and the quiet resonance of her voice drifted on the evening air. "I love you both, but tomorrow is my last day."

Chapter Four

Katherine dragged a sleeve across her forehead and squinted into the sun that had crept to the middle of the sky, beating down upon her with a relentless heat.

The last gasp of summer, Mr. McCorkindale from the bakery had called it, right before he told her that while he appreciated she needed the work, he simply wasn't hiring.

It was the same answer at every other shop in town. She had been to each of them, until they all began to resemble one another and she could recite the shopkeeper's answer verbatim before she even asked the question. No one seemed interested in employing a stranger, especially not one who had made a spectacle of herself at the train station the day before.

Oh, they all tut-tutted and clucked their tongues over her predicament. A few even gave her an encouraging pat on the hand before sending her on her way. But, despite the sympathetic shakes of their heads, no one had any use for her.

Now the day was near spent and she was no closer to solving the pickle she found herself in than when she'd left the boardinghouse earlier that morning. Her shoes pinched her feet, dust covered her skirt, her stomach growled to be fed and her head buzzed with the knowledge that her options had dwindled down to one.

Katherine stood outside The Last Chance Saloon. She twisted her mouth to one side. Aptly named.

The hum of masculine voices, mixed with the tinkling of glasses and ladies' ribald laughter, filtered out onto the boarded sidewalk. If no reputable business would hire her, the disreputable ones surely would. Hadn't the man at the boardinghouse yesterday stated he needed new girls?

Bile rushed up from her belly. She didn't want to do this, to turn out like her mother. But what choice did she have? She couldn't leave town, not without fulfilling her promise. Her word was the only thing of value she owned. If she gave it up, she'd be left with nothing.

Maybe the owner would be content to let her serve drinks? She could put up with having her backside pinched and dodging the groping hands of drunken men. Anything would be preferable to tossing her skirts up for anyone willing to pay the price.

Tears burned her eyes and another wave of nausea roiled in her belly. Katherine swallowed and straightened her shoulders. With trembling hands, she gripped the shuttered wood of the swinging door and pushed it open.

Bart peered through the smoky haze of his cheroot. "You any closer to findin' someone to take care of Jenny? Day's almost over."

Connor gave a dejected shake of his head and stared down at the scarred tabletop. He toyed with the idea of begging Amelia to give him more time, but he knew the plea would fall on deaf ears. Once she made her mind up, God himself couldn't budge her.

"No." The word dragged a weary sigh out with it. Lord, but he felt old. At barely thirty, tired and worn out had become his closest friends. Even a simple conversation became a taxing event.

A drink plunked down in front of him.

"Here you go, Sheriff. Anythin' else I can get ya?"

Connor glanced up into the painted face of Lucy Mae. Though younger than him, she had the hard, beaten-down appearance of a woman well beyond her years.

He shook his head. "No, thanks."

"You sure? You're lookin' a little tense, Sheriff. I can take care of that for ya. Jus' give lil' ole Lucy a chance and I'll have you singin' a new tune in no time."

Connor stared down at the whiskey she had brought him, tipping the glass one way then the other. The amber liquid sloshed back and forth, nearly overrunning the rim.

"I think I'll pass, Lucy Mae." He'd never learned a graceful way to turn down such a proposition.

The barmaid pouted, but it lacked the sincerity of someone truly hurt. "Suit yourself, honey."

She whirled away in a froth of lace, feathers and stale perfume to work her wares on a more receptive table of customers.

Bart took a drag on his cheroot and tapped the ashes onto the floor of the saloon. He raised his voice just enough to be heard over the tinny strains of an out-of-tune piano. "You still got one option left. My guess is Miss Stockdale'd be willing if'n you'd just ask her."

"I'm not asking her. Besides, once she earned the money, she'd be gone. And having one more person leave is the last thing Jenny needs."

"Why would she leave? She lost everything back in Kansas. Seems to me she'd be lookin' to set down some roots and start over. You sure it's Jenny you're worried about being left behind, and not yourself?"

Connor glowered at Bart, but left the question unanswered. Unfortunately his silence was not enough to deter the old man from continuing.

"Eight years is a long time to be nursin' a grudge. You plannin' on spending the rest of your life alone?"

The notion had appealed to Connor at one time. Now, he wasn't so sure. Lately, the idea of living the rest of his life on his own seemed a rather lonely proposition. Still, loneliness wasn't enough to convince him to trust, to give his heart again.

"Leave it alone, Bart."

Bart crossed his arms over his narrow chest and tilted his head to one side. "You been gittin' right ornery day after day. Maybe Amelia's right. Maybe you do need a woman." He pointed a finger at Connor's chest. "And I ain't talkin' about havin' her clean your house."

Connor shifted uncomfortably in his seat. The stink of sweat and cheap women closed in on him. "And what do you suppose I do about that? Call Lucy Mae back and take her up on her offer, so I can spend the next six months listening to everyone hash it over like they had some right?" Hell, a man couldn't pass gas around here without the town discussing what he'd had for dinner.

Bart took one last drag of his smoke and eased the chair back onto all fours. With a flick of his thumb and finger, the butt hit the floor next to him. He ground it into the sawdust with the heel of his boot.

"Well, maybe Garrett's new girl will be a little more discreet."

"What new girl?"

Bart nodded toward the bar. "The one he's about to hire."

Ice invaded Connor's veins. He knew what he'd find even before he turned around. His stomach jolted at the sight of her standing at the bar, Garrett hovering over her like a hungry wolf about to pounce. Though her limp felt hat prevented him from seeing her face, Miss Stockdale's hands were clasped so tightly against her stomach he could see the whites of her knuckles from nearly halfway across the room.

"What the hell is she doing in here?"

Bart shrugged. "I 'spect she's lookin' for a job. Word is everyone else in town turned her down. Guess they thought if they said no, you'd have to say yes."

Connor's attention snapped back to Bart. "What?"

"Maybe you don't want to admit you need a wife, but this town has other ideas. Far as they're concerned, you get yourself a wife, get settled, less chance of you wandering off again for years on end, less chance they'll have to go lookin' for a new sheriff."

Connor relaxed a little. "Then Garrett won't hire her?"

"Garrett Bentley don't much care if you stay or go. He jus' cares about makin' money. And a pretty lil' thing like that tending to his customers will draw men in here like bees to honey."

A band tightened around Connor's neck, cutting off his air. "She can't work here."

"She ain't got much choice now, does she? Seems some mean ole sheriff told her she had to repay Oliver."

He swung around and gave Bart an incredulous look. "This is my fault?"

Bart shrugged again. "Maybe. Maybe not. Question is, are you going to help the lil' lady out? Or are you gonna leave her to the likes of Bentley?"

His heart hammered in his chest. He turned in his chair to look at her. He didn't think he'd ever seen someone look more alone. Dammit.

Dammit, dammit, dammit.

"This is blackmail."

"Ain't no such thing. You don't have to do anything. She ain't your responsibility. I'm just sayin', if'n you don't want a wife, you still need a housekeeper, and she needs a job. Seems like a winning proposition all the way around."

"I can't have her living up at the house with me. People would talk. It—it would ruin her reputation." He sat back with a satisfied nod.

Bart lifted one bushy eyebrow. "And workin' here won't?"

Connor's satisfaction fizzled. "I can't—"

"You can. You can and ain't no one gonna look funny at her for acceptin'. Everyone knows the situation. They know you're an honorable man. And if someone makes a stink 'bout it, tell them you're sleeping in the barn."

"I'm not sleeping in the barn!"

Bart gave a self-satisfied smirk. "I didn't say you *had* to, I said you can tell people that."

"So I'm honorable, but I should lie?"

"No, you should stop mincing words with me and get up there before Garrett has her dressed up in feathers and lace and prancing around offering men drinks and *whatnot*."

Connor closed his eyes and pressed his fingers against the lids but the image refused to be rubbed away and a sick sensation pooled in his gut. He'd been painted into a corner but good and Bart damn well knew it. No man with an ounce of self-respect would let a woman like Miss Stockdale prostitute herself for the sake of a train fare. Especially not a train fare he'd ordered her to repay.

Connor lifted the whiskey to his lips and took a sip. It slid down his throat with a welcome burn. "Fine. I'll do it. But I want it noted I am not happy about it."

Bart grinned, his dark eyes sparkling with victory. "Duly noted, son."

With a scowl firmly planted on his features, Connor

slammed back the remainder of the whiskey in one searing gulp and pushed back his chair.

Miss Stockdale had her narrow back to him, remaining oblivious to his approach. Only Garrett noticed and issued a warning look. One Connor promptly ignored.

"I realize your, uh, clientele expect a certain type of, um, service, Mr. Bentley, but if I could maybe just serve the drinks and leave the...the..." She rolled her hand, as if she could grab the appropriate word out of the air.

"That won't be necessary," Connor cut in, saving Miss Stockdale from finishing her sentence.

She jumped a little at the sound of his voice and whirled around. Embarrassment tinged her cheeks a pretty shade of rose.

Though his eyes hardened, Garrett's voice remained smooth and friendly. "You mind, Sheriff? Me and the lady are discussing business."

"The lady doesn't have any business with you."

"I—I don't?" Miss Stockdale bit her lower lip, dragging her teeth over its fullness. God, he wished she wouldn't do that.

Connor shook his head. He had to be ten times the fool to go through with this. He rushed the words out before his brain caught up to his mouth and he changed his mind. "I've decided I could use a housekeeper after all."

Before Miss Stockdale could thank him properly, Garrett cut in. "Now wait just a minute, Langston. I got first dibs on her. She's willing to serve my customers drinks and I'm willing to have her do so. We've already agreed to it."

"We have?" Miss Stockdale spun back to face the bar owner, the pale yellow calico moving loosely against her small frame. She really was a little wisp of a thing. No match for the drunken louts that filled this place after dark.

"Yes ma'am. Job's yours if you want it."

Connor pictured his hands reaching out and squeezing the width of Garrett's neck, choking him. "That won't be necessary. Like I said, I've hired her."

"And I said I've hired her as—"

"Gentlemen!"

Connor glanced down at Miss Stockdale in surprise. She tossed her gaze between the two of them. "While I appreciate that you both want to hire me, I think in the end it comes down to one thing."

"Which is?" Frustration edged Connor's voice. How could she not jump at his offer? Did she really want to be working here? Had he misjudged her?

"Money," Garrett finished, with a grin. "And I'm willing to pay ten dollars a month, with room and board. Any tips the customers throw your way are yours to keep."

Miss Stockdale turned to Connor, expectation rife in her pretty green eyes. He did a quick calculation. He'd saved a tidy sum over the years bounty hunting and his current salary afforded him a decent living if not a spectacular one.

"Twelve dollars a month, plus room and board."

"Fifteen," Garrett piped up.

Connor gritted his teeth. He couldn't go much higher. He had Jenny to think of. "Fifteen," he ground out, pulling his lips into a grim line. "And you can keep your reputation intact and work without the threat of being groped and propositioned every two minutes."

"How's she going to keep her reputation intact living out on the edge of town with you?"

"I'll sleep in the barn," Connor answered, the lie slipping easily off his tongue. So much for honor.

"We have a deal."

She stuck out her hand. Reluctantly, Connor took it and tried to ignore the uncomfortable sense of foreboding as her fingers squeezed his hand.

∼

K atherine still couldn't believe her luck, or the insanity it took to accept a job that brought her in such close proximity to the law. And exactly what was this lawman's connection to Grant Langston? It was too much of a coincidence to think there wasn't one. Brothers, maybe? Possible, though she couldn't see any hint of a resemblance between the two men. It would be just her luck if they were.

When Grant had told her to tell "Con" he was sorry and pass along the letter he'd given her, she assumed "Con" was a shortened form for Constance, that she was searching for the girl he mentioned, for a wife or sweetheart. She never dreamed there would be two separate people she needed to track down.

Or that one of them would have a sheriff's badge pinned to his chest.

The horse's easy gait carried them away from town. Even in her acceptance, Katherine had never once considered she and Connor would be this close. She kept her arms wrapped securely around Connor's middle. Her fisted hands rested against the hard ridges of his stomach while her body burned from the friction of bouncing against his back. Heat melted into her and the total effect left her senses reeling. A fact she found more than a little disconcerting.

The harder she tried to keep her mind on other things, the more her traitorous thoughts drifted to the days ahead. What would it be like spending her days alone with this man? She had little experience in that regard. Though married for eight years, Rogan rarely stayed home for more than a few days at a time, leaving her alone for long stretches. The loneliness had been unbearable, but being with him had been even worse.

The rhythm of the horse and the warmth from Connor's body slowly lulled her into a doze. She tried to keep her eyes open, but it felt as if lead weights had been tied to her lashes.

She told herself she'd close them for only a moment. That was the last thing she remembered until Connor's voice penetrated the fog clouding her mind.

"Miss Stockdale?"

She heard a throat clearing but it seemed far off in the distance. The fading warmth of the sun acted like a blanket, tucking her in for the night. She ignored the sound, quite content with where she was. She snuggled in further.

"Miss Stockdale?"

A hand touched hers, rough yet comforting. It squeezed and she stretched slightly, nuzzling further into her pillow, taking a deep breath. Lord, it smelled good. She wondered if this Miss Stockdale knew someone was calling her.

"Hannah?"

The hand squeezed again, harder this time, dragging her unwilling mind back to the surface. Was he talking to her? Her name wasn't Hannah.

"Kate," she mumbled, attempting to burrow back into the comforting warmth, to recapture the sleep that had eluded her for days. "My name is Kate."

"What?"

The sudden crack of the tone broke through her sleeping brain with the effectiveness of a dash of cold water. Her head shot up and heat burned her cheeks when she realized she'd been resting it on the sheriff's back. "What?"

He turned his head just far enough to give her an appreciative view of his profile. Dark lashes contrasted with the pale blue of his eyes, the golden tone of his skin the perfect backdrop to set it all off. Lord liftin', but he was one handsome man.

"You said your name was Kate."

The tiny voice inside her head that had known taking this job was a bad idea came back to mock her now. Her mama always said when it came to lying she didn't have a lick of talent. Why hadn't she taken that into account before assuming another woman's identity?

"It's—I—that is to say—" Her mind worked furiously to concoct a plausible explanation, grasping at any wisp of an idea that spun through her brain. "Kate is my nickname...uh, short for...Kathleen. Which is my middle name." She forced her smile wider, hoping that would make her words more believable. She should have stopped there, but words kept tumbling out. "Hannah was my mother's name too. So they called me Kate to...to avoid confusion."

There. That wasn't so hard.

Connor nodded slowly and turned to face the small clapboard house in front of them. "Alright then." His tone gave nothing away. Had he believed her?

He patted her hands. "You want to let go now, so we can get down?"

"Oh!" Embarrassed, Katherine snatched her hands away as if scalded.

Connor held her arm in a firm grip and helped her ease herself down from the horse's back. The horse snorted and Katherine stepped away, allowing Connor room to swing his legs over and dismount.

"That you, Connor?"

Another voice carried out through the door of the house. A second later Amelia Holkum's top half appeared through the screened-in portion of the door.

"Evening, Amelia," Connor answered, untying Katherine's satchel from behind the saddle.

"Why, Miss Stockdale!" The door opened and the woman stepped outside, her arms thrown wide. Before Katherine knew what she was about, she'd been swallowed up in a pair of sturdy arms then quickly released. "It's good to see Connor came to his senses and hired you. That is what he's done, isn't it? Unless he's gone and married you to make it permanent?" Hope eased the lines in her face.

Katherine shook her head, catching Connor's scowl from the corner of her eye. "I've agreed to be his housekeeper for the time being," she explained, ignoring the sinking disappointment his scowl brought on. What did she care if the man had no interest in marrying her? She was hardly in the market for a husband. And if she was, a lawman would be the last man she'd pick. That would be the closest thing to suicide she could think of, short of letting Rogan catch up with her.

"Well, either way," Amelia said, "it's good to have you here. C'mon inside and get settled."

"Put her in my room. I'll take the sofa," Connor said, taking hold of the horse's reins.

Katherine stopped. "What happened to sleeping in the barn?"

Connor half turned. A smirk twitched the corners of his mouth. "I lied."

She wasn't sure how she felt about that, but the tiny thrill that rushed through her veins didn't bode well. "Oh."

"Unless that's a problem?"

"The lying part or the sleeping in the barn part?"

"Pick one." His hand slowly caressed the neck of his horse.

Katherine swallowed. "It's fine." She was hardly in a position to call the man on lying, especially when he fessed up to it. And she wasn't about to kick him out of his own home after he'd rescued her from working in a saloon. She forced a smile, hoping it masked the uncertainty crowding her insides.

His hand stalled on the horse as if he'd forgotten he'd been moving it in the first place. Sunlight caught his eyes and the blue lightened to silver. The space that stretched between them filled with a strange sizzle, one that would have burned the tips of her fingers if she'd had a mind to reach out and touch it.

Amelia cleared her throat, interrupting the silence that engulfed them. "Let me show you the room. You must be exhausted."

Thankful for the diversion, Katherine nodded and forced her attention to the other woman. Her heart pounded an erratic beat. What had just happened?

Picking up her satchel, she followed Amelia through a door that opened directly into the kitchen. A table that easily sat six and a good-sized cookstove warred for dominance on the left side of the room. She paid them little heed. Her gaze stuck on the one thing she had not expected to see.

On the opposite side of the room, standing on a chair pulled up to the counter, was a little girl, maybe six or seven years old. Her hands methodically snapped a bowl of yellow beans. The screened door shut behind them and the girl peeked over her shoulder. She blinked twice and then returned to the task at hand.

The child's eyes were cornflower blue, just like Connor's.

Shock rendered her momentarily speechless. She hadn't known there was a child. With the way the townspeople talked about getting Connor married off, she had assumed he was a bachelor. But he wasn't. He was a widower. And a father. The change in dynamic shifted the landscape of what she was dealing with, raising the stakes to a new level.

Katherine offered a tentative smile, even though the girl had turned away. "Hello."

"Jenny." Connor's voice startled her. She'd thought he'd taken the horse down to the barn. "Jenny," he called her name again. The snapping stopped and the girl turned her head. Wisps of wheat-blond hair trailed down the side of her face, having escaped the misshapen braid at her back. "This is Miss Stockdale. She's going to be staying with us awhile."

Katherine smiled nervously. She didn't have much experience around children, though she had always yearned for one of her own. Someone to hold and watch grow, another little body to care for, to fill the void in her empty life and stave off the loneliness that had become synonymous to her very existence. But Katherine had refused to bring a child into her world. With an outlaw for a husband, what kind of life would she be able to offer a child? So, on the rare nights Rogan had been home, she'd been careful, employing the methods her mother had used to prevent conception.

"How do you do, Jenny? You can call me Kate," she offered, sticking with the variation of her own name. It made her feel less like a liar.

Jenny didn't answer. She snapped one last bean then crawled down from the chair and brought the bowl with her. Her dress, faded and a tad too short, swirled around thin legs as she crossed the room and held the bowl out.

Katherine set her satchel on the floor and took the offering. Without a word, Jenny's hands slid away and she quietly glided from the room like a shadow slipping across the walls.

Katherine stared after her, not sure of what to say, or what to do with the bowl.

"Well," Amelia said, wiping her hands on the apron tied around her waist. "Perhaps I'll let you get her settled, Connor. It's getting late and I'm sure Bart will be wonderin' where his supper is. It's lovely to have you here, Miss Stockdale."

"Please, call me Kate."

"Kate it is then." Amelia leaned up and kissed Connor on the cheek, giving his arm an affectionate pat.

"I'll be down to the barn in a minute to give you a hand with the buggy," he said. The door closed behind Amelia. Connor cleared his throat and stepped out from behind Katherine. He took the bowl from her and set it on the table. "Jenny doesn't talk much."

"You have a daughter?" The silence of the little girl hadn't startled her nearly as much as the fact she existed at all.

47

Katherine understood now why the townspeople had urged him to take a wife. Obviously they thought the little girl needed a motherly influence. How long had she been without? And what had happened?

"Caring for her is part of the job. That's non-negotiable." He slipped his hands into the back pockets of his denims and rocked back on his heels. "I should have mentioned that, I guess." He hesitated. "You still want the job?"

Katherine nodded, unable to resist the hope she saw flicker in his eyes. Caring for a child was a far sight better than serving drinks and *whatnot.*

"Yes, yes of course." She needed him every bit as much as he needed her. He remained the one and only link to Grant Langston she had stumbled upon.

"Tell Con...I'm sorry." Those had been Grant's last words as the life ebbed from his body, his breath coming in rasps. She'd pressed her hands against the mortal wound in his chest, his heart slowing with each beat. He had used the last of his strength to pull a letter from his jacket pocket. *"Give Con the letter...tell my girl...tell her I love her. Make sure she's okay... promise?"* And she had. She'd had no other choice. The man had saved her life. Keeping his dying wish was the least she could do in return.

"Good," Connor said, startling her out of her memories. The broad line of his shoulders relaxed a little. "I'll show you to your room. You can get settled while I help Amelia hook up the buggy."

Katherine waited for the door to shut behind Connor before she sat down on the bed, its soft, feather mattress an inviting temptation after the hard surfaces she'd been sleeping on for over half a year. Being on the run didn't allow one to be choosy about comfort.

Nor should she get it in her mind to become so now. This

was a temporary stopover until she could pay back the Hewitts and keep her promise to Grant.

Although, keeping that promise just became a whole lot more difficult. How she planned on keeping up the ruse she'd taken on for an entire month she had no idea.

And what if the real Hannah Stockdale decided to suddenly put in an appearance? What then?

She had no answer.

Fear raced through her and she flopped back onto the bed, staring up at the exposed beams above her.

"Oh, Katy, you've managed to wedge yourself between a rock and a hard place this time," she whispered to herself.

If the real Hannah Stockdale arrived in Fatal Bluff, or the sheriff discovered her true identity before she could pay off her debt, the jig would be up.

And no amount of dancing would save her then.

Chapter Five

C onnor knocked softly on the oak door. "Miss Stockdale?" He waited a moment. No response. Another rap. "Miss Stockdale?"

Still nothing. Connor twisted his mouth to one side. What was she doing in there? Amelia had left over an hour ago, the sunlight had long since faded, and he and Jenny were famished.

He tried again. "Kate?"

Silence answered back. Leaning his forehead against the wood, Connor surveyed his options, which basically consisted of barging into the room—his room, really—to discover why she ignored his repeated summons, or standing out here banging on the door like a fool.

Connor chose the former. With a twist of the brass knob he pushed open the door. "Miss Stock—" He stopped short and squinted into the dimness. Was she—?

He took a step closer. "Miss Stockdale?"

Good Lord.

Kate had curled up on the bed and nestled into the pillows, the soft down feathers providing a sanctuary from the day. There had been plenty of days when he'd wished to do the same, crawl into bed and pull the covers over his head. But he hadn't. Afraid if he did, he might not get up.

Quietly, Connor stepped to the side of the bed and turned up the lamp on the bedside table. The flame cast a warm glow across her face. Fear and worry had eased from her expression, leaving behind half-mooned shadows beneath her eyes.

Fiery curls spilled over the stark white pillow. Autumn, Connor realized suddenly. That's what her hair reminded him of. Vibrant strands of red, orange and gold, all entwined together to create a vivid display of color.

A quiet snore emanated from his new houseguest, a testament to her exhaustion. He rubbed a hand down his face in an attempt to chafe away the day. It just figured. Only he could be forced into hiring a housekeeper—a far too beautiful one at that—who spent her first hours on the job in fitful slumber. It amazed him just how far one man's bad luck could stretch.

"What am I supposed to do with you," he muttered, not that he expected her to bolt awake and give him the answer. Though it would have been nice, because damned if he had one.

He let out a long, slow sigh. "Alright then, guess I'm cooking supper tonight." He reached down for the patchwork quilt his mother had made years before and drew it up around Kate's shoulders.

She snuggled further into the warmth, a stray curl draped over her face. Without thinking, Connor lifted it away, tucking it behind her ear. It felt like silken threads between his fingers. The urge to sink his hand into its full softness jolted through him. He snatched his hand away and buried it beneath his armpit.

What the hell was he doing? He had no business even entertaining such thoughts. It didn't matter how long it'd been since he'd had a woman. This one was off limits. With hurried steps he retreated from the room.

By the time his sleepy housekeeper finally roused herself from his bed, Connor had things well in hand. Sort of. Their supplies were dangerously low and his cooking skills did not extend beyond anything that could be burned over a campfire.

"I fell asleep," Kate said.

Connor glanced over his shoulder from the counter where he was busy slicing up what was left of the ham and hoping it would stretch between three people. She looked rumpled, dazed and even a little apologetic, but having spent the past half hour trying to pull together a meal with his belly gnawing at his backbone, Connor wasn't in the mood to be charitable.

"I believe that's stating the obvious."

She flushed, or maybe that was just from the sleep. "I—I can help now."

Connor turned and walked to the table, setting the platter of ham down in the center with a little more force than he intended. "Now is too late. The work is done."

Her face pinched and she twisted her fingers about each other. Connor had noticed her doing the same thing when she stood in Garrett Bentley's saloon looking for work, and again when she lay on the sofa at Amelia's while Oliver railed at her about his lost train fare. She'd had a rough couple of days, he allowed. But he'd had a rough six months.

He pointed to an empty chair. "Sit."

With hesitant steps, she came further into the kitchen and slid into the offered chair. She smiled at Jenny and said a timid hello. Jenny didn't respond but Connor caught a flicker of interest when her gaze flitted over Kate.

The meal itself proved only marginally edible. The biscuits were burned on the bottom, the ham hardly enough to stick to the ribs, and the carrots might as well have been served raw. Only the coffee had turned out well, but by the time he'd served Kate a cup, there was barely enough left to fill his own. He supposed he would have to get used to brewing for two. Or she would. The thought left him unsettled. He couldn't quite wrap his head around the idea of a strange woman tending to his needs.

He gave his head a shake but the thought lingered, conjuring up the reminder of far too many other needs that were going unattended.

When everyone had finished their meal, Kate stood and began clearing the table. "I hear you've only recently returned to Fatal Bluff."

Connor hesitated. "From who?"

It never ceased to amaze him the way the people in this town discussed everyone else's business. Having been gone for so long, he'd almost forgotten the rampant grinding of the gossip mill that kept the townspeople entertained.

Kate reached for his empty plate, her arm hovering just inches from his face while she contemplated his question. He could smell the heady scent of lavender. He closed his eyes for just an instant and breathed it in, then caught himself and straightened in his chair. Dammit!

"I forget his name." She turned her head slightly toward him. Curls bounced around her temples and cheekbones. Soft, shiny and mesmerizing. She'd attempted to tie her hair back, but half of it had escaped. Connor couldn't help but want to lift a hand and—

Oh God...this was wrong. Wrong, wrong, wrong. He forced his gaze to the corner of the table—the one square inch of his vision that wasn't filled with her tousled loveliness.

She lifted his plate and leaned away, oblivious to the machinations of his overworked mind. "The gentleman with the bushy moustache that owns the haberdashery."

"Milo," Connor croaked. The sound made him wince.

"Yes, that was it." Her face brightened in the flickering lamplight. "So did you?"

"Did I what?" He couldn't remember the question. In fact, his own name escaped him at the moment. He needed some air.

She smiled at him. He really wished she wouldn't do that.

"Did you just return to town?"

He nodded. "Last April. Did—" He hesitated. He really didn't want to discuss this, especially not in front of Jenny. "Did he say why?"

She made a face. "I'm not sure. I could barely make him out with that heavy accent. I spent a lot of time smiling and nodding."

Connor issued a silent thank you for Milo's European heritage.

Kate set the dishes on the counter and pumped water into the tin washbasin on the counter. Connor watched her move about the kitchen, confident and capable now that she had something to do. And too damn pretty while she was doing it.

He wished he could have hired a woman far less pleasing to the eye, perhaps one with hair on her chin and a wart growing out of the side of her nose. Older too, with enough extra padding on her person so that every movement she made didn't draw his attention to the lithe form beneath her dress, teasing him with thoughts he didn't need, or want, to be having.

Connor exhaled slowly and concentrated on the coffee cup he'd pulled into his hands. His fingers tapped against the warm curve of the earthenware mug. He should have stuck to his guns and let Garrett Bentley hire her. At least then she'd be someone else's problem and not his. And that's what she would be—a problem. He could feel it in his bones with shocking clarity. Kate Stockdale had trouble stamped all over that delectable little body in big bold letters.

"Sheriff, you haven't heard a word I've said, have you?"

Connor gave himself a mental shake. "Sorry, no."

"I asked where you were before returning to Fatal Bluff." She walked to the stove and lightly touched the kettle, testing its warmth.

He tried to keep his focus fixed on the table, but every time she moved it strayed in her direction. The yellow calico caught the light, swishing and swirling about her legs. The length appeared shorter than he'd seen other women wear, and every now and then, he'd catch a glimpse of her stockings. Stockings encased in the ugliest pair of boots he'd ever seen. Flat heeled, scuffed and worn thin in some spots, they looked more like something he'd see one of the poor Patterson boys wearing as they schlepped about town begging for work to support their pa's drinking habit.

Why would someone with Kate Stockdale's background be wearing boots like that?

Connor cleared his throat and lassoed his thoughts, dragging them away from Kate's legs and forcibly back to her question. "Nevada, for a bit. Arizona Territory a while after that."

"Were you the sheriff down there too?" She poured water into the basin. Once filled, she rolled up her sleeves, exposing her skin from wrist to elbow.

Connor started. Smooth, supple skin. Oliver Hewitt's words echoed in his memory. He angled his body to get a better look before she plunged her hands into the water. Not a burn scar in sight.

Perhaps they were hidden elsewhere.

His gaze drifted slowly over the soft curves of her body and he tried to imagine where the scars were. She glanced over her shoulder and he flushed. "Uh, no. Bounty hunting, mostly." He took a sip of his coffee and leaned back in his chair, determined that was the last time he would look at her. "How long ago did your parents pass away?"

A dish clanged against the metal ridge of the basin and toppled into the water with a splash. His determination fled and his gaze flew back to her. Kate's shoulders went rigid.

Connor winced. "I'm sorry. I shouldn't have asked." He silently cursed his stupidity. It had been so long since he'd lost both his parents that the rawness of their passing had been tempered and softened by time and fond memories.

"No, no, that's fine," she said quickly, shooting him a forced smile over her shoulder. She picked up the dish and turned back to her task. "It...uh...it was a little while ago. A year or so."

Or so. Her choice of words struck him as odd for something so significant. He could never forget the date and time of Grant's death. Late afternoon, March 5, 1873. The memory had been carved into his soul.

"It must have been difficult to find yourself alone. Did you have any people at all?"

She shook her head and continued scrubbing the dishes with a vigor that would have made Amelia proud. But sadness tinged her tone when she answered. "No. No family. I'm alone."

"I'm sorry." In the gaping absence of her family, his words sounded wholly inadequate.

"Thank you," she whispered. Her shoulders relaxed a little and the intense scrubbing eased. She pulled the dish from the pan and set it on the counter. "I guess we all have our burdens. What about you? Is your family nearby?"

Connor's gaze drifted over to Jenny, who up until now had been sitting quietly in her chair. Whether she had been listening to them or not, he couldn't say. Connor smiled warmly at her. "It's just Jenny and me."

Kate squeezed the excess water from the washcloth and set it aside. Picking up the dishtowel, she turned and leaned her back against the counter. Amelia had done the same thing countless times, stood there talking to him while she cleared and cleaned the dishes. But somehow this was different. The air felt charged around them. And sure as shootin' he had never once considered crossing the room and gathering Amelia up in his arms to plant a good solid—

Connor pushed out his chair and stood abruptly. "I should get Jenny ready for bed."

The floorboard creaked beneath her weight. Katherine shifted her stance. She cringed and crouched down, trying to mesh with the shadows. A hesitant peek at the sofa revealed Connor had turned onto his side, away from her. The quilt had slipped down to bunch at his waist, revealing the bare expanse of his broad back. Its muscled smoothness teased the dim morning light, creating a display of light and dark. Connor inhaled.

She pursed her lips and forced her gaze toward the kitchen. *Focus, Katy. You've a job to do.* She'd failed miserably last night, falling asleep on the job and leaving Connor to fix the meal on his own. The results had been rather horrifying. No wonder Jenny was so thin if that was what she'd survived on. But this morning she would make up for that. She'd fix a big breakfast and prove to the sheriff she could earn her keep and maybe then the doubt and apprehension that riddled his handsome features would ease.

Letting the first weak strands of sunlight guide her, she carefully picked her way to the lantern sitting atop the cook-stove. Her hand groped for the matches on a small, narrow shelf bolted to the wall behind it. The scrape of the match against the rough surface of the stove tore through the morning hush. Katherine held her breath until the quiet snoring from the other room continued undisturbed.

With deft swiftness Katherine built up a fire and then searched the pantry to determine what she had to work with. Supplies were running low and a trip to the mercantile would soon be in order. Did she do that? Or did she just give him a list, since he would be in town anyway? She'd never been a housekeeper before; though for eight years she'd managed whatever hovel Rogan holed her up in. She'd always tried to create a sense of home in each one, a definite chore when they were little more than shacks. But it had given her something to do to break the monotony.

But it wasn't just herself she needed to look after now. There was Connor and Jenny. And if last night was any indication, they were in desperate need of her help. She pulled ingredients from the pantry with renewed purpose and set to work.

An economy of movement kept the noise to a minimum as she fixed breakfast. Once the biscuit dough had been rolled out and cut, she placed the biscuits in the oven and took the last of the fresh eggs from the larder. The cracking of the shells against the crockery bowl echoed like a gunshot through the kitchen.

A quick check of the sofa revealed Connor had not budged. Either he was a heavy sleeper, or too exhausted by events of yesterday to allow small sounds to disturb his slumber. She had barely slept a wink last night, tossing and turning, thinking about the promise she'd made to Grant Langston. She'd found the Con he spoke of, of that she was certain. How many Connor Langstons could there be, after all? But she'd held off passing on Grant's apology.

She could hardly blurt out her story now, or tell Connor the truth without putting her own freedom in jeopardy.

Connor was the law. She was an outlaw's wife. The two were hardly compatible. And the last thing she needed was for him to toss her out, or worse, lock her up, before she had a chance to make good on her promise.

The best plan she could come up with was to get him to open up to her about Grant and see if she couldn't ferret out the information she needed to track down Grant's girl.

Connor proved reticent to talk about his family, maybe because they had just met, or maybe that was simply the way he was. What she did know was he had come to town a month after Grant's death. Was that significant or just coincidence?

She needed answers to these questions. Preferably, before the real Hannah Stockdale arrived in town and her ruse was discovered.

As things stood now, she had no idea where or even who this girl was. All she knew was she had to be in Fatal Bluff. Before Rogan and his gang attacked the stagecoach, Grant had spoken of returning home to Fatal Bluff. And if this was his home, then his girl had to be here somewhere. It was just a matter of finding out where without giving herself up in the process. Promises were hard to keep from the wrong side of a jail cell.

Katherine stopped stirring the eggs, the wooden spoon going still in her hand. Was it possible Jenny could be—?

But no. She shook her head.

The little girl was the picture of Connor. Which begged the other question—who cared for Jenny while he was off bounty hunting? Had his wife only died recently, forcing him to settle down and take a more stable job? One would think the itinerant nature of bounty hunting was not conducive to raising a family.

She let out a breath and continued whisking the eggs. She would just have to dig a little deeper until she discovered the truth.

A dash of salt finished the eggs. She gave one last swirl with the wooden spoon then picked up the bowl to empty it into the hot skillet waiting on the stove.

A terrifying screech rent the air.

Katherine screamed and whirled in the direction of the sound. The bowl slipped out of her flour-dusted hands and hit the floor with a resounding crash. Crockery and noise scattered about the room.

The window provided a clear view of a proud rooster strutting across the top of the chicken coop. He puffed out his feathered chest and crowed again.

"What's wrong?"

Katherine spun back around. "No, wait—!" She threw her hand up but it was too late. Connor's foot hit the slippery egg mixture. He skidded, his arms flinging wildly for balance until his body collided with hers.

Strong bands of muscle wrapped around her, pressing her cheek against the warm, solid flesh of his chest. The force knocked the wind out of her and set her off balance. She tried to hold her footing, but it was no use. The eggs had slicked the floor until it had the consistency of ice. She braced for the impact.

It never came. Connor rolled them, using his body to buffer her fall. She wasn't sure which was harder, his chest or the floor, but she appreciated the chivalrous attempt just the same. Connor grunted as they hit and then rolled again, pinning her beneath him.

He pushed himself up on his elbow, hovering over her by mere inches. The heat from his body seared through her clothes. She didn't know where to look. He was naked from the waist up, giving her a close-up view of a well-muscled chest, strong arms and a set of shoulders that blocked out everything beyond them. She didn't want to look, didn't want that image imprinted on her mind so that forever after, no matter what he had on, that would be how she envisioned him. But the only alternative was to look up into those damnable blue eyes, and that could be equally dangerous.

"Are you hurt?"

She forced a smile. "Does my pride count?"

She had failed yet again at a job she was sure she could do well. Their breakfast, the one she planned to surprise Connor and Jenny with, lay smeared all over the floor.

A quiet chuckle rumbled from his chest. "I reckon that type of injury heals much slower than others."

Connor's smile transformed him, startling her. His eyes sparkled like a thousand tiny jewels kissed by sunlight and in that brief moment, the weight of the world slid off his shoulders. Katherine took in a breath to calm her rattled nerves. It did little good. He smelled of sleep, that warm, comforting scent that wrapped itself around a body nestled in the warmth beneath the covers. The image of crawling under the quilt with him shot unbidden and unwanted into her mind.

Outside, the malevolent bird let out one last contemptuous squawk as if it had read her mind.

"The rooster startled me," she said, trying to put her thoughts to rights.

Connor lifted his gaze to the small window over the counter, his hip lifting off hers just a little, enough to make her realize the full predicament she found herself in—pinned to the kitchen floor with the half-naked sheriff hovering over her. She tried not to look at the sun-bronzed skin stretched over ridged muscle. A thin line of hair meandered downward from the light smattering on his chest and disappeared beneath the open waistband.

"He does that every morning."

She jerked her gaze away from him, from his body. "Good to know."

Connor looked down at her. Heat slowly pooled in her belly. Even with his hair mussed from sleep, flattened in some areas, sticking up and out in others, he was a good looking man. He seemed more relaxed than yesterday. Lighter somehow. Maybe home had that effect on a body. A real home. Not the sad, beaten-down shacks Rogan had stuck her in while he hid from the law, but a place with furniture, pictures and keepsakes accumulated over the span of years. And memories soaked into the walls and the floorboards so they reverberated through you with each step you took. What she wouldn't give for a home like that.

She waited for him to say something, anything to interrupt the silence growing between them. But he just stayed there, his body pressing intimately into hers while he stared at her, as if he could see into her soul. The effect rattled her.

"I—I should clean this up," she stammered, looking away, searching for anything that would lessen the pull he had on her. She'd known him less than two days. This was ridiculous. She'd known Rogan eight years and never once in that time had he ever looked at her and made her body tremble like it did now.

Slowly, Connor rolled away from her, disengaging their tangled legs and pushing himself to his feet. He reached down and helped her up.

"I'm sorry. I didn't mean to break the bowl. I wanted to fix breakfast before you had to leave. And then the rooster—"

"It's just a bowl."

"Still...I'll fix this mess." She wasn't altogether sure which one she meant—the remnants of their breakfast scattered about the floor, or the disastrous disarray his closeness wreaked on her good sense.

Connor peered down at her bare feet, then at the broken glass surrounding them. "Not without shoes on, you won't. Last thing I need is you getting cut up."

Before Katherine could protest, he'd scooped her up in his arms.

"Oh!" She looked down, then back at him.

Mistake. His mouth was only inches from hers. One

wrong move on either of their parts and their lips would touch.

"I can walk," she whispered.

"Not without hurting yourself." His breath brushed against her skin, setting it on fire.

"What about you?"

His head gave an almost imperceptible shake, his gaze searing hers. "I have no intention of getting cut up."

For some reason, Katherine had the sense he was not talking about the glass on the floor, but then he looked away and whatever emotions she thought she'd seen were quickly locked up and put away.

He strode through the kitchen and into the main room, not stopping until he reached the doorway to her bedroom. His foot kicked the door open, barely breaking his stride. Then he unceremoniously dumped her in a heap atop the soft feather mattress.

He didn't stay. "Change your clothes," he said. The surliness had returned. "I'll clean up the mess."

"I—I can do it," she called after his retreating back. He didn't answer, closing the bedroom door and leaving her behind to stare at the four walls and wonder what the hell had just happened.

Chapter Six

Katherine's first week passed in a blur of activity. Plenty of work needed to be done from dusting to scrubbing to the laundry. The latter alone took two straight days. Only now did she see an end in sight as she wrung the water from one of Jenny's dresses, her arms numb from the strain. Connor had offered to take it into town to be done, but Katherine insisted she could do it. She needed to redeem herself. To prove her worth. Already she could see Connor eyeing her as if he'd made a huge mistake that needed rectifying.

She couldn't afford to lose this job. She didn't even want to think what would happen if she couldn't repay the Hewitts their blasted money. No doubt they would lynch her in the middle of town. Probably even sell tickets to the affair to recoup their losses.

Her nerves had eased somewhat with seven days passing and no sign or word from the real Hannah Stockdale. But the possibility of her showing up in the future always lurked in the back of Katherine's mind like a ticking clock, reminding her she walked on a very narrow edge, and that one wrong move could send her toppling over into an abyss.

This little family was her one link to finding Grant Langston's girl, whoever and wherever she might be. She had tried each evening to get Connor to talk to her about his family, but it was like conversing with a stone wall.

Last night proved no different. She had met with the same lack of success as every evening before that.

"And Jenny is your only family?" she'd asked Connor.

He'd nodded and then shoved a mouthful of baked beans into his mouth, likely hoping she would stop asking questions and leave him alone to eat in peace.

The man was harder to crack than a bank vault. "No mother, father, or siblings living elsewhere?"

His eyes had drifted over to the silent little girl and a niggling voice in Katherine's head told her to pay attention. There was something in Connor's expression, something lingering just beneath the surface she couldn't quite read. But she silenced the voice with a forceful shove to the background. Jenny was Connor's daughter. Not Grant's. If she was Grant's then that would mean—

No. She wouldn't allow her mind to go there; to contemplate the notion her husband had left a little girl orphaned. She couldn't. Her life wasn't worth the price paid.

Besides, Jenny and Connor hadn't even been in Fatal Bluff at the time of Grant's death. They'd arrived afterward. But every attempt she made to discover something about his life that extended beyond these four walls was met with a change of subject or an answer so vague it meant nothing and led nowhere.

"You got any more of them biscuits?"

Katherine forced a smile. She got up from the table and placed several biscuits on a plate before returning to her seat and setting it in front of Connor like an offering, hoping to soften him toward her.

"Where are your people from originally?"

"Here and there."

His lack of detail was astounding. His ability to answer each one of her questions without answering it at all exasperated her.

"And have any of your people from *here and there* ended up here? As in Fatal Bluff?" she'd added, in case he thought by *here,* she meant some nebulous location with no fixed address.

"You sure do ask a lot of questions for a housekeeper." He eyed her with barely concealed irritation. She recognized the look. It meant the conversation was about to be shut down.

Katherine had tried to soothe his ruffled feathers. She needed to find out what he knew about Grant Langston. She couldn't risk lingering here for longer than necessary waiting for him to give up the information. She needed to pay off the Hewitts, keep her promise to Grant and then get out of town before Rogan or the real Hannah Stockdale arrived.

"Isn't it natural to want to know something about the people you're living with?"

He'd shrugged. "Can't say I gave it much thought."

Katherine pulled her lips into a tight line. The man was infuriating. He made no effort to disguise the fact he didn't want her here, and even less of an effort to make her stay agreeable in any way, as if by being as ornery as possible it would drive her away.

She had wanted to remind him it was *he* who had hired *her,* luring her away from accepting a job at The Last Chance Saloon, but she refrained. With her luck, he'd change his mind, suggest she pack her bags, and see if Garrett Bentley was still hiring.

Any hope she had harbored of probing further was abruptly cut off as Connor stood, pushing his chair back.

"Got chores to do," he'd said, grabbing up the last biscuit and heading for the door, plucking his hat off the peg as he went.

Katherine shook off her irritation from the previous night and flapped the dress out, hanging it on the line. Maybe she should just stop asking. Maybe if she held her tongue, Connor would let the information slip out in normal conversation. If they ever had a normal conversation. Connor was the master at single word responses that were grunted as he retreated from the room.

Maybe she should march into town and start asking around. The townspeople seemed far less reticent about nosing into his business. Surely, they had plenty of information to impart. If she could find a reason to go into town, that is. So far, Connor had picked up any supplies they needed, leaving her and Jenny to stay at the homestead.

However, going into town had its own perils. The vaguer her memory was in the minds of the townspeople, the better for her should Rogan show up asking about her. She didn't want anyone having a clear enough recollection to point him in her direction. Although, that hope was likely just a pipe dream now given her less than auspicious arrival in town.

A tired sigh escaped her lips. She stretched, her hands pressing against the small of her back. Her body ached and a thick film of sweat coated her skin from the day's exertion. She wanted a bath in the worst kind of way. She'd managed to wash herself as best she could in her room each morning, but it wasn't enough. Not after the week she'd had.

"Jenny?"

The little girl peeled back one of the sheets hanging from the line and peeked around it.

"When you take a bath where do you go?"

Jenny stood up and went into the house. Taking that as her cue to follow, Katherine weaved around the laundry flapping in the light breeze. Inside, Jenny opened the door to a small storeroom off the kitchen.

"In here, huh?" She'd been in the room enough times for supplies. It hardly seemed big enough to fit the tub in, but she had little choice. She wasn't about to strip down to her altogether in the middle of the kitchen.

With the last bit of strength in her muscles, she dragged the hip bath inside, until it was nestled between shelves of canned goods, one of Connor's coats, brooms and mops. She filled up the tub with hot water, carefully unfolded the lavender-scented soap Amelia had given her, and slipped into the bath. With vigorous strokes, she washed the day's grime from her body until the delicate scent of lavender drifted up from her skin and she felt clean once again.

From the crack left in the doorway, Katherine spied Jenny sitting near the door playing quietly with her wooden animals, moving them about the floor. She wondered if there was some type of dialogue or conversation running through the girl's head when she played. Every now and then, Katherine thought she saw her lips move, but no sound came out.

Katherine wondered why Jenny didn't speak. She certainly didn't appear slow or confused, or incapable in any way.

She supposed she could ask Connor, but given his penchant for leaving the room whenever the conversation turned personal, she didn't think she'd get very far. Besides, the more time she spent around the handsome sheriff, the more it stirred up a bees' nest of emotion inside of her. If it kept up, she was liable to get stung.

There was something about that man that set her blood on fire. Something deep and elemental, like a lightning strike. She couldn't put her finger on it. He was handsome, but she'd seen handsome before. It had never made her feel this way, tingly and prickly, like an itch she couldn't reach.

Whatever it was, she knew better than to keep scratching

at it. She'd come here for one purpose and one purpose only. Once she'd saved up enough money to pay off the Hewitts, she would deliver the letter to Connor and be on the first train out of town. If she stayed any longer than that, the risks were too high. To both her heart, and her safety. Maybe she could have Connor relay the message to Grant's girl.

Provided he even knew who she was. At this point, she'd failed at even discovering the link between the two men. It wasn't as if she could just up and ask, given that she would then have to explain how she knew.

She closed her eyes and let out a long sigh. The whole thing was one big conundrum.

Drawing her knees up, Katherine rested her head against them and let the hot water soothe her aching muscles. It had been a long time since she'd worked this hard. Katherine decided she liked it. Time hadn't crawled by. She hadn't spent her days staring at the sun, counting the hours until it descended in the sky, watching her life plod past her. Each day she'd done something useful, accomplished something. It was a good feeling.

Katherine didn't recall drifting off, but she must have. The snap of the screen door caused her body to jerk. Water sloshed over the side and splashed against the floor with a wet splat. For a moment she couldn't remember where she was. Her gaze flew to the crack in the door and her heart stuttered to a dead stop.

Connor, his arms weighed down with a box of supplies, stood frozen in place, staring at her, eyes wide.

"Oh!" She hugged her arms across her breasts.

He spun on his heel. "Sorry!"

The mortification in his voice made her cheeks flame even hotter. She couldn't move. Her legs would not work. His heated gaze had all but locked them in place. "I thought you weren't going to be home until later." She looked around for the towel. It hung on the hook next to Connor's old coat, right where she had left it. She would need to stand up to reach it. Her clothes lay draped over the chair at the kitchen table. The small storage room was too small to dry off in. Katherine swallowed. She would have to leave the storeroom wrapped only in the cotton towel.

"I—I—you said you needed supplies. For supper." With jerky movements he set the box on the counter. He didn't turn around.

What now? She could hardly stay in here all day and Connor had yet to do the polite thing and leave the room. Steeling herself, Katherine eased quietly out of the lukewarm water and reached for the towel, keeping one eye on Connor, who stood rigid, his back to her.

"I, uh, got the molasses and sugar that you asked for, but the mercantile was all out of cinnamon."

"Oh..." What had she wanted the cinnamon for? She wrapped herself in the towel. Apple crumble. Of course. She made a wonderful apple crumble. A recipe passed down to her from her mother. She'd planned to dazzle Connor with it, to show him he was right to have hired her. Instead she'd made a spectacle of herself. She wondered if her predicament could get much worse.

She had her answer when he turned around to face her, keeping his eyes averted.

～

Sweet Mother of all that was good and holy!

The blood in Connor's head rushed out, leaving him dizzy and disoriented. It wasn't enough that he'd seen the naked length of her leg where it stuck out of the tub, or the delicate curve of her waist where it emerged from the soapy water when she sat up in shock. She'd thrown her arms across her body, but not before he got a healthy view of one glorious breast.

Now she stood before him, wrapped in a thin sheet that clung to her in spots where the water had seeped through. Her hair had been piled haphazardly atop her head and frizzed from the steam. And her face. Good Lord, that face—flushed from the heat of the bath and delicately framed by damp curls. Her mouth parted slightly in surprise when he turned and Lord if it didn't beg to be kissed.

God help him, he wanted to cross the room and take them up on their offer. He could still feel the imprint of her body from that first morning. All week he'd tried to erase it, tried to think of something else—anything else. But not one single thing grabbed his attention away from the soft cushion of her body.

He could smell the sweet scent of lavender, stronger now than before. She must bathe with it, he thought, then wished he hadn't. He didn't want to think about Kate rubbing sweet scented soap all over her delectable skin—

Dang it all to hell!

He turned back to the counter and gripped its edges, digging his fingers into the wood surface.

"You best go get dressed," he croaked out. Desire had reached up swiftly and grabbed him by the throat, robbed him of breath and thought and sense until need and unmitigated lust were the only things left swirling in his brain. Not to mention other areas.

He couldn't keep her, he realized, listening to her bare feet pad hurriedly over the hardwood floor through the main room to the bedroom. He didn't need this kind of complication. A man could only take so much torment before he did something to end it. And the only thing that would end this was to have Kate Stockdale beneath him, her legs wrapped around his hips with him buried deep within her.

Enticing an idea as that was, it wouldn't end there. Kate wasn't some cheap doxy you just bedded, paid for, and went on your merry way. She had come to Fatal Bluff looking for a husband. Hell, he'd be surprised if she didn't demand he make an honest woman of her after what had just transpired between them. What would he do then?

The slam of the bedroom door cut that thought off before it had a chance to take root. He would not marry her. He had no intentions of marrying anyone. He'd tried that once and it had ended in disaster.

Connor straightened and rubbed his hands over his face.

She definitely had to go.

Supper came and went. If Connor was impressed with the meal she had prepared, he didn't say. Katherine supposed she could take the fact that he wolfed it down in record time as a good sign, but she suspected that had more to do with his wanting to get away from her than any culinary skills she possessed.

No sooner had he pushed his plate away then he stood from the table and turned to reach for his hat by the door, mumbling something about chores. She wasn't quite sure what he did down in the barn but he'd certainly spent a lot of time there this week.

Connor stopped at the door, worrying the brim of his hat in his fingers. He didn't look at her. Hadn't looked at her since she'd practically shown him her altogether earlier that evening. The memory caused her skin to flush anew. His gaze had raked over every exposed inch of her before he turned away.

"Did you want something else?"

He winced and took a deep breath. "Bart and Amelia asked us to dinner this Saturday."

"Oh, how nice." Katherine smiled, her embarrassment quickly forgotten. She'd never been invited anywhere before. Pleasure washed over her. Even if the Holkums were only inviting her out of courtesy, it was nice to be included just the same. "Should I prepare something?"

Connor looked up, startled. "Prepare something?"

Katherine nodded. "Something to bring with us. A dessert, perhaps?"

"I—I don't know. See the thing is…" He shuffled his feet. "The thing is, after that, on Monday, I'll be taking you back into town."

To town? Katherine glanced around the kitchen. "Do we need more supplies?"

"Uh…no…" Connor looked pained. For the life of her Katherine couldn't find the reason, but a sickly feeling developed in her belly. Something was wrong. Her stomach coiled in anticipation.

"Why?" The word whispered out of her.

Connor cleared his throat. Looked at Jenny, then back to her. "See, the thing is I don't think this is going to work. It's not proper you living here like this, and I don't want you getting any ideas that it's going to lead to marriage—"

Katherine laughed, relief flooding her. "Marriage?" Is that what he was worried about?

"Yes," he answered crossly. "And I'll have nothing to do with it."

"Nor will I."

Connor's face crinkled in confusion. "Isn't that what you came to Fatal Bluff for?"

"Oh!" Drat. "Yes, right…" Katherine bit her bottom lip. Hannah Stockdale had come to Fatal Bluff with the intention to marry Walter Figg. A sure sign the woman was desperate. "Well, I've changed my mind."

He arched one skeptical eyebrow. "Just like that?"

"I'm not saying someday I won't entertain the idea again," she said, thinking that day would have to be after Rogan Slade was dead and buried and no longer chased her from town to town. "But right now I have more pressing concerns." Like not falling for the likes of Connor Langston.

"So do I, and I can't be worrying about what the towns-folk are suspecting. It isn't fair to risk your reputation. It was a foolish idea from the start and I mean to rectify it."

Reputation? When had she ever had a reputation worth saving? But Hannah Stockdale apparently did. "I don't need you protecting my reputation."

He continued on as if she hadn't spoken. "I'll keep you on 'til Sunday. That'll give me a few days to find someone else. And I'll pay you like we agreed, with a bit extra to get you on your feet."

Silverware slammed on the table. Katherine turned to Jenny, who sat glaring at Connor with all the fury of a small storm. Her breath came in short gasps and twin dots of pink burned in her cheeks. Stunned, Katherine reached out a hand to comfort the child, but before she could reach her, Jenny pushed her chair out, hopped down and ran from the room.

They stared at the empty space left behind. Katherine blinked in amazement. Connor flinched as Jenny's bedroom door slammed shut. Though the child hadn't spoken, her feel-ings were clear. In her own silent way, she'd stood up for Katherine. No one had ever done that before. Katherine's heart swelled and tears stung her eyes. For some reason, Jenny wanted her here. She needed her. It was a new feeling, one Katherine couldn't quite wrap her mind around. But her heart spoke up in spades.

She turned and met Connor's tortured gaze. "I'm not going anywhere."

～

"Seems Eli's gettin' a bit off in his head," Bart said, leaning against the post at the front of the stall.

He'd stopped by after checking in on Eli Gillis, one of the prospectors who lived up on the bluff behind Connor's property. Word was he'd been causing some ruckus with the neighboring farms, stealing their chickens and raiding their storehouses. Bart had spoken with the man. Warned him off.

"Hardly surprising," Connor muttered, his mind only half on what Bart was saying. He finished mucking out the stall and then dragged in a fresh bale of hay.

"Guess livin' up on the mountain alone for all those years was bound to make a man a bit squirrelly."

"I reckon."

"Said he was talkin' to the fairy folk. Introduced me to 'em and everything. Nice people. Bit small, though."

"Good...good..." Connor stopped, the prongs of the pitchfork buried in the hay. "What?"

Bart chuckled. "Didn't think you were listenin'. You want to tell me what's on your mind?"

Connor scowled. "I can't get rid of her. Jenny won't have it. Going on two weeks and already she's attached. This is what I was afraid of."

"I take it we're talking 'bout Miss Stockdale?"

Frustration poured out of him. "And this is your fault." Connor let go of the pitchfork long enough to jab an accusing finger at Bart.

"My fault, huh?"

"Fine then—it's Grant's fault. What the hell was he thinking tangling with the likes of Rogan Slade?" Anger surged through him and he jabbed at the hay again. The prongs of the pitchfork vibrated as they missed the bale and stuck in the planked flooring. "Dammit."

He yanked the prongs free. "The man screwed up my life

eight years ago and now he's doing it all over again. Only this time he didn't even have the decency to stick around and answer for it."

"If I remember correctly," Bart said, crossing his arms, an unlit cheroot tucked in the corner of his mouth. "It was you that took off eight years ago. Not your brother."

Connor glared at the man who was like a father to him. Bart's words hit home and knocked the bluster out of his sails. He slumped against the stall and slid to the floor.

"Look at me, Bart." He threw his hands up. "I'm not cut out for this. I'm making a mess of it. I can't find the damn Slade Gang—can't even go out and look for them because of Jenny. I've got a housekeeper that drives me crazy, a town that wants me married, and I'm hiding out in the barn trying to avoid it all."

"Sounds like you got your hands full." But the older man's voice held more humor than sympathy.

Connor rubbed his hands over his face and then stared up at the ceiling. He was quiet for a moment, trying to digest all of what had happened. "Why couldn't Grant have let Compton make the trip to Mercury? Was it so damn important to collect the bounty himself?"

"He thought so."

When Bart had told him why Grant went to Mercury, Connor could have torn his hair out. The damn fool didn't even take along a deputy to watch his back while dragging Finster Jutes back to Mercury for trial. The man had been caught rustling horses just inside the county limits and when Grant heard of the hefty reward being offered, he insisted on collecting the bounty himself. He wanted a safety net for Jenny, in case anything ever happened to him.

And then something did. And Connor was left to pick up the pieces of a life he'd abandoned eight years before. Only this one had a housekeeper in it. A housekeeper that drove him near mad with want and fueled his desire like a lightning rod to dry brush.

If he had half a brain, he'd ride into town and take Lucy Mae up on her offer to take care of his needs, but he knew he wouldn't. Thing of it was, he didn't want Lucy Mae. He hadn't woken up in a fever every night for the past two weeks dreaming about Lucy Mae. And he sure as hell didn't imagine gathering Lucy Mae in his arms and kissing that fool mouth of hers every time she pried into his family business.

But even this unwanted desire Kate provoked in him couldn't overpower the feeling something was not quite right. He couldn't put his finger on it precisely, but she seemed... what? Afraid? Nervous? Desperate?

"It just feels like she's hiding something," he said, voicing his thoughts.

Bart lifted one bushy eyebrow. "Miss Stockdale? What would she have to hide?"

"I don't know." Connor pushed himself to his feet. "Maybe it's time I found out."

∽

Much to Katherine's relief, Connor hadn't mentioned anything further about firing her and sending her on her way. Jenny's reaction to the idea put an end to it, at least for the time being.

Katherine spent the next few days working even harder, more determined than ever to prove her worth. Along with her regular chores, she'd also taken time out to play with Jenny. Just yesterday they'd had a tea party. Granted, Katherine had carried the conversation, but given that she'd spent the past eight years holed up with no one to talk to but herself, she'd become quite adept at it.

Guilt flared in Katherine's gut as the hoe hit the dirt and

she unearthed a section of potatoes. Eventually she would have to leave, she knew that. What would happen to Jenny then? She'd been at the house now for two weeks, and had developed a fondness for the quiet little girl whose blue eyes were filled with heartbreak.

Was it because she missed her mama? The woman was obviously gone, yet was never mentioned. Why? Had it happened a long time ago, or just before their return to Fatal Bluff? And why were there no photos of her? No remembrance?

"Grab the potatoes, sweetie, and put them in the bucket," Katherine said, stepping aside while Jenny did her part. The brief respite offered her a chance to look around. Overhead, the sun beamed brilliant in an azure sky and a faint breeze brushed the leaves on the old oak, its branches casting shade over the chicken coop. Lucifer—as she had taken to calling the rooster—strutted about, every now and again stopping to puff out his chest when one of the chickens passed by.

The thought of leaving here drove a sharp pain into her heart. What she wouldn't give to stay. But she knew better. Staying wasn't an option. The mistakes of her past wouldn't allow it.

She closed her eyes against the bucolic scene surrounding her. The sound of potatoes dropping into the bucket stopped. Even without opening her eyes and looking, Katherine knew Connor approached. The air changed when he drew near. It crackled and sizzled until her hair stood on end.

"Miss Stockdale." Bart Holkum tipped his hat. "Lookin' forward to seeing you this evening."

She opened her eyes and forced a smile. "Thank you for inviting me."

Connor winked at Jenny then walked on without acknowledging her. Once Bart left, Connor disappeared into the house.

Katherine breathed a sigh of relief. She didn't have the strength to fight against her growing attraction today.

But her relief was short lived.

A moment later Connor reappeared, kitchen chair in one hand, knife and chunk of wood in another. He settled near the end of the garden, his feet propped up on an overturned bucket. The brim of his hat left all but his mouth and chin hidden in shadow.

Lord, but he had the most beautiful mouth.

Temptation. That's what he was. Surely she wasn't the first woman to face it. But just because it stepped in her path didn't mean she had to stop and chat with it like an old friend. No, she would just stick her nose in the air and march right past it like she never even noticed. That's what she'd do.

Katherine returned to the potatoes. She wanted to finish harvesting this row before she readied herself for dinner. This time, she would take the tub into her room. This time she would try to forget the feeling of Connor's gaze searing her flesh like a physical touch.

She gritted her teeth as the hoe sliced through a potato with a jerk.

Pay attention. Quit letting this man get to you. He's just a man. Puts his pants on one leg at a time. No, don't think about him putting his pants on.

She squeezed her eyes shut and tried to close her mind to the image, to the sensation of him watching her from behind, to everything that had anything to do with Connor Langston.

"I'm curious," Connor said, his voice mocking her attempt to block him out.

Katherine stopped digging. Jenny moved in and scooped up a few unearthed potatoes.

"About what?" She glanced behind her. Connor slid the blade of his knife along the piece of wood he held in his hand. Another animal for Jenny. An elephant, she guessed, based on the outward curve of the snout. She didn't have one of those yet.

Connor hesitated then continued on. "That day we met, Oliver said you had been burned in the fire, that it had left you scarred. I assume you must have told him as much when you answered his ad for mail-order brides."

He lifted his head. The sun behind her caused him to squint. Katherine could feel his eyes running over the length of her. She tingled with warmth as if he had reached out and laid his hand upon her skin.

"Yes?" She had gathered from the questions Connor had asked earlier that there had been a fire, but the scars were a new detail she hadn't been aware of. Trepidation tiptoed up her spine.

"It's just that I haven't seen any evidence of them." He motioned at her person with the knife.

Heat rolled over her like a cresting wave. What could she say? He'd seen a healthy portion of her the other day when she'd tried to bathe. She grabbed the hoe and attacked the earth again, her brain working furiously to come up with a plausible explanation.

"So where are they? The scars?"

"They healed."

"Healed?" He uncrossed his feet at the ankles and leaned forward. "Isn't it the nature of scars not to heal? That's what makes them scars."

She turned her back on him, working up a reasonable scenario to satisfy his sudden curiosity about the supposed marks on her body.

"Mr. Hewitt must have misunderstood. When I answered his ad, my burns were not fully healed. I suggested to him there may be some scarring. I wanted to make him aware of the possibility, so he wouldn't feel I had tried to sell him a false bill of goods."

Connor resumed his carving. She could hear the scrape of the blade against the wood.

"How long does it take burns to heal and disappear?"

"How long? Uh...a while." How was she supposed to know? But she supposed the real Hannah Stockdale would, having experienced it firsthand.

"How long is *a while?*"

Tarnation! Could the man not leave well enough alone? What did it matter?

"It's a while. I didn't exactly mark the days off on a calendar and count them up."

Katherine swung the hoe in frustration, wishing Connor's questions would cease. She hated lying. The hoe caught on a root and stuck in the earth. She yanked hard but her grip slid against the smooth wooden handle and sent her stumbling. "Oh!"

A strong hand on the small of her back kept her from landing on her bottom in the dirt, but didn't stop her momentum. Not until her back hit the solid strength of Connor's chest. His hand slipped around to the curve of her waist.

"Careful there." The low tenor of his voice in her ear sent a shiver coursing down to her toes and back up again.

"Thank you." She wished he would step away. She'd do it herself but her knees felt a bit wobbly and she feared any movement would cause them to buckle.

He stayed put. "You're welcome."

One arm reached around her and his fingers slowly encircled her wrist. She didn't stop him. She knew she should, but she couldn't. His touch cast a spell over her. His chest warmed her back. She couldn't breathe, couldn't think beyond the pounding of her pulse or the ache beginning low in her belly.

Connor's hand slipped into hers. The rough texture of his calloused palm sent a shiver up her arm. He turned her wrist over, exposing the underside of her arm, then turned it back the other way, stretching his hand to straighten her fingers.

"Amazing," he whispered, though he didn't sound amazed. He sounded skeptical.

She glanced over her shoulder, tilting her head up to catch his expression. Eyebrows arched over sinfully blue eyes. This close she could almost count the shards of black that flecked the irises. "What is?"

"The body's ability to heal itself. I've seen some burn scars in my day. Nasty things. Most don't heal so well. But you... there's not a scar in sight."

Katherine trembled, from his words. From his touch. If she turned a little more, leaned back another inch, their lips would touch. Fear mixed with a complicated need to turn in his arms and nestle herself—

No! her conscience screamed and Katherine took an abrupt step away, then another for good measure. If her sudden departure had any effect on him, it didn't show. His arms fell to his sides.

"I—I guess I was lucky. They weren't too serious."

Funny, she didn't feel lucky. In fact, she and luck had parted company more years back than she could count.

"Guess so."

Connor stared a little longer. She had the sickening feeling he didn't believe a word out of her mouth. She waited for him to call her on it, but he remained silent. And she remained unnerved.

"I need to go get ready for dinner," she stammered, backing away from him despite her mutinous body's need to move back into those arms. She spun on her heel and hurried back to the safety of the house, feeling his gaze on her with every step she took.

Chapter Seven

The bath had done little to soothe Katherine's agitated nerves. The warm, shallow water of the tub could not erase the heat of Connor's touch. It had scorched into her skin, branding her. If she were smart, she'd resurrect his offer to drive her into town tomorrow morning. She'd take the next train out of Fatal Bluff and get far away from this madness.

But she couldn't. With no money, she was stuck here. Even if she had the money to move on, her promise to Grant tied her to Fatal Bluff until it was kept.

Katherine's shoulders slumped as she sat on the edge of the bed and looked around the room. It was a good-sized room. One large window framed with pretty, blue floral curtains brought in plenty of light.

She stopped. Floral curtains?

Katherine got up from the bed and walked over to the window, touching the material. The cotton slid through her fingers. Forget-me-nots printed against a white background. Not exactly the choice she expected from a man like Connor. She turned and stared at the rest of the room, studying it more closely for the first time.

A large bed, tall bureau, nightstand, a chest against the far wall. Only one item seemed out of place. Why hadn't she noticed it before? She had seen it, passed by it, even dusted the top of it, but it had never registered.

Katherine left the window and crossed the room. Her fingers trailed over the smooth mahogany of the vanity's surface. It was a well-crafted piece of furniture with scrolled edging, but what did a man like Connor need with a vanity?

If it belonged to his dead wife, did it hold such sentimental value that he could not bring himself to part with it, or move it into Jenny's room where it would be of more use as the girl grew older?

The thought of him having such a strong attachment to another woman caused weeds of jealousy to twist around her heart.

Foolishness! She had no right to feel anything in that regard. She was nothing to Connor. And she could not allow him to be anything to her. Thoughts like that led to nothing but trouble. Best she nip those in the bud and concentrate on what she came here to do.

She shoved the thoughts to the side and stared down at the vanity, her fingers hovering on the top drawer.

Should she look inside?

Trying to pry information from Connor about his family had proven fruitless. Maybe she needed to resort to more drastic measures.

She hesitated, tapping the wooden knob with her short nails. Would it be so wrong?

After all, he had given the room to her. Maybe she just wanted to put some of her things in the drawer. She thought of the few hairpins she hadn't lost when Walter Figg upended her in the middle of town and realized that was all she had, and those were currently stuck in her hair, trying to hold her mass of curls in place.

"Oh, just do it," she whispered, and her fingers moved greedily to obey.

She slid the drawer open quietly, glancing nervously at the door. Her compromised conscience feared Connor would break in at any moment and arrest her for...for...she squinted. Was snooping an actual crime? If so, she would definitely have no defense to offer.

Why yes, your Honor, I realize snooping is wrong, but you see, this man I was living with was driving me crazy by refusing to answer my questions and I thought if I could just learn a little more about him, I could rid myself of these traitorous thoughts and get on with the business of keeping my promise.

Sure, Katherine snorted, she'd get off no problem. She peered down into the drawer's contents. Two bottles of perfume jostled together, making a musical clinking noise.

Her heart pounded in her chest. Perfume? Her fingers touched the smooth glass. She stopped. Sunlight poured in from the window and glinted off silver. Katherine reached beyond the bottles and pulled out a framed photograph. Air locked in her lungs and she couldn't breathe. Blindly, she groped behind her for the small stool, stumbling until it hit the back of her knees. She sank into it with a thud, unable to take her eyes off the photograph.

Grant Langston.

Her breath came in shallow gasps. His intense gaze stared back at her. Solemn and dark, his mouth pulled into a grim line.

The horror of that day seven months ago rushed back. The screams, the chaos, the acrid scent of blood and gun smoke. And the dying man whose life had been cut short because of her. Because he'd gotten in Rogan's way and tried to save her. She should have just gone with Rogan. Maybe then nobody would have died. But every life on that stagecoach was forfeited the moment she stepped onto it and he came after her.

Her eyes slid past Grant to the woman seated in front of him. Fat dark curls framed the dainty features on her pretty face. Her rosebud lips were pulled tight, her eyes conveying a sense of...of what? Katherine pulled the photograph closer. The woman looked trapped. Like a cornered animal too frightened to find a means of escape. Grant's hand rested on her shoulder. Neither of them looked very happy.

Katherine touched the photo gently. A curl slipped over her shoulder and dangled downward, brushing the edge of the frame. This had to be the girl she sought. His wife. Her heart pounded in her chest. Where was she now? And how would she find her?

"Kate!" The door flew open and Katherine froze. "Dammit woman, I thought you'd hurt yourself. I've been standing on the other side of this door knocking for at least—" Connor stopped, the rest of what he was going to say lost in the silence of the room. He looked at Katherine, the picture, then the open drawer of the vanity. Anger rolled over his features like a descending storm.

Katherine had no time to react as he stepped forward and snatched the photograph from her hand.

"What the hell are you doing?"

Katherine opened her mouth but nothing came out. What could she say?

"What were you doing going through my things?"

His things? But they weren't *his* things. She looked again at the curtains and back to the vanity. Her brain whirled and spiralled until she thought she might topple and fall off the stool. It made more sense now. Connor had moved back to Fatal Bluff only six months ago. He'd said so himself. Someone had lived here before then. The woman in the photograph had lived here. With Grant. But then where was she now and when had she left?

"The woman in the photograph...is she—"

Connor tossed the photograph in the drawer and slammed it shut with a flick of his wrist. Katherine jumped as wood slammed into wood. He spun the stool around and planted his hands on either side of her, pushing her spine into the edge of the vanity.

"Let's get one thing straight, Miss Stockdale. I hired you to clean, to cook, and to look after Jenny. I didn't hire you to snoop through my belongings like you had some right."

She nodded because it was all she could do. Words had deserted her.

He leaned a little closer. She could smell the scent of fresh air and leather on him.

His gaze tore through and touched every part of her. She couldn't move, couldn't speak, couldn't do anything but stare back, lost in him, her chest rising and falling in tandem with his. The sudden urge to grab the front of his shirt and haul him into her until that mouth descended on hers rocked her senses. Katherine squeezed the edge of the stool to keep her hands from betraying her. Something flickered beyond his anger, shoving it out of the way, something equally as frightening.

Desire.

She drew in a breath. He felt it too. She could see it in his eyes.

His gaze dropped to her mouth. For a fleeting instant, she thought he might kiss her. Hoped he would. Anything to end this desperate longing that fired up her insides whenever he came close. Maybe then she could rid herself of it, make it go away.

Her lips parted. Connor's jaw twitched, his mouth tightened. Then, without warning, the storm passed and he stepped away, turning his back.

Katherine stared at the rigid line of his broad shoulders. His fingers drove through thick sun-kissed waves. "This was a mistake. This whole thing was a mistake," he muttered.

"I—I'm sorry." Her voice echoed off the walls, small and ineffectual. "I didn't mean—"

He cut her off. "Jenny and I will be waiting in the buggy. Get what you need and come on." He strode to the door then stopped, turning just enough to reveal the strong lines of his profile. "And stay the hell out of my things."

Tension crackled between them on the drive over to the Holkums. Neither said a word. Kate did not even attempt to converse with Jenny, something Connor noted she had begun doing on a regular basis even though the little girl never answered back. He knew he should say something, apologize. He hadn't meant to blow up, but seeing her holding that photograph, the questions rife in those green eyes, questions he would have to answer...

Connor shook his head. It had set him off. He didn't want to think about it. And he didn't want her of all people asking him about the past. Because he'd probably spill his guts if she did. She'd look at him with that expectant expression, stand close enough to make his mind stop working, his carefully constructed defenses would hit the trail and that would be that. She'd have the whole sordid story laid at her feet. He couldn't think right when she was around. It'd been two weeks and she had him so damn addled he didn't know if he was coming or going. Hell, mad as he was, he'd still almost kissed her right there in the bedroom.

She had the curiosity of a cat, the way she kept nosing into his business, asking her endless stream of questions and now snooping around in his things. He'd tried to turn the tables, to learn something about her. For some reason what little information Oliver had given him about Kate just didn't seem to match the woman he lived with. And the vague bits of her past she meted out came stilted and unsure, as if she were making it up as she went along.

But why? What could she be hiding? He wasn't sure which infuriated him more—that he couldn't uncover her secrets, or that he cared enough to try.

Either way, erupting in anger when all she did was open a damned drawer was no way to go about finding out. She'd never trust him if he acted like a complete ass. He owed her an apology.

He pulled on the reins as they arrived at Bart and Amelia's and then set the brake. With a deep breath, he turned to her.

"Kate?"

She sat staring straight ahead, so still he wanted to touch her to see if she was made of stone. Or he just wanted to touch her and was looking for an excuse. He couldn't tell anymore.

The door opened and Amelia appeared on the step. "Well land sakes, don't just sit there—get down and come inside."

Connor looked at Kate once more. She had bent to gather the pies she'd made and handed them down to Amelia, who stepped forward, clearing the doorway for the rest of the family to filter out. He sighed. The apology would have to wait. No way was he about to do it in front of Bart, Amelia, their daughters, their daughters' husbands and a gaggle of kids. He'd rather strip bare and run through the middle of town.

Once herded inside the children went off to one corner, the men sat at the table, and the women worked their magic in the kitchen. The house quickly filled with laughter and conversation and Connor felt the tension of the day draining out of him. He missed this, he realized, this sense of family and belonging.

His gaze traveled the kitchen where everyone congregated and he tried to see it through Kate's eyes. To him it was commonplace. Even after being away for so long, he'd slipped back into the rhythm of his old life with the Holkums as if he'd been gone a day and not eight years. There were changes, of course. New children, new spouses. Grant's absence. Connor pinched the thought off before it got too far. He couldn't think about that. Hell, he could hardly think about anything with the noise level thirteen people crammed into one room could generate.

Beth and Joyce, Bart's daughters, had joined them, both bringing their husbands and four children between them. It gave Connor a sense of ease to see Jenny playing quietly with Beth's two girls. That she hardly spoke didn't seem to matter. They set their dolls around a makeshift table and held their own pre-dinner tea party.

At the counter, the women worked in companionable collaboration. Every now and again Connor would hear Kate's laughter trickle up over the voices and his gaze would be drawn to her. She had tied her hair back in a loose knot at the base of her neck. Even subdued it possessed a wild quality, as if it would break out of its moorings at any moment. He kind of wished it would. A part of him longed to see it as it had appeared on that first day, fiery curls flying freely about.

Dammit. He closed his eyes and squeezed the bridge of his nose.

"You okay, son?"

Bart's voice cut through the muddle in his brain. Was he okay? No, he realized. He was a hard day's ride from okay. His brother had been murdered, his own life had been turned upside down, Jenny wouldn't speak and now he had to contend with Kate and the unwanted emotions she stirred within him.

"I'm fine," he lied. "Just tired, I guess." That part was only a half-lie. He was tired. Tired of feeling as if he was swimming to the surface only to be tugged back under by the current. Maybe he should just let go, let it sweep him away.

He opened his eyes and looked at Jenny. No. He couldn't let that happen. Jenny needed him. It was one thing to fail himself, it was something else entirely to fail Jenny. She'd had enough tragedy in her short life without him adding more to the pile.

"Guess you've got a lot on your plate, Con," Beth's husband said. Reverend Will Sangster leaned back in his chair. He crossed his arms over his broad chest and the wood creaked beneath his weight. Connor had been friends with Will since they were boys. It seemed strange sometimes to think of him as Reverend, especially after all the scrapes they'd gotten into in their youth.

"I guess," Connor allowed.

"Could be you need some guidance," Will mentioned, a sly grin crossing his features. Connor braced himself for what was next. "The kind you might get at, oh, I don't know, Sunday service perhaps."

Connor lifted one eyebrow and crossed his own arms over his chest. Here it comes, he thought. The pitch to get him back to church. Hell, he'd only ever gone before because Grant dragged him, and the last time because Emily—

He clenched his jaw. "I'm not goin' to church, Will. It ain't a place I want to be." Too many memories—all of them bad. He was pretty sure God would understand.

"And Jenny? Or Kate?"

"Kate can go to church any time she pleases. She's an employee, not a prisoner," Connor ground out. At the sound of her name, Kate glanced over her shoulder. He caught her gaze. She still looked ready to spit fire at him. Hell! He wasn't the one in the wrong here. She was the one caught snooping!

"That woman is far more than an employee," Will said, lowering his voice and nodding in Kate's direction once she'd turned back around.

Connor's heart lurched. Did Will know the lusty thoughts that kept invading his mind? Was he that obvious? "What do you mean?"

"I mean she's a good woman. She has a warm heart. I've only just met her and I can see that. And Jenny is obviously taken with her. She's a jewel in the rough. Seems to me God sent you an angel when you needed one most. You'd best not take such a gift lightly."

"She's no angel, believe me," he muttered. The devil seemed more likely. Temptation and sin rolled into one delectable body that begged to be touched. Kate was the proverbial forbidden fruit.

Will shook his head. "Sometimes when good things arrive, we need to take the time to unwrap them before we see how truly special they are."

Connor groaned and dropped his forehead to rest against the tabletop. The idea of unwrapping Kate ran roughshod over the rest of his thoughts.

"Why don't you boys round up the young 'ins while we dish out the plates," Amelia said, leaning over the table to set fresh bread in the middle.

"Yes ma'am!" Connor jumped up, thankful for the timely intervention, and made a beeline for the children.

With the children seated at their own table and their meals served, the adults filled the seats at the larger table. Amelia sat Katherine next to her with the Reverend on the other side. Connor took the spot directly across from her. At first, the distance pleased her, until she realized she'd have to spend the entire meal trying not to glance over at him.

Katherine tried to ignore Connor and concentrate on the others. If some families thought silence at the dinner table was proper, the Holkums were not one of them. Will had no sooner finished saying grace than conversations picked up around the table and the noise level rose to a cacophony of voices and laughter. Katherine didn't think she'd ever seen the like before. Even Connor, who had been sullen the entire ride over, came back to life. His vivid blue eyes danced as he sparred back and forth with Bart and Joyce's husband, Anthony. She loved to watch him laugh. Everything about him altered when he did. His smile had the power to light up an entire room and chase away the shadows in her heart.

She wished she could freeze this moment in time.

Her mama's voice echoed in her memory. *Wishes are for those that can afford them, Katy.*

She hadn't believed her for the longest time, but now she knew the truth of it. She'd made her choices—most of them bad. She'd hastily married Rogan to avoid the hardships and indignities her mother had suffered. But what had it gotten her? A life on the run, and no hope of ever having the love and family she'd dreamed of.

She looked away from Connor and stared at the contents of her plate.

"I hear it tastes better in your belly than on your plate," Will suggested, leaning toward her so she could hear him over the din.

Katherine smiled. Reverend Will was a nice man. A good man. He probably wouldn't have yelled at her if she'd inadvertently found a photograph in a drawer. Fine, maybe she had been snooping a little, but what else was she supposed to do? She needed to find Grant's wife and deliver his last message to her, but Connor was no help in that department at all. She was no closer to finding Grant's wife now than when she'd first arrived. Time was running out.

"I guess I'm not hungry."

Will lifted his eyebrows. "Troubles?"

She considered lying, but he was a man of God. She had enough strikes against her. "Is it that obvious?"

"Only two things I can think of that would keep someone from filling their boots on Amelia's beef stew. Troubles, or death. Now, you seem fit as a fiddle, so I'm guessing it isn't the latter."

She laughed in spite of herself and caught Connor eyeing her with something akin to suspicion. The unspoken accusation rankled her. What did he think she was doing? Wasn't she allowed to laugh?

"No, I'm not dead." Not yet, anyway.

She returned Connor's glare until he looked away, but the effect of his gaze lingered liked a longed-for touch. Heat burned her cheeks.

"Worried about the Hewitts?"

"Yes, a little," she said, thankful for the distraction. What kind of woman entertained such lustful thoughts when talking to a reverend?

"Well, I wouldn't give it a second thought," Will said. "Connor would never let any harm come to you. He'll keep the Hewitts off your back."

Katherine grimaced. "Connor would throw me to the wolves, given half a chance." Especially after tonight.

A deep chuckle rumbled in Will's chest. "Oh, don't be too sure. He's as stubborn as the day is long, but he's fiercely loyal to family. You've nothing to worry about."

Katherine toyed with the succulent piece of beef drowned in gravy and vegetables. She tried to force a smile, but it didn't take. "I'm not family, Reverend. I'm just his housekeeper."

She'd heard him say so earlier, qualifying her place in the scheme of things. It had hurt more than she wanted to admit.

Will shook his head. "Then why can't he take his eyes off you? Heck, every time I lean down to say something, he looks like he wants to stab me with his fork."

Katherine's lips twitched at the humor in Will's tone, and the weight pressing down on her heart lifted a fraction. "Maybe he just doesn't like you much."

Will laughed and slapped his hand on the table between them. Katherine looked across the table at Connor. He ignored her, too busy strangling his fork and glaring daggers at his friend.

"Kate, I think poor Connor was a goner from the moment you stepped off that train." Before she could contradict him, or set him straight on the fact that nothing would be developing between her and Connor, Will said, "Now, how about the three of you come to Sunday service tomorrow? Jenny can spend some time with the girls and you can meet some of the people in town. I think you'd enjoy it."

She brightened at the idea. Jenny seemed much more animated around the other children. It would do her good. They'd both been stuck in seclusion for too long. Despite her earlier misgivings about going to town, perhaps she could use the opportunity to ask around about Connor's family. Surely, the Hewitts wouldn't make a scene at church. Would they?

"I think I'd like that, Reverend. I'll bring it up with Connor." When she wasn't so angry at him for yelling at her. Or he at her for snooping.

Dinner didn't last nearly long enough for Katherine's liking. She loved being surrounded by the laughter and cama-raderie of the Holkums. Even Connor's mood had changed. The rigid tension in his shoulders disappeared. He sat in the rocking chair talking to Bart in low tones, with Joyce and Anthony's youngest boy, Davy, asleep in the crook of his arm.

Connor used his toe to push the chair back and forth in a steady rhythm.

"Makes for a nice picture, doesn't it?" Amelia came up from behind, wiping her hands on the dishtowel and glancing over Katherine's shoulder to her husband and Connor.

"He's good with the children." Katherine had watched Connor throughout the evening. He rough-housed with the boys, teased the girls until they giggled and squealed, and all the while kept an eye on Jenny. Now and then his hand would softly touch the back of her head, or tug gently on one of the braids Katherine had plaited before they left.

"A natural born father, we tell him, but he doesn't believe us. Thinks he's failing miserably," Amelia said with a sigh and turned back to the counter.

Katherine took her eyes off Connor and set the vase of fresh wildflowers back on the cleared table before following after Amelia. "Failing? Why?"

"He worries about Jenny. She won't speak and the longer it goes on, the more he fears it's because of something he's doing, or worse—not doing."

She recalled the tense lines around Connor's eyes and mouth over the past week whenever he watched Jenny. Lines that deepened each time he spoke to her and received no reply.

"Did Jenny ever speak?"

"Oh yes," Amelia said, turning and folding the dishtowel. "Used to be you couldn't shut her up. She'd talk a mile a minute about whatever was in her head. Much like Connor was at that age."

Katherine tried to imagine a talkative Connor but the image failed to take root. There were times he could rival Jenny for silence. Maybe it was hereditary.

Katherine suddenly realized she had been barking up the wrong tree as far as discovering the nature of Connor's relationship with Grant. With all the effort she had put into trying to drag the information out of Connor, she could have just paid Amelia a visit and had a nice little chat with the woman.

Watching the interaction between Connor and the Holkums, it was obvious they had a longstanding relationship —one that had lasted longer than the six months he'd been in Fatal Bluff. If they had known Jenny before, when she spoke nonstop, Connor and Jenny could not have been gone from Fatal Bluff for very long. Still, the mystery lingered—what had brought them back, and why had they left in the first place?

After finding the picture, Katherine had a strong suspicion Grant and Connor were brothers. It was the only thing that made sense, though she found it strange Connor never mentioned him. He was as tight-lipped about his family as a priest was about confession.

But perhaps Amelia would be more willing to open up about Grant and his wife. Heck, maybe she could even give her specific directions on where to find the woman in the photograph and save Katherine a world of trouble.

But before she could ask Amelia about the photo, the niggling voice in her head demanded she satisfy her curiosity about Jenny and the sudden silence she had imposed on herself.

"What happened to make Jenny change?"

Amelia's expression darkened and her hands smoothed across the dishtowel. "Oh well..." Her voice trailed off. Katherine's neck prickled and awareness skipped down her spine. She knew Connor stood behind her without having to look. But she couldn't help herself.

She glanced over her shoulder and stared straight into the open collar of Connor's red shirt, softened and faded from repeated washings. Warm, tanned skin lay exposed at the base of his throat. Smooth and inviting. He stood close enough that if she leaned back just a few inches her head would rest on his shoulder. For a brief second she let her mind wander there, let herself imagine what it would be like. His arms would come around hers and pull her full against him, a protective cocoon from the rest of the world. His mouth would rest near her ear. He'd laugh softly at something she said and squeeze her tight in response. Every muscle, every hard ridge moving against her back. His lips would find that tender spot, just behind her ear and—

"Kate?"

Katherine jumped and her face burned. God help her, she was losing her mind where this man was concerned! "What?"

Connor lifted one eyebrow. "I said, we should head on out. It's getting late."

"Oh, yes. Of course." She grabbed the dishtowel Amelia had already folded and redid it. Anything to avoid looking at Connor.

"Thank you for the pies, dear," Amelia said, taking the towel from her. "They were quite delicious."

"It was my pleasure," Katherine said. "Thank you for a lovely time." One of the best she'd had for as long as she could remember. She would hold the memory close for years to come.

"And don't forget about next Saturday's social." Amelia looked past her to Connor. "It'll give Kate a chance to get to know some new people and have some fun. Can't work all the time, can she?"

Connor shrugged and looked away. "She can go if she wants."

"Well land sakes, Con, you can't expect her to go by herself!"

Katherine wanted to interject, to say she didn't have to go, but she couldn't get the words out. She'd never been to a town social before, and part of her really wanted to go to experience what it was like to belong to a community that didn't turn its back on her. Just this once.

"She can go with you and Bart."

"Bart and I will be in town that day," Amelia stated, lifting her chin. "She'll need a way in."

Katherine's hopes plummeted. One look at Connor told her all she needed to know. He didn't want to go. More importantly, he didn't want to go with her. An employee. "I-I don't have to go. It's not that important—"

"Nonsense." Amelia set her hands on her hips and fixed a steady glare on Connor, waiting. Katherine had the sense the woman would have stood rooted to the spot for the rest of the night if she had to in order to get the response she wanted.

Connor scowled and his hand pressed against Katherine's lower back, pushing her gently toward the door. Tingles of sensation spread through her body at the small, innocent touch. "I'll think about it," he growled.

The ride home proved no less tense than the ride over, but for altogether different reasons. Katherine could not hold on to her anger for the way Connor had treated her. The man had a right to be put out with her snooping through his things. But without her anger providing a barrier, her growing awareness of him threatened to get out of control.

Katherine was thankful Jenny had wedged herself between them. The warmth of her little body nestled against her filled Katherine with an unexpected sense of contentment. She glanced down at Jenny's face. Thick lashes lay in crescent moons against her cheek while she dozed. She really was a dear thing. A rush of protectiveness washed over Katherine without warning. She wanted to see Jenny happy. She wanted to erase the haunted look in her eyes. She wanted to hear her chatter non-stop like Amelia said she used to.

The desire to know the reason behind Jenny's silence pulled at Katherine. Perhaps if she knew its origins, she could better help the little girl find her way out of it. But Connor would never confide such details to her. He viewed her as an employee. Nothing more.

"Will asked us to Sunday service tomorrow," Katherine ventured, keeping her voice low. The house rose in the distance, painted orange and purple by the sun as it sank beneath the bluff. An unexpected sense of coming home filled her.

Connor kept his gaze focused on the rutted road ahead of them. For a moment, he said nothing, and she thought he hadn't heard her, or worse, ignored her. Then he sighed. "I know."

"I—I thought it might be nice to go. To take Jenny."

Conflicting emotions crossed Connor's face in the dimming light until finally he shook his head. "No."

"Why not?"

His jaw tensed and he adjusted his grip on the reins. "Because I said so."

Katherine took a breath and attempted another route. "I thought it might be good for Jenny to be around other children."

He turned to look at her, anger dipping his brow. The setting sun reflected in his eyes like a burning fire. "*You* think?"

His words struck her, as if he didn't think she deserved an opinion on the matter. Maybe he was right. Maybe she didn't. Who was she anyway but the hired help? Yet he had hired her to care for Jenny. That meant something to her. She couldn't just sit in silence if she thought she could help.

"Yes, I do," she said, whispering the words quickly before her courage failed her.

"Oh, well then." He shook his head. "If *you* think so. I mean you've been here all of what—fifteen days?"

She swallowed. "Sixteen."

"Sixteen. Well, I guess that makes you even more of an expert on what's good for Jenny. Far more than me, because

I've only had six months. But you, no, you've had sixteen whole days."

Katherine sat stunned. Had she heard him wrong? "What do you mean you've only had six months?"

Connor's mouth pulled tight and he glanced down at Jenny before shifting his angry gaze at Katherine. "Never mind."

Again the niggling voice poked her, demanding attention, but Connor's expression clearly indicated he was far from amenable to further conversation. Frustration boiled inside of Katherine. Well, if Connor wouldn't talk to her, she would go to town for Sunday services with or without him, and she'd find out what she needed to know from the people in town, just see if she wouldn't.

"Well, I'm going to church on Sunday," she stated, staring straight ahead. Purple smudged the skyline as the sun slipped beneath the bluff.

She could feel Connor's gaze as it landed on her, and the cool absence of it when he finally looked away.

"Do what you want."

"I will."

"Fine."

Silence descended, awkward and thorny. Connor drove the buggy up to the house, yanking harder on the brake than was necessary. He climbed down and walked around to her side, jerking his hand toward her. "Hand me Jenny."

Katherine put her arm around the little girl as she rubbed her eyes and looked around, dazed from sleep.

"Jenny, sweetheart, go to your pa."

Jenny's brow crinkled and tears filled her eyes as she looked from Katherine to Connor.

"Don't say that," Connor said, his voice curt. He reached for Jenny.

"Why not?" Trepidation crept over Katherine.

Jenny climbed into Connor's waiting arms and hugged his neck, nuzzling into the curve. Grief etched deeper into Connor's features.

"Just don't."

His tone warned her to leave it, but her conscience wouldn't allow it. Too many things did not add up. "What did you mean you had been gone until six months ago? Gone where?"

Connor glared at her. "Away."

"Who looked after Jenny while you were away?" Blood pulsed in her ears. It couldn't be true. Please don't let it be true.

Connor hesitated, his hand cupping the back of Jenny's head where it rested on his shoulder. "Her father. Jenny is Grant's daughter, not mine."

"Grant?"

"My brother."

Chapter Eight

Katherine paced the kitchen floor, her hands twisting around each other. She had put Jenny to bed while Connor took the buggy down to the barn and unhitched the horses. Exhausted from a full day, Jenny had fallen asleep quickly, but Katherine didn't fool herself into thinking it would come that easy for her.

Jenny was Grant's daughter.

Connor's words reverberated in her mind.

His girl. *She* was the one Katherine had been searching for. Right under her nose the entire time and she'd been too blind or stupid to see it. Maybe she hadn't wanted to.

The knowledge sickened her.

Her husband had orphaned a little girl. And he'd done it because of her.

What did she do now?

The door behind her opened and Katherine spun around. Connor cast her a quick glance before turning his back and hanging his coat and hat on the peg by the door. His broad shoulders slumped. "Guess you're waiting up for some kind of explanation."

She nodded, half expecting him to tell her it was none of her business. But he didn't. He motioned her to a chair at the kitchen table. Once she was seated he sat down across from her, his hands splayed flat against the smooth wood.

"Jenny's my niece."

Katherine pursed her lips, wrestling her emotions under control. Connor and Grant were brothers. A part of her had suspected it all along, she just hadn't wanted to see it, to acknowledge how close to home the man's death had hit for these people. The guilt of it was almost too much to bear.

"What happened to Jenny's father?" The part that had turned a blind eye to the obvious resurrected itself as she prayed for a miracle, prayed she had the wrong house, the wrong people. That the telltale signs of tragedy that lurked in every nook and cranny of this house did not point back to her. That the responsibility for the sadness coating everything and everyone that stepped across the threshold did not rest at her door.

But it did. She knew it. And Connor's words only confirmed it.

"He's dead. Murdered." His finger traced the outline of the wood grain. "Stagecoach robbery seven months back."

Thick tears filled her eyes until she was afraid to blink for fear they would trip over her lids and fall down her cheeks. She covered her mouth and smothered a sob. There would be a reckoning. She would be judged and held accountable. She may not have orchestrated Rogan's attack on the stagecoach, but maybe, just maybe if she'd agreed to go with him willingly he might have left the others alive.

But she hadn't. She'd resisted. And now Grant was dead and buried and only Jenny remained. And Connor.

Tell Con I'm sorry.

Sorry for what? For leaving them? For ripping Connor

away from the life he had been leading to take on the mantle of father and sheriff once worn by his brother?

Guilt flooded her. How many other families like Grant's were out there? How many more lives had been destroyed by the man she'd married? What if she had turned him in to the authorities? Could she have prevented this?

"Kate?"

"How long has Jenny been—" She stopped her question. She already knew. Amelia said Jenny used to be a little chatterbox. Used to be.

Connor bowed his head. "I didn't know her before. I left Fatal Bluff eight years ago. Amelia and Bart said before Grant's murder she was full of life. By the time I got here though she was—" he paused and looked up, worry paling his skin and leaching the life from his eyes. "Well, you see how she is now."

"Has she said anything?"

Connor shook his head. "No. It's like she's crawled inside herself and won't come out. Or can't. I don't know which."

Quiet filled the room. Katherine's stomach burned and she wondered if she might be sick.

"What will you do?"

"What can I do?" The sound of his voice matched the bleakness of his features.

"Children are resilient," she offered, wanting to erase his pain and replace it with hope. "I lost my own father in an accident at Jenny's age. It was horrible, but you get through it. Maybe she just—"

Connor cut her off, his gaze narrowing. "What do you mean you lost your father when you were Jenny's age? I thought he died in a fire. *A year or so ago*, wasn't it?"

The blood drained from her face, leaving her lightheaded.

"M—my father died when I was nine," she said, stumbling her way around the truth and meshing it with the lie. "Mama remarried shortly after that. Mr. Stockdale was my stepfather."

105

Connor nodded slowly. His gaze pinned her, left her cornered, trapped and on the verge of confessing. She hated lying. More than that, she hated lying to him. He deserved far better than this. But better was the truth, and the truth brought with it a pain all its own.

"How did your father die?"

"His wagon overturned. It had been full of supplies, and he was crushed beneath the weight." She didn't bother filling in more details than that. Didn't bother elaborating that the supplies contained an accumulation of their lives to that point, or that they were traveling west from Missouri to start a new life after the war. The horror of that day had never left her, watching her father gasp for air. The other men struggling to pull him free. Her mother's screams when their efforts were in vain.

"What was your name before that?"

The hair on the back of her neck prickled with unease. "Before what?"

"Before your mother remarried."

"Mackenzie," she told him, using her maiden name. At least that wasn't a lie.

He stared at her for a moment until his gaze made her skin burn and sizzle. The air between them seemed charged with an undercurrent of awareness. Then Connor abruptly looked away, breaking the spell weaving its way around them.

"I'm sorry about your pa."

Katherine nodded and pushed the ugly memories away. "It was a long time ago. And I survived. Jenny will too. It just takes time."

He nodded. "I can take you to church tomorrow, if you want."

The small concession surprised her, but while he had been busy unhitching the horses and she had been wrestling with the consequences of the crime perpetrated in her name, she knew she could never show her face in church.

She didn't belong there.

Too much blood colored her conscience and stained her soul.

"No. That won't be necessary."

He lifted an eyebrow. "Thought you said you were going."

Katherine shook her head. She couldn't imagine facing the Holkums now, knowing what her actions had wrought. They treated her like family, but all she had done was destroy those close to them.

"No. I—" *I* what? "I don't have anything to wear," she finally said. "Nothing suitable, anyway."

Connor took her explanation at face value. How easily the lies were beginning to slip from her tongue. She wondered if there would come a time when the lies became so abundant they outnumbered the truths.

"Fine." He rose from his chair and looked down at her. "It's been a long day. We should turn in."

Her gaze flitted away like a hummingbird, not resting on anything for more than a few seconds and avoiding Connor altogether. She wanted to turn in. She wanted to slip beneath the covers and find him there. Curl into his long, hard body and find solace.

But she didn't deserve it.

She never would.

A sinking sadness filled her. Just returning the letter and ring would never be enough.

Grant's words haunted her.

"...make sure she's okay...promise."

But she wasn't okay. She wasn't even in the same territory as okay. And Katherine couldn't leave here until she was. She had made a promise, and this time she would not fail.

~

Connor stood over the chest nestled against the far wall of the bedroom, his back to the door. Sun streaked through the window and soaked into the aged cedar. The key dangled in his hand. He jostled it against his palm, debating what to do. It wasn't that big a deal really. He'd never even seen Emily in these clothes, so what did it matter? It wasn't as if she was coming back to get them. They were just sitting there, waiting to be eaten through by moths if they hadn't been already.

Exasperated with himself, Connor crouched down and jammed the key into the lock before he could think on it any more. He'd put it off long enough. The minute he'd walked into the house he'd erased every hint of her, not that there was much left after all these years. But what he'd found he'd put away, out of sight.

The key turned with ease. Connor's heart picked up its pace. He thought he could avoid the memories forever, just shove them aside and pretend they had never happened. Maybe he could have continued on that way too, but Kate had looked so damned distressed last night when she refused to go to church, too embarrassed by how she would look.

It had touched him somehow.

Something about Kate had slipped beneath his defenses. He couldn't pinpoint the exact moment the change had happened, but it had. Swiftly and completely. And he was hooked. He knew it, and he hated it. But he couldn't help it. All she had to do was look at him with those sea green eyes and he was done for.

Connor groaned and rubbed a hand down his face, letting it come to rest on the curved top of the chest. He could feel the ridges of the carvings he'd shaped into the wood all those years ago. Different flowers he'd found pictures of in books but couldn't remember the names of after all this time. He was surprised she'd kept it, given how things had ended.

Inwardly bracing himself, Connor pushed the top open. Its hinges creaked in the quiet, the sound scraping along his nerves. He waited for her scent to waft up and assault him, but time and the cedar wood had done their job. He realized then that he couldn't even remember Emily's scent. Or the sound of her laughter. Every time he tried it was Kate's sparkling laughter he heard.

Connor dug a hand deep into the chest and pulled out a soft green shirtwaist. With hesitant movements, he lifted the material and held it against his nose and mouth. He inhaled, slowly at first, then more deeply. Waited for her essence to fill his senses, for the bitterness and betrayal to overwhelm him.

Nothing.

"Connor?"

At the sound of Kate's voice, Connor spun on his heel and sprang upward, the shirtwaist still in his hand. He stared, blinking, and stood there like a kid with his hand caught in the cookie jar.

"I thought you were in the garden."

"I was." She leaned a little to her left to peer around him. "What are you doing in here?"

He cleared his throat. "It is my room," he said, throwing out the only justification he could think of for his being in her room fishing through an old trunk.

Hurt pinched her expression. "I know."

"I mean...that is..." Dammit! Why did she always get him so tongue-tied? He was trying to do something nice and he couldn't even get the words out without mucking it up.

"I'll just leave you then." She started to back out of the room.

"Wait." He held a hand out, the shirtwaist dangling from it like a peace offering. He waved his other hand at the chest behind him, trying to get his brain and tongue to work in tandem. "There are clothes in here. I thought maybe you could make use of them."

There. He'd said it. The deed was done.

Kate took a step forward and leaned to her right to peer around him. Her eyes widened, and then she turned on him. "Where did they come from?"

"Come from?" She would have to ask that question. "From...they belonged to Jenny's mother."

An emotion he couldn't place rippled across her features. She shook her head. "Oh no. I couldn't take her things."

"She's not going to mind. It isn't like she's got need of them. She passed on a while back." He waited for the words to put a chokehold on his heart. They didn't. Just a dull ache that faded with each passing beat.

Perhaps he should tell her the truth about Emily. It wasn't any big secret. Not in this town. Besides, better she hear it from him, rather than the embellished version of the truth she'd pick up in town. The one that portrayed him as some kind of hero, swooping in and taking responsibility for Jenny.

He was no hero. If there had been a heroic bone in his body he would have returned long before and made amends with his brother, instead of riding in after Grant was already dead to pick up the pieces of his life.

Maybe if he told her that, it would build a bridge between them and give her reason to confide in him. He knew she was hiding something. She was far too evasive whenever the subject of her past came up.

In the end, he let the moment pass. He was not looking to get involved, regardless of his feelings. He'd done that once. It had ended in disaster.

"Anyway," he said, closing the subject with a brusque tone. "The clothes are yours. You may as well make use of them."

Chapter Nine

The next day dawned bright and cool. Katherine could feel the first nip of autumn against her skin as she wrapped her shawl around her shoulders and ventured out of the bedroom.

The couch was empty; the patchwork quilt tossed carelessly over the top. Connor had been in a rush to leave. He'd barely said a word to her since gifting her with a trunk full of clothes yesterday. He seemed almost embarrassed with his own generosity, and Katherine felt too guilty to consider what to do with the dresses.

She wandered to the kitchen, where she found the remnants of a fire crackling in the wood stove and a pot of coffee warmed on the burner. Connor's hat was gone from the peg near the door. He'd left without saying good-bye.

She tried to beat back the sense of rejection that slithered into her heart. It was foolish really. He was under no obligation to keep her company.

But the mornings were one of her favorite times. She liked cooking him breakfast and sitting at the table over coffee while he made short work of whatever she'd fixed him. They rarely spoke. Katherine had to work to coax a few words out of him, but when she did the thrill was far more intense than it should have been. Like winning an unexpected prize. So much of her life had been spent alone, fending for herself, that she revelled in the companionship now afforded her, even if that companionship was given reluctantly, or would soon end.

She moved to the stove and lifted the coffee pot, testing its weight. He'd left her enough for two cups. She smiled. At least that was something.

As she set about preparing breakfast, Jenny appeared in the kitchen, rubbing sleep from her eyes. Her mussed hair hung loose about her face. Draped over her arms, two baskets they used for collecting eggs banged against each other. It had become their routine. Each morning after Connor ate and left for work, she and Jenny would gather the eggs. Katherine still had a healthy respect for Lucifer, but she no longer feared venturing into the coop, worried he might swoop down from his perch and peck her to bits.

Katherine took the two baskets from Jenny, glancing down at the child's feet.

"I think you had best put on a pair of shoes, sweetie. It's getting colder in the mornings. If I keep letting you traipse about in your bare feet, you'll catch a chill."

Jenny glanced down and wriggled her toes.

In the time Katherine had been here, she couldn't recall a time Jenny hadn't been running around barefoot. Even the pair of shoes she wore to the Holkums for supper had ended up coming off once they arrived. She seemed to have an aversion to footwear.

"Go get me your shoes and bring them here."

Jenny set the baskets down on the floor and skipped back to the bedroom, blond hair bouncing against her back. A moment later she reappeared, a shoe in each hand. She walked up in front of Katherine and dropped them to the floor, looking up at her with expectant eyes.

"Can you put them on for me?"

Jenny scrunched up her nose and sat on the floor. She made no move to put the shoes on.

"Jenny?" Katherine crouched next to her.

With a bit of a huff, Jenny jammed her foot into one shoe then held it out to Katherine.

Placing Jenny's foot in her lap, Katherine's fingers pressed at the toe and felt the shape of her foot filling it to capacity. They winced in unison.

"Your shoes don't fit." No wonder the poor girl had been running around without them.

Jenny reached back and placed her weight on her hands. Her eyebrows lifted skyward, like a small replica of her uncle.

"Well, this won't do." Katherine pulled the shoe off with a bit of effort and set it on the floor. "Do you have another pair?"

Jenny shook her head once.

Katherine sighed. What was she to do? She couldn't let Jenny walk about in bare feet with cooler weather coming. She thought of the trunk and the clothing she had yet to sift through. They wouldn't fit, of course, but they could make do until she got Jenny to town to purchase a proper pair.

Katherine stood up and held out her hand. "Come with me, Jenny. I think I have an idea."

Jenny scrambled to her feet and slipped her hand into Katherine's, surprising her. The small hand resting in hers touched a part of her deep inside, easing the sense of rejection Connor's early exodus from the house had created.

A search of the trunk produced only one pair of shoes in brand-new condition. Unfortunately, neither Jenny nor Katherine had feet large enough to fit into them properly.

Katherine clucked her tongue. There was no way around

it. "I think we're going to have to make a trip into town, Jenny."

The shoe shopping proved an easy task. Everyone had been pleased to see Jenny, waving at her from their storefronts and issuing greetings back to Katherine. For a moment, it allowed her to dream, to imagine what it would be like to be a part of that, to be accepted. But she cut the dream off before it got too far.

Best not to think about what she couldn't have. Or grow too comfortable with the way things were. She wasn't staying.

After purchasing Jenny a new pair of shoes on Connor's account at the mercantile, they stopped at the boardinghouse to see Amelia. They found her in the kitchen, packing up a basket.

"Well land sakes, look what the wind blew in," she said, coming forward and giving Jenny a hug. "And just in time. I made a fresh batch of ice cream this morning. It's been waiting in the icebox for some little girl to show up and demand a dish with some lemonade. How does that sound?"

Jenny's eyes glowed and Katherine salivated at the thought. The cool morning had burned off, leaving in its wake another warm September afternoon. They had walked into town, Jenny in Katherine's old boots, the toes stuffed with socks. Katherine wore the pair from the trunk in much the same way. It took almost two hours to reach the main street and by early afternoon, she was tired and famished and not quite ready for the walk back. A bowl of ice cream sounded just the thing. She'd been about seven the last time she'd tasted it, but even now, she could remember the seductive cool of the creamy substance sliding down her throat. Ice was not an easy commodity to come by at this time of year, making it a rare treat indeed, and not one Katherine wanted to pass up.

"That sounds—"

Amelia thrust the basket she'd been filling into Katherine's arms before she could finish, a warm smile still creasing the lines of her face. She had no choice but to wrap her arms around the basket's girth.

"Kate, could you be a dear and run this over to the boys at the sheriff's office while I dish Jenny up some ice cream? I always provide the boys with a hearty lunch and I'm well past due this afternoon."

Katherine's heart pounded. "The sheriff's office?"

"Do you mind?"

Katherine swallowed. She still smarted from Connor sneaking away that morning without a word. After he opened up to her about Jenny and his brother, she thought maybe he had begun to trust her. That maybe he had stopped resenting her presence as something he had been forced into accepting.

It was foolish really, to let such a small thing irritate her. It was his house. He could come and go as he pleased. They weren't married—God forbid! She had no claim on what he did or when he did it.

"Kate?"

Katherine gave herself a mental shake and saw Amelia waiting expectantly. "Oh...yes. Of course. I can do that."

Amelia winked. "Jenny and I will have a nice little visit and I'll be sure and save you an extra scoop for when you return."

Katherine perked up. An extra scoop? Perhaps she could just drop the basket on Connor's desk and hurry back. "I won't be long."

When she arrived, Katherine found the ageing deputy sitting behind the desk. Bart had his feet propped up and hat pulled low over his brow. The deep rumble of a snore drifted from beneath the brim. She stopped at the opposite side of the desk and cleared her throat.

Booted feet slammed to the floor and his wiry body

jumped out of the chair. The swift movement surprised Katherine and she stumbled back several steps.

"Ma'am!" Bart readjusted his hat, pushing it back off his forehead. Then, apparently thinking better of it, he swiped it off his head entirely, exposing a disheveled snarl of thin grey curls.

"Mr.—I mean, Deputy Holkum."

"Oh, just call me Bart," he offered. "Why, we're practically neighbors." His small brown eyes twinkled and the heavy creases in the corners deepened.

"Yes, of course." The idea warmed her. Neighbors. She'd never had those before. Unless you counted the butcher shop next to the shanty she and her mother occupied. But the butcher had spoken an entirely different language she couldn't make heads or tails out of and he didn't seem the friendly sort. Not like the people in Fatal Bluff.

"So what can I do for you, Kate? You bring that basket of goodies for Con?"

Katherine resented the lump of disappointment that settled itself in her stomach at Connor's absence.

"Your wife asked that I bring this over to both of you."

She set the basket down on the desk and then moved to wipe her hands against her skirt but quickly thought better of it. Vanity had overpowered her guilt, and she'd donned one of the dresses from the trunk. She didn't want to mess up the dark green and black plaid. She would have to return them when she left.

"Well now, lookee here." Bart lifted up one corner of the checkered cloth and took a deep breath. "That wife of mine is one mighty fine—"

The slam of the door drowned out the rest of his recitation of his wife's skills.

"Dang it all! Get in there, you fool!"

Katherine spun around. Two men clambered through the

entrance. The man in front faltered, nearly dropping to his knees before catching himself and surging back to his feet. From behind, a man shorter in stature but loud in voice followed, giving the first man another shove.

Bart moved, partially blocking her view, but not before she saw the iron bands shackled around the man's wrists and ankles.

"Oh, pardon me, ma'am."

As Bart had done earlier, the man doing the pushing grabbed his hat from his head and held it against his chest. He shot her a sheepish grin. Thick brown hair spilled over his shoulders in a haphazard fashion. A sun-bleached leather duster nearly swept the ground, swallowing up the man's compact body.

But it was the prisoner with manacled hands glaring at her with hate in his eyes that caused Katherine's heart to slam against her ribs with such force she thought it would bust through and fly clear across the room.

Frank Beesom.

One of Rogan's men.

Chapter Ten

Katherine gave the brim of her hat a swift yank, pulling it down to shadow her face. Her skin crawled as Beesom's menacing glare reached out and brushed against her. She needed to get out of there, but the man doing the pushing still blocked the door.

When Bart stepped forward she shifted behind him.

"Haven't seen you in these parts for a bit, Devers. What've you brought us today?"

"This here's Frank Beesom. The law in Bakers is waitin' on him. Seems he shot some men down there a while back. I'll be collectin' a nice bounty from the sheriff once I get 'im there."

Bart waved a finger at the irons connecting the man's legs. "He ride in like that?"

"Nah." Devers grinned. Two small dimples revealed themselves, giving him an almost boyish look. "Gave me some trouble just outside 'a town, so's I slapped them on him and rode him in arse end up on the back of his horse."

Just outside of town? Was Rogan closing in on her? Did he know she was here? Katherine couldn't breathe.

Devers lowered his voice and she had to strain to hear what

he said next. "Heard he rode a bit with Slade and his boys. Thought Con might wanna have a word with 'im before I took him in."

The air drained out of Katherine's lungs. Oh no. Oh no, oh no, oh no. She chanced a quick glance at Beesom. Had he gotten a good look at her?

The man's eyes pierced hers and a slow, malevolent smile stretched his leathery skin. The room closed in on her. Her fingers groped blindly for the desk behind her, gripping the smooth wood to keep her knees from buckling beneath her.

Bart nodded gravely. "Any word on Slade?"

"Rumor has it Slade's huntin' down some woman. Think it's the one that run off after the stagecoach attack, but I can't figure why. The sheriff in Mercury thinks it might be to keep the law from gittin' to her first. Maybe he don't know she already sent him up the river with her letter."

Katherine had written down what had happened that day, making sure to detail how Grant had died heroically saving her, and that Rogan's younger brother had been killed in the shoot out. She'd left the letter on Grant's body, knowing it would get into the right hands, and then she had made a run for it in the middle of the night. She couldn't stay. If Rogan had found her there, the farmer who had taken them in would have suffered a fate similar to Grant's. She'd had to keep moving.

"You thinkin' Slade wants her for different reasons?" Bart asked, interrupting her memories.

Devers shrugged. "I got a sense maybe she was the reason he came after the stagecoach in the first place. He let her live. He ain't one for leavin' live bodies behind. And there weren't nothin' on that coach worth stealing. Doesn't make no sense any other way."

"Hmph." Bart rubbed at his grizzled beard. "Bit of a mystery on that one."

Katherine struggled for composure. The bounty hunter's words bounced around in her head until it ached. Rogan continued his search. How close was he? How long before she had to run again? Would it never end?

Rogan and his men had killed everyone on the stagecoach save her, leaving behind no other witnesses. If Grant hadn't killed Rogan's brother in the shootout, no doubt Rogan would have caught up with them and it would have ended there. But she and Grant had been given a reprieve, limited as it was, allowing them to find a safe haven before Grant succumbed to his wounds.

Now one of Rogan's men stood a few feet away.

"I don't know spit about no Slade and I ain't never shot nobody!" Frank tried to pull away from the bounty hunter, but the smaller man's grip held him firm. "You got the wrong man."

"Oh sure," Devers said. His eyes lifted heavenward. "You're innocent as a babe. Happens all the time, don't it, Bart?"

Bart chuckled and walked over to the key ring hanging from a nail on the wall. He lifted it off the makeshift hook and unlocked the first cell door, opening it wide. With short, quick shoves, Devers prodded the man toward the cell. Frank staggered past, his uneven steps causing the irons around his ankles to chink against each other.

With his prisoner locked behind bars, Devers turned to Bart. "Con around?"

Bart shook his head. "Nope. Sheriff's over seein' to an altercation at Garrett's."

"Townsfolk found that boy a wife yet?"

Bart chuckled and shook his head. A smile quirked beneath the whiskers of his scruffy beard. "Not for lack of trying. Got himself a housekeeper though." Bart acknowledged Katherine with a brief nod. She wished he hadn't. She didn't want any attention brought on her, not with Frank Beesom glaring through the bars of his cell at her. Her head spun and fear spiralled through her. Beesom recognized her. She could see it in the cold, calculating way he took her measure, the malicious glint in his dark eyes. Why didn't he say something?

"Ed Devers, this here is Miss Stockdale. Oliver tried to marry her off to Walter Figg. Con saved her from that onerous fate and hired her to help him out."

Devers nodded. "Pleased as punch to meet you, ma'am."

"Thank you," Katherine whispered, keeping her eyes fixed on the floor. No need letting a bounty hunter get a good look at her. She had enough trouble on her doorstep without courting more.

"Con should be back shortly," Bart said.

Devers shrugged, apparently unconcerned at the delay. "No rush. Beesom's not goin' anywhere. I'll just drop into the hotel and get me a room. Figure I'll be around a day or two while Con questions ole Frank here."

With a quick grin, Devers replaced his hat and tipped the brim in Katherine's direction. "Ma'am."

Katherine returned his smile, barely conscious of the effort.

"Miss Stockdale." Bart's hand touched her elbow and she jumped, her nerves teetering on a sharp edge. Part of her wanted to forget about her promise and run, to move on to the next town, or the one after that. But how far would she have to go before she was truly safe? Before Rogan gave up and the law lost interest in her? She doubted there was a place that far.

"I need to get Jenny and go home."

Bart's calm voice did little to slow the blood pounding in her ears. "Sounds like a fine idea. And don't you worry none about Beesom. He's locked up safe and not going anywhere."

"Thank you, Deputy. Bart. Thank you." Words tumbled out of Katherine's mouth. She had to get Jenny home. And then...and then what? Run? Abandon Jenny?

She couldn't, even if she wanted to. Not yet. Until Connor paid her, Katherine didn't have two nickels to spit on to get her anywhere.

Maybe Beesom hadn't recognized her. Maybe she was just being overly fearful. The piercing stare Frank had given her resurrected itself in her mind's eye and sent a shiver of pure fear streaking down her spine.

No. He knew.

Her time was running out. Beesom might keep her identity a secret from the law for now—he couldn't reveal her identity without indicting himself as a member of Rogan's gang. But he was set to hang. It was entirely plausible he would trade information to gain his freedom if given the option. Would he use her identity as a bargaining chip?

Or worse, what if he broke out? She'd lost count of the number of jails that had tried to contain Frank Beesom and failed. She knew without a doubt as soon as he gained his freedom, he'd hightail it back to Rogan and give up her whereabouts to stay in the man's good graces.

"I'll see that Con makes it home for dinner tonight," Bart said, interrupting her thoughts. "I suspect he'll need a good meal and pleasant company after spending the afternoon with Beesom."

Katherine didn't fool herself on that account. Once Connor learned he'd been housing the wife of Rogan Slade, her company would be the last thing he wanted.

She plastered a bright smile on her face and loosened the grip she had on the sides of her skirt. "That would be nice. I'll be sure and make up something special."

If things didn't go in her favor, it may be the last decent meal she'd have for a good long time.

~

"Good afternoon, Sheriff. How's that housekeeper of yours working out?"

Connor tipped his hat at Mrs. Greevy as he left the street, taking the steps to his office in one leap. "Just fine, Mrs. Greevy," he answered, gritting his teeth together.

He settled his hat back on his head and quickly stepped into his office to avoid any further questioning on the subject. Seemed he could barely stick his head out the door without someone asking him that same question and hinting that perhaps he should change her status to one of a more permanent nature.

He was halfway to his desk when he realized his seat was occupied. He stopped, the tune he'd been whistling abruptly cut off.

Ed Devers sat behind the desk, his feet propped up on the corner while he leafed through a pile of Wanted posters. His duster lay in a heap by the chair.

"Afternoon, Con."

Connor nodded at his old friend. It had been months since they'd crossed paths. They'd met years earlier at the Lazy M Ranch in Arizona Territory, where they both ran cattle. The two had become friends, and after a while, when Ed decided it was time to move on and go back to bounty hunting, Connor had gone with him, restless and looking to put more distance between himself and the memories he'd left behind. In the time they rode together, Ed had proven to be a loyal friend. Outside of Bart and Amelia and their family, he was about the only other person Connor truly trusted.

When Connor got the news about Grant, it was Ed that promised to keep his ear to the ground and help track down any leads on Slade.

His gaze slipped to the form resting on the cot in the first cell. Whoever it was had his head dipped down as if in a doze. "Good to see you, Ed. What brings you by?"

"More like *who* brought me by." He set the leaflets down and wiggled the toe of his boot toward the cell. "Let me introduce you to the soon-to-be-extinct Mr. Frank Beesom."

Connor sauntered further into the office. "He of any interest to me?"

"The man runs with Slade. Thought you might have a thing or two to ask 'im."

Slade.

A violent need to retaliate against his brother's death tore through Connor's veins. His hands shook with the force of it. He curled his fingers into a fist and took several slow breaths. He wanted every member of the Slade Gang to pay for what they'd done to his brother. And if that payment turned out to be long, drawn out, and extremely painful, all the better.

Connor swallowed his need for vengeance like a bitter pill. Justice, he reminded himself. He sought justice. Anger lodged in his throat and he couldn't speak. All the things he wanted to say rushed through his mind.

He approached the cell slowly, taking a closer measure of the man behind the bars. Beesom sat with his legs stretched out on the narrow cot. Filthy boots, crossed at the ankle, rested on the thin wool blanket. The man appeared relaxed, as if the noose would never find its way around his neck.

"Beesom." Connor nodded at the man.

The man lifted his head and stared back at him. A snarl crept over his unshaven features, accentuating cold, beady eyes.

"What can you tell me about Rogan Slade?"

Beesom shrugged. "Never heard of 'im."

Connor flexed his fists. He wanted to reach through the bars and strangle the answers out of Beesom, but he had a sinking feeling it would do little good. Beesom would probably enjoy goading him to violence. His type usually thrived on it, and Connor refused to give him the satisfaction. He loosened his fists and crossed his arms over his chest.

"Where is he now?"

"Who?"

Aggravation twitched the muscles in his jaw. "Rogan Slade."

"Told you, I ain't never heard of the man, so I don't rightly know where he'd be."

Ed's boots dropped to the wide-planked flooring and he pushed himself out of the chair to face the cell. His hand rested against the six-shooter strapped to his hip.

"You want me to shoot him? I can put one in his leg. Maybe then he'll be more amenable to answering your questions."

The offer was tempting, but Connor shook his head. "Not right now." He forced a grin he didn't feel. "Maybe later."

Beesom eased himself off the cot and sauntered toward the bars. The stench of stale tobacco and sweat wafted through the heavy air. He stopped just out of Connor's reach and sank his hands deep into the front pockets of his worn wool trousers.

"Things might go easier for you in Baker if you answer my questions," Connor said. "I can put in a word for you with the judge."

"And what?" Beesom turned his head and spat. "I'll be a little less dead? I'm gonna swing. Ain't nothin' gonna change that and we both know it. You got nothin' to bargain with."

The tang of bitterness left a bad taste in Connor's mouth. Beesom wouldn't help. The man had no incentive and nothing left to lose. A sinking helplessness clenched his guts.

Ed turned to Connor, hope lighting his eyes. "You sure you don't want me to shoot him? 'Cause I can take him in dead or alive. It don't matter none to the folks in Baker."

Connor stared at Frank Beesom. The man's eyes were cold and hard. The temptation to put a gun to the outlaw's head and pull the trigger was strong. But what would that do? Unlike Rogan Slade, he couldn't just kill someone and walk away like it meant nothing. Beesom would die soon enough.

"You want me to talk? How's about you bring back that pretty lil' redhead you had in here earlier?" Beesom leaned closer to the bars. "I think maybe another look at her is jus' what I need."

Connor's gaze snapped to Ed. "What redhead?"

"Nice lady," Ed said to Connor. Then he sneered at Beesom. "And she sure as hell wouldn't have anything to do with the likes of you." He turned back to Connor. "Bart said she's your new housekeeper."

Beesom snorted. "Is that what they're calling it these days?"

Connor lost his battle with his will. His arm shot through the bars and grabbed the front of Beesom's wool jacket. With a swift jerk he yanked the man against his bars, feeling a sense of satisfaction as the outlaw's forehead cracked against hard steel. Beesom staggered back onto the bed, cursing.

Ed leaned closer to the bars and snickered. "Nice."

Connor ignored the praise. "Kate was here? With Jenny?"

Without waiting for an answer, he spun on his heel and stalked to the door, jerking it open. It flew back and hit the wall with a resounding slam.

Katherine pushed the hot iron over the wrinkles in Connor's shirt and hummed a quiet tune, one she remembered her mother often sang before the music went out of her. Funny how despair could do that to a person; rob them of so much joy they couldn't even work up the gumption to hum. Maybe if she kept singing, things wouldn't seem so all-fired bad. Maybe the worrisome sickness eating its way through her middle would go away, and Frank Beesom would make it all the way to Baker and hang, her whereabouts dying with him.

And maybe pigs would fly past the moon at midnight.

She set the iron on its end. Closing her eyes, she dug her fingers into the small of her back and stretched. What if she was wrong? What if Beesom gave her up? Her chance to make amends would come to a staggering halt.

Blast that man! Why couldn't he have stayed hidden in a cave somewhere? And blast Grant Langston for jumping in front of that bullet. Why did he have to save her? It seemed a wasted effort. She was no good at all this lying business, and what did she know about fixing little girls with broken hearts? It would have been best for all concerned if she had been the one to die that day.

But she hadn't.

Her gratefulness over Grant's heroic deed tangled with her guilt until she didn't know where one left off and the other began. All she knew was she had to keep her promise. Otherwise, Grant Langston would have died for nothing. She couldn't allow that to be his legacy. Or hers.

Katherine opened her eyes. "Oh!"

Connor stood silently in the doorway staring at her, his eyes a stormy blue. After several heartbeats, he walked into the room and lowered his weight to the corner of the kitchen table, crossing his arms.

"You scared me. I didn't hear you," she said.

"You seemed lost in thought." A hardness altered his features, like a bitter wind blowing in across the plains.

She shivered despite the warmth from the stove. "I guess I was." She tried to read him. Did he know? Had Frank given her up? She couldn't tell. A curtain had dropped over his expression.

"I heard you were in town today." He lifted his hand to his jaw. Long fingers rubbed the stubble on his chin in slow steady strokes.

Katherine swallowed. He knew. He must. She could feel his anger sizzling in the air, see it in his tightly controlled movements. Would he haul her off now and throw her into the cell next to Frank, thinking she had some part in his brother's murder? The idea of sharing space with that man curdled her insides.

"Y-yes, I needed to get—"

"You went to my office?"

Her skin prickled. The need to run overwhelmed her.

Maybe she should throw herself on Connor's mercy. Make him see that she didn't know what she was getting into, marrying Rogan. She had been young and scared and desperate. If she could go back and change things, she would. Oh Lord, how she would.

"Connor..." She forced a smile she didn't feel, a sad attempt to charm. "Let me explain. I—I know Mr. Hewitt told you that my family owned a restaurant and yes, I went along—"

His hand cut sideways through the air and his eyes blazed. "Just answer my question—did you or did you not take Jenny into town?"

Katherine blinked. Jenny? What did Jenny have to do with this? An ember of hope flared to life, touched by the gentle breeze of possible reprieve. "I beg your pardon?"

"Are you hard of hearing, Miss Stockdale?"

Miss Stockdale. Not Slade. Her breath caught. Had Frank kept his miserable mouth shut?

I don't know spit about no Slade.

She prayed Frank Beesom's sense of self-preservation, his

denial he knew anything about Rogan Slade, would be her saving grace. Her heartbeat slowed to almost normal.

"No," she swallowed, "I hear just fine."

"Then answer my question."

"Yes, I took Jenny into town."

He nodded, an agitated jerk of his head.

"Jenny needed—"

He pushed away from the table and came around the ironing board, stopping in front of her. "Jenny needed to be protected and I trusted you to do that. You had no business taking her to my office. That's no place for a little girl, especially with—"

"I never had her anywhere near your office!"

"What?"

"I left her with Amelia while I delivered the basket of food. How could you think I would take her there?" She swatted a hand at his chest. Connor grabbed it and held tight.

His eyes bore into her, searching. She wanted to look away but his eyes held her mesmerized. Warm breath brushed her skin and sent little ripples of sensation skipping down her spine. Another inch and her body would be flush against his.

The air around them sparked like lightning bugs on a clear summer's night.

His hold on her hand loosened. "She wasn't at the office?"

Katherine shook her head. "No. I would never take her there."

He had yet to step away. His closeness rattled her. If she just leaned in—

Footsteps echoed behind them and interrupted the direction of her thoughts. Jenny walked through the door and into the kitchen, lifting her feet high like a newborn colt.

Connor relinquished his hold on Katherine and half turned. She had a close view of his chiseled profile. Confusion turned to comprehension as he stared down at Jenny's feet.

"I bought her new shoes today," Katherine explained. "Her old pair didn't fit. That's why she was always running around barefoot. I took her into town to buy a new pair."

Connor paled. For a moment he said nothing, then, "I should have known that. I should have seen it." Guilt smothered his tone, keeping his voice barely above a whisper.

Jenny marched across the kitchen, the steady clomp, clomp, clomp of her new shoes resonating through the room. Connor flinched with each step.

Sympathy tightened Katherine's throat. "How could you have known? I've been here nearly three weeks and I just realized it this morning."

Connor shook his head. "I should have known. Grant would have."

Katherine didn't know what to say, what words would reach past the gnawing sense of failure riddling his handsome features. He seemed lost.

She placed a hand on his arm, the only bit of comfort she had to give. The only bit she thought he would accept. "I'll see to supper," she said.

He nodded, but she wasn't sure he heard her. A moment later the door shut again, and when she peered out the small window over the counter, Connor was halfway to the barn, his long strides carrying him swiftly over the beaten path.

Chapter Eleven

C onnor did not return for supper. Instead, he hid out in the barn, doing mindless chores until the lights in the house dimmed and he knew Kate and Jenny had turned in.

He'd never considered himself a yellow-bellied coward, but he could not bring himself to face Kate. He'd behaved like an ass, accusing her without first hearing her out, automatically assuming the worst of her. He should have known she'd never drag Jenny into his office. She'd shown nothing but the greatest concern for his niece. Lord only knew she was a far cry better at the job than he'd proven to be. Hell, he hadn't even noticed Jenny needed new shoes.

If he had any sense at all, he'd leave Jenny with Bart and Amelia and hightail it out of Fatal Bluff. The idea slithered up from a dark corner of his mind on a regular basis. He ignored it now as he had every other time. Regardless of how bad he was at the job, he couldn't bring himself to abandon the little girl. She'd already lost too much for him to take away the one person she had left. Even if that person was an abysmal failure when it came to filling her father's shoes.

When he finally slunk back to the house, all was quiet.

Connor glanced at the closed bedroom door and tried not to think of Kate, curled up on the soft feather mattress, her hair fanned out against his pillow. He pulled his boots off and tossed them aside with a muttered curse. He spent way too much energy avoiding thoughts of his pretty housekeeper.

Connor shrugged off his shirt and flung it over the back of the sofa before crawling beneath the quilt and trying to find a comfortable position. He missed his bed. It was a sad thing to admit. He'd spent the past eight years sleeping in one bunk after another, or out under the stars, but six months back home had softened him. He longed for the comforts he'd quickly become reacquainted with, and others he wished to—

No! Connor flopped over onto his side, hoping the sudden movement would dislodge the unwelcome thoughts. He didn't need that sort of entanglement. One slip, one lapse in judgment and no doubt Kate would haul him kicking and screaming to the altar. She had come to Fatal Bluff to get married, after all. He needed to remember that.

Sleep proved an elusive bedmate. Though exhaustion slowly claimed his body, his mind refused to rest. Worse, it refused to let go of the image of Kate's face only inches from his own as he berated her, those delectable lips pursed into an angry line. He had grabbed her hand to prevent her from leaving before he had his say, and it took all of his willpower not to scoop her up in his arms and kiss her senseless. To peel away the layers of clothing that separated them.

Dammit! His body went hard just thinking about her. He surged up from the sofa, wrapping the quilt around his shoulders to ward off the chill.

Walk it off. Just walk it off.

He paced the room, eventually stopping near the back window. Clouds smothered the stars and covered the moon, which burned a hazy glow through the mist, giving just enough light to cast the room in shadows. He leaned against the wall that separated the bedroom from the main room. He wasn't sure how much more of this madness he was expected to endure. He had to do something. He had to figure out a way to—

He stopped. What was that?

His body stilled, his senses attuned to the sound he'd heard.

It came again. Muffled, but unmistakable. The sound pierced a part of his heart he thought dead and gone. He rubbed a hand over his chest. The quilt slipped off his shoulders and puddled on the floor at his feet.

What now?

The sob rent the air again, louder this time, shuddering through him.

Damn.

Should he just pretend he didn't hear it? Crawl back to the sofa and bury his head beneath the blankets until it passed? Connor glanced down the length of the wall to the door. Another sob ripped at his insides.

You were an ass. That's why she's crying. This is your fault.

The accusation rushed at him. The sob grew louder. Hell, at this rate he'd have a full-fledged wail on his hands in no time. His gaze shot across the room to Jenny's bedroom door. It was closed, but his niece had proven to be a light sleeper. The last thing he wanted was her popping out of bed, worried or upset because Kate had decided to have herself a good cry.

Connor inched his way to the door and gently touched a hand to the door knob. "Kate?"

Silence.

He rested his head against the door. Tension eased out of his shoulders.

There. That was simple.

His smugness was short-lived as another sob broke through the hush and cut the night air.

Connor pressed a hand over his face and groaned but it wasn't loud enough to drown out her crying. God, the sound was pitiful. It made his chest ache. How had it come to this? Just seven months ago he had lived a life of freedom, worried about nobody but himself. Now here he was, back home in Fatal Bluff with two females to contend with and not the first clue how to do it. One was too silent, the other too dangerous.

He sighed and reached for the doorknob. The smooth brass was cool beneath his palm. With great reluctance he twisted it, a bit surprised when it opened. She hadn't locked him out. Probably hadn't felt the need to. Connor guessed come morning she'd have a different view on that.

The hinges creaked, cutting off her cry mid-sob.

"Kate?" Her back was to him, her arm hugged around the pillow. His pillow. He eased the door open a little further. Strands of misty moonlight spilled across the bed. He closed his eyes. It'd be fine if he didn't have to look at her. "Are you okay? I heard you crying."

She sniffed, and for a moment he thought she wouldn't answer. When she did, her hoarse voice betrayed her. "I wasn't crying."

His eyes snapped opened at the bald-faced lie and he stepped further into the room, finding the lamp on the bureau. Fumbling for the matches, he lit the wick and turned it down low until a faint glow chased away the darkness.

"I heard you."

She pulled away from the pillow just enough to glare over her shoulder at him.

Loose curls splayed over the stark whiteness of the pillowcase and trailed away from her like gold and red streamers caught in a gentle breeze. The blankets pooled about her waist, revealing a plain cotton nightdress that had slipped down, exposing the warm curve of her shoulder. Good Lord, she was more beautiful than anybody had a right to be. Her scent drifted up to taunt him.

Connor swallowed, barricading his heart against the onslaught of unwanted emotion that made his hand twitch to reach out and run along the exposed line of her collarbone, or trace the dangerously low, scooped neckline where several buttons had come loose of their moorings. The memory of her naked in the tub resurrected itself with a vengeance.

His fingers folded into his palm and he crossed his arms over his chest, realizing his shirt remained slung over the back of the sofa. Damn. He shouldn't be here.

"Go away," she whispered, echoing his thoughts. "I'm fine."

"Your crying is going to wake Jenny."

She suddenly seemed more alert. She pulled herself up. "Did I wake her?"

"I didn't say you woke her, I said you would if you kept crying."

"I was not crying."

Shadows flickered over the thin material of her nightdress, outlining the curves beneath it. The opening at the neck gaped and he could see the gentle swell of her breasts.

"Jesus," he whispered, slapping a hand over his eyes. The silhouette of her small, perfectly rounded breasts seared into the back of his lids so there was no escaping the image.

He had to get out of there. It was sheer insanity to stay. He tried to move his feet, but the limbs remained rooted to the spot.

"You may want to, uh—" he cleared his throat and waved his hand in her general direction, "—cover yourself up."

A soft gasp reached his ears and his insides somersaulted and twisted themselves into knots. He waited a moment before sliding two fingers apart to peer through them. Kate had pulled the quilt up and tucked it under her arms, her belligerent chin jutting into the air.

She narrowed her gaze, her green eyes almost disappearing into slits. "Satisfied?"

Not nearly, he thought, but kept it to himself.

"I'm fine. Sorry if I disturbed you," she said.

Disturbed didn't even begin to cover the effect she had on him.

"You can leave now."

Except his legs still wouldn't move. "You wanna tell me what turned on the waterworks?"

One shoulder lifted in a shrug. She dropped her gaze, fingering the design on the quilt. The edge of the nightgown came perilously close to dropping over her shoulder once again. Like the rest of her things, it seemed made for someone much larger.

"Was it about your parents?" He hated the hopeful note that entered his voice, the pathetic desire that maybe he wasn't responsible after all.

She shook her head.

"Are you worried about the money you owe the Hewitts?"

Mr. Hewitt told you that my family owned a restaurant and yes, I went along with it.

He crinkled his brow. He'd heard it when she'd said it, but he had been too wrapped up in his own anger for it to register then. Now it rattled around in his head, demanding his attention.

What had she meant by that? Had Oliver concocted some story to make one of his brides more appealing? It didn't make sense. A man like Walter Figg wouldn't have given two licks about his bride's background. He just wanted someone to cook his meals and warm his bed.

Connor moved to the bed and sat down.

"What are you doing?"

"Looking for answers," he said, taking her arm. She tried to pull away but she was no match for his strength. He turned her arm over in his hand, much as he had that day in the garden. No burn scars. Not one. Nor did she seem to have any idea of the actual date the fire occurred and her family perished. How could she not?

"Get off the bed!" Katherine kicked from beneath the blanket, her foot hitting his hip. He grabbed her leg, winding his hand around her ankle, while his brain worked to wind around the growing inconsistencies he had forced himself to ignore. Until now.

"Quiet down, you'll wake, Jenny," he admonished her, feeling only a small prick of conscience at using his niece to silence Kate.

"I'll wake the whole town if you think for one minute I'm just going to fall back on the sheets and let you have your way!" She tried to dislodge her leg from his grip but his fingers tightened.

"While your assessment of my character is less than flattering, I can assure you, I'm not in the habit of forcing myself on women." She had the chagrin to blush at least a little. "Answer this—you said you went along with Oliver when he said your parents owned a restaurant. What did you mean?"

K atherine squirmed. How she wished she had kept her mouth shut. When she looked up, her gaze collided with Connor's and then quickly skidded away, unable to spar with the intensity found in their depths.

"You were angry and I just...I just..." Her words trailed off. She just what? She had no suitable answer and she was too tired to make up another lie.

He studied her, saying nothing. Seconds passed. The clock

on the bureau ticked out a static beat. "Is it the truth? Did your parents own a restaurant?"

She evaded the question with one of her own. "Why would I lie?"

Connor shrugged and shook his head, his eyes boring into her, searching for answers. "There's something you're not telling me."

"I expect there's a lot I'm not telling you. We barely know each other."

"Then enlighten me."

Katherine picked at a loose thread jutting up from one of the colorful squares of the quilt. The room lapsed into silence. She thought of any number of scenarios she could concoct to keep him from discovering the truth, but she knew he'd see right through them for the lies they were.

The pressure on her ankle ceased and for a fleeting second, Katherine knew a sense of relief and loss. It didn't last long. His calloused hand encompassed hers. Strong fingers wrapped around and pressed into her palm. Heat swept through her body.

"Look at me," he commanded, his voice soft but firm, tripping over her nerves like a feather tickling her skin.

Katherine shook her head, her attention riveted to the hand holding hers. She knew better than to look up into those eyes. They had a way of confusing the issue, making her forget herself. They had captivated her the first time Walter Figg threw her into Connor's arms, and every time since. It was dangerous territory. Whenever she looked into those eyes, she had the urge to blurt out the truth.

"You shouldn't be here. I can't—" She stopped. "Please, just go."

A coyote wailed in the distance, a high, mournful sound that shattered the still night. A wave of helplessness stole over her.

"You can't what?"

I can't have you touch me. I can't stand that I want to touch you back.

She should tell him to go, but every fiber of her being wanted him to stay. Madness had invaded her senses and taken over.

"Nothing," she said, and shook her head. Several curls fell forward, partially blocking her view of him. It didn't help. His presence coiled its way around her, encompassing her in a cozy cocoon she feared she wouldn't be able to break out of. Or didn't want to.

"Kate, look at me."

She started as he tucked his fingertips beneath her chin, forcing her to meet his gaze. His touch branded her skin, but it was the tenor of his voice that was her undoing.

Her heart pounded with such ferocity she feared it would explode. His gentleness startled her. How long had it been since someone had taken her hand in a gentle embrace and simply held it? How long since someone touched her face in a caress? Tears stung her eyes. Too long? Never?

But now was not the time, and this was not the man. The truth wouldn't allow it. Her husband had killed his brother, left Jenny locked up in her grief. If Connor knew, he would hate her, toss her out in the middle of the night, or worse, haul her off to jail to face a judge, figuring she had a part in it. He would not be sitting here at her bedside, his touch inciting a riot within her she couldn't quell.

She should have never come here. Never promised a dying man she'd make things right. It was too hard. It hurt too much.

She couldn't hide the truth forever. Sooner or later it would come out. If Beesom didn't talk, or the real Hannah Stockdale didn't eventually show up, then likely she would trip herself up and Connor would catch her in one of the many lies she had told since she arrived here. And then what? Already she teetered on the edge. He knew she was hiding something, that she had secrets. But oh, the destruction that truth would bring once it was revealed. The pain her secrets would cause.

Tears rushed back and poured over her lashes. Katherine twisted her head and tried to turn away, mortified by the moisture cascading down her face, yet unable to staunch the flow.

She let go of the quilt long enough to swipe the back of her hand over her cheeks, her movement forcing him to drop his hold on her chin. She hadn't cried since her mama died. Now it seemed she couldn't stop, as if a dam had burst inside of her.

"Tell me what's wrong." Something elemental blazed in the depth of his eyes, creating a light of their own that burned brighter than the moon.

A strangled sob burst from inside, harsh and bitter. She fought to find a reasonable explanation that would satisfy him. "What's wrong? What could possibly be right? I'm in a strange town, surrounded by people I don't know. I owe money to a couple who have threatened to haul me before a judge if I don't pay it back. I don't have a penny to my name and no one to turn to."

The muscle in his jaw flinched. He glanced at the door. No doubt he wished he'd left her alone. Yet every inch of her wanted him to stay, to gather her in his arms and tell her everything would be okay. She didn't care if it was a lie. She just needed to hear the words.

He did none of those things.

"You're not alone," he said. "You have...me, and you have Jenny."

"I work for you, that's all."

He didn't correct her, a silent omission that cut her to the core. "And because of that you'll have some money in your pocket and be able to pay off Oliver Hewitt."

"And then what?" The question popped out and lingered in the air between them. Katherine studied him, taking in every detail of his face, the straight nose and steady gaze, the way his hair flipped out slightly at the ends, the stubble that shadowed his jaw.

"What do you want?" he asked.

You, her pesky heart whispered. *I want you*. But those were words she could never say.

"I want to repay Mr. Hewitt, then I'll be on my way."

What other choice did she have? Staying much longer in Fatal Bluff, in this house, could only result in her ruin.

"Where will you go?"

"I don't know." Her mind didn't stretch that far into the future. She'd spent too long living day by day.

An array of emotions traveled across Connor's features. She couldn't read any of them, save for a hint of loneliness. That one she recognized. She saw it every time she looked in a mirror. Somehow, having it reflected back at her in this way was far different. A knifing pain cut through her heart. This wasn't how it was supposed to be.

He shook his head and stared at her. "Who are you, Kate Stockdale?"

A ripple of dread danced across each nerve in her body. Her heart pounded inside her chest with deafening blows. She couldn't lie to him. And she couldn't tell him the truth.

"Nobody," she whispered. "I'm nobody."

His grip loosened and she pulled her hand away. The tips of his fingers grazed her flesh, sending tiny pinpricks of sensation shooting up her arm.

He didn't believe her. She could see it even beneath the mask. The concern he'd shown earlier vanished, replaced by suspicion and mistrust. Tears burned her eyes but she blinked them back.

Connor stood and stared down at her. Moonlight cascaded over his bronzed chest and the lamplight danced shadows across the corded muscles in his shoulders.

"This conversation isn't over." He turned and walked to the door. She wanted to call him back. Suddenly the prospect of his leaving made the loneliness and desperation choke her. But she couldn't. She'd made her bed, now she had to lie in it. Alone. "Get some sleep. We'll talk more in the morning."

"There's nothing more to talk about," she said.

"I disagree." She had no chance to protest. The door shut behind him.

For several long moments, Katherine stared at the rudimentary carvings on the oak door until her eyes burned and she closed her lids.

Chapter Twelve

Connor hesitated outside the door to Oliver Hewitt's office, trying to convince himself he was not out of line. He had the right to know everything he could about the woman who lived under his roof, caring for his niece.

He knew she was lying to him; he just couldn't get her to admit it. He had tried to raise the subject again this morning, but she became as tight-lipped and evasive as any outlaw he'd come up against. Hell, he had a better chance of cracking Frank Beesom before he got Kate to fess up about why everything about her seemed to contradict what he had been told by Hewitt. And it didn't help any that Jenny was glued to her side. He didn't want to have the conversation in front of his niece. He didn't want to upset her. But he had to know the truth.

With a sense of righteousness wrapped around his conscience, Connor pushed the door open and stepped inside.

Oliver glanced up from the papers scattered about his large mahogany desk. He removed the spectacles perched on the end of his bulbous nose and leaned back, surprised. The leather chair creaked as his ample frame shifted between the armrests.

Despite the oppressive heat outside, Oliver wore a fancy wool suit, fit with all the flashy trimmings of a man trying to remind everyone of his worth. It never made much sense to Connor. A fancy waistcoat or shiny cufflinks couldn't replace a lack of character, no matter how much money you paid for them. A quick scan around the office with its expensive furnishings and ostentatious design told Connor that was a lesson this businessman had never learned.

Oliver pressed his fingertips together and rested them beneath his layer of chins. "Sheriff Langston, what a nice surprise. What can I do for you this afternoon?"

Connor cleared his throat. Now that he was here, the conscience he had successfully silenced outside the door needled him once again. What did Kate's past matter? She didn't plan on staying. She said so herself. She would repay the Hewitts and leave town. But to where?

And why did the idea of her going anywhere leave him with a sick, empty feeling?

He pushed the thought aside. Buried it down deep with all the other things he didn't like to think about. It barely fit. The space had become rather crowded.

"Sheriff?"

Connor bit down on his emotions. "What do you know about Kate Stockdale?"

Oliver blinked and lowered his hands to his desk, splaying his fingers over the papers. "Kate?"

"I mean Hannah."

"Stockdale?"

"Yes."

"The bride?"

Connor's patience snapped. "Yes, Oliver, the bride! The

woman you brought here and tried to foist off on Walter Figg. *That* Hannah Stockdale."

"Well pardon me, Sheriff, if I seem confused," Oliver said, puffing his chest out with indignation. "But you called her Kate. I can't be blamed if you can't keep your housekeeper's name straight."

Connor pulled off his hat and gripped the stiff brim with his fingers to keep from reaching across the desk and doing something similar to Oliver's fleshy neck. "She said most people call her Kate. From her middle name, Kathleen. Now what do you know about this woman?"

Oliver scrunched his face up. "I know her middle name isn't Kathleen. It's Elizabeth. Hannah Elizabeth Stockdale."

An uncomfortable chill swept over Connor's bones. He forced himself to remain expressionless. "What else?"

"She's from Dodge City in Kansas. Only daughter of Maureen and William Stockdale who perished in a fire almost two years past."

"Maureen?"

"Yes."

"Not Hannah?"

"No, Hannah is Hannah." Oliver drummed his fingers again and the sound reverberated through the stillness of the room, thrumming in concert with Connor's pulse. "Sheriff, have you been drinking?"

"What? No!" One whiskey was hardly enough to addle his brain. One Kate Stockdale, on the other hand—well, that was an entirely different matter. "I'm just trying to get the facts straight."

"Why all the questions, Sheriff? Perhaps you're rethinking my offer to marry her, hmm? The discounted commission still stands. A special rate for such a dedicated lawman." A wolfish smile spread across the man's face.

Connor gritted his teeth. "No, Oliver. I am merely inquiring after her character."

Oliver's smile faded. "Why in heaven's name would you hire her when you can marry her and get her for free?"

"Save for your commission, of course."

"Of course," he answered with an oily grin.

"Just tell me what you know."

Oliver grumbled and yanked open a side drawer on his desk, fishing around inside until he found a small packet of letters. "Guess you can take these. They were for Mr. Figg, but they're no use to him now. Man can't read anyway."

Connor took the offered letters, three in all, and turned them over in his hand. The faint scent of roses drifted up to tickle his nose. Other than that, the small pink envelopes gave nothing away, save for the feminine scrawl addressed to Walter Figg, care of Oliver Hewitt.

"What are these?" He flapped the letters.

"Letters Miss Stockdale sent. We exchanged correspondence before the lady—" Oliver made a face, clearly indicating he used the term loosely, "—decided to make the trip from Kansas to marry Mr. Figg."

Connor tucked the letters into the breast pocket of his shirt and settled his hat on his head. The letters burned through the cotton material and he marvelled the badge pinned on his chest didn't melt and ooze down the front of his shirt.

"Obliged." He nodded.

"You'll let me know if you change your mind on marrying her, Sheriff?"

Connor ignored the man's parting comment, shutting the door behind him with more force than necessary and made his way back to the office.

"Where you been? Lunch is here."

Bart's words greeted Connor as he walked through the

door. He left it open, in the hopes a small breeze might find its way into the room and freshen the stale air polluted by Beesom's unwashed stench. If he didn't think the prisoner would make a break for it, he would dunk him in the nearest trough.

"Had to talk to Oliver."

Bart bit into a piece of succulent roast pork. Amelia made sure the two of them had at least one hearty meal delivered each day, and Connor knew if he didn't grab his when it arrived, Bart would plow through the two plates in short order. For a small man, he sure ate a lot.

Connor flipped up the gingham cloth covering. One plate still remained.

Bart winked. "Got here just in the nick of time, son." He sucked the grease off the end of his fingers with a loud smacking noise.

"Why don't you go on over and see that wife of yours for a spell?" Connor needed time alone to digest what Oliver had told him.

Bart stuffed a last piece of biscuit into his mouth and stared at Connor while he chewed.

"Guess I could do that," he said. He eased his old bones out of the chair and stretched. "Maybe she's got some tasty treat for me." Bart wiggled his bushy brow and chuckled, leading Connor to think it wasn't food he was hoping to find when he arrived at the boardinghouse.

Bart walked around the desk and fetched his hat from the hook on the wall. "I'll stop by the post office on my way back," he said. "Maybe Doby has somethin' new for us. Ed says Nate Thompson was gonna pay a visit to the stagecoach office in Mercury, see if he couldn't scare something up on this mystery woman. Maybe he's sent word."

"Maybe." Nate was one of the network of bounty hunters helping him track down the Slade Gang. Connor slid into the empty chair behind his desk and pulled the plate from the basket.

He didn't hold out much hope. News on the woman had proven scarce and the few eye witness accounts of her remained vague. She'd kept herself covered from head to toe, leaving little to remember. He wondered if she was purposely trying to disguise herself. It made Ed's theory more plausible. Maybe Slade *had* been after the woman.

It made sense. Stagecoaches weren't Slade's style. Banks or trains were more to his liking. About the only thing consistent with Slade's behavior that day was when he killed everyone in sight.

Everyone except the woman.

A woman his brother had been intent on protecting.

But why? Had she needed protection from Slade? And why had she disappeared?

Connor couldn't shake the sense there was more to this woman than met the eye. But before he could unravel that conundrum, he had his own mystery woman to deal with.

His stomach rumbled. Connor set aside the letters and dispatched his hunger. For all he knew, he wouldn't have much of an appetite left once he finished perusing the contents of the pink envelopes.

It took only a few minutes to make short work of the roast pork, cheese and biscuits. Connor pushed the empty plate aside and reached for the letters. A hint of rose still clung to the envelopes. Strange, he didn't recall Kate ever smelling like roses.

"Letters from your sweetheart, Sheriff? Ain't that sweet."

Connor scowled. Frank Beesom had raised his sorry ass off the thin cot and pressed his face through the bars, one hand gripping them on either side.

"Shut up, Beesom. Unless you've got something to tell me

about Slade, I'm not interested in listening to you yammer on."

Beesom clucked his tongue. "Now, is that any way to treat a guest?"

"Keep it up and I might just rethink my decision to let Devers take you in dead rather than alive."

The man chuckled, a cold, derisive sound that scraped over Connor's nerves like the jagged blade of a rusty knife. "Don't get too cozy with the idea of me getting planted in the bone orchard. I ain't dead yet." He walked back into the cell and leaned against the stone wall. "And I ain't planning to be any time soon."

Ed had told him on his first day that there hadn't been a jail made yet that could hold Beesom. Every time he'd been caught, he managed to escape. The news only fired Connor's determination that it wouldn't happen on his watch. He'd hired a few extra deputies to keep an eye on the prisoner through the night and he rarely ventured far from his office when he was in town. If Beesom thought he was going to escape, he'd find himself on the business end of a bullet before he reached the town limits.

With an aggravated growl, Connor slipped the envelopes into the back pocket of his denims. He would read them later, at a time when Frank Beesom wasn't heckling him from his cell, disturbing his thoughts.

He had plenty of time to unravel the mystery of his new housekeeper. With the money she owed to the Hewitts, she had to stay with him until at least month end. He smiled. For now at least, she wasn't going anywhere.

K atherine set the picnic basket down next to the thick trunk of a cottonwood and handed Jenny one of the fishing poles she'd found in the barn. She needed a break, a diversion that would get her out of the house and away from the confusion whirling like a tempest inside of her. Last night had nearly been her undoing, having Connor in her bedroom half-naked asking his infernal questions while the moonlight glistened off his muscled chest.

Katherine pinched the bridge of her nose, trying desperately to rid her mind of the image. She didn't want it there. Didn't want the insufferable ache that invaded her insides every time she thought of it.

"Jenny, have you ever hooked a worm before?" Her forced cheerfulness trilled brightly over the gurgle of the creek flowing down from the bluff. Just on the other side, a steep rock face jutted into the sky, rivaling the redwoods for supremacy. Shards of sunlight cut through the trees and slashed the ground around them. It was a beautiful afternoon. A perfect day to beg off from chores and go fishing.

Jenny's small fingers dug through the tin of dirt they'd brought with them and scooped up a fat worm. Katherine steeled herself for the job ahead. This was the part she hated.

"Sorry worm, looks like today's your last day." She winced as she hooked it, then quickly cast the line into the water and handed the pole to Jenny. She did the same with her own and the two settled down on the shaded grass.

Katherine leaned against the boulder next to her and reached down with one hand to loosen the ties on her boots. Within moments, she had kicked them free and draped her stockings carelessly over the rock. Grass tickled the bottom of her feet, the cool ground wonderfully decadent. Jenny copied her movements and tossed her new boots behind her away from the water.

It didn't take long before Jenny's line tugged and the girl's eyes widened. The threat of a smile dimpled the corners of her mouth. Katherine shimmied over next to her and helped pull the first trout out of the creek. Several more followed, and by midday the covered basket submerged at the creek's edge held four trout.

"We've managed to catch our supper, Jenny. Isn't that something? I'll bet your uncle will be surprised." Drat. She hadn't meant to think about him this afternoon. She gritted her teeth and stood. "Hungry?"

Jenny looked up and nodded.

It pleased Katherine to no end that the little girl was becoming more responsive with each passing day. Gone were the blank stares and that dead-eyed sorrowful look that sliced through Katherine's heart like a hundred tiny daggers.

"That's good. Because I packed a big lunch. Ham, biscuits, apple pie, some of those pickled beets you like." Katherine laid an old quilt on the ground and set the picnic basket on top. All around them tufts of wildflowers grew in colorful bunches and filled the air with their sweet scent. If there was a prettier place in the entire world, Katherine couldn't think where it might be. Jenny had picked the perfect spot.

They enjoyed their picnic, making short work of their provisions. By the end of it, Jenny's face and hands were stained with beet juice.

"I think you need a bath, sweetie." Along with lunch, Katherine had packed a cake of lavender soap and towels. The creek had much more elbow room than the hip bath. Not to mention less chance of Connor wandering in unexpectedly while she tried to bathe. No doubt he was in town, questioning Frank Beesom. Her stomach churned at the thought. The only comfort she found was in the fact that Beesom could not reveal who she was without linking himself to Slade, something he would never do. People who gave up information on her husband had a nasty way of turning up dead. And Beesom had always had a predilection toward self-preservation. That alone might be the only thing that saved her while they held him in that jail cell.

Jenny picked up one of the towels and motioned with her arm, skipping further downstream. Katherine grabbed the cake of soap and hurried after her charge. Following the curve of the creek, Jenny stopped at a spot where the water calmed and sun shone straight down onto the gentle pool.

They threw modesty to the wind, stripped down to their underthings and ran in. The cold water sent ripples of goose bumps over Katherine's skin, but she quickly acclimated. Jenny paddled in a circle, dunking herself underwater and bobbing back up with a shake of her head. She had no fear of the water. Somewhere along the way, someone had taught her to swim. Her father, perhaps? A cloud of guilt loomed. Katherine dunked her head, letting the cool water wash it away. Nothing was going to darken her afternoon.

"Oh! Sorry, ma'am!"

Katherine spun around at the sound of a gruff voice at her back. Her arm reached out to shield Jenny and pull her behind her. A man stood on the bank, his arm thrown over his eyes. Raggedy clothes hung off a bone-thin frame and grizzled hair brushed his shoulders. A large dog, whose gray fur mirrored the state of the man, sat next to him, his tongue lolling out the side of his mouth.

Katherine sank lower in the water and held Jenny firm. The little girl squirmed, trying to see around her. "W—what do you want?"

"Don't mean to intrude, ma'am. Surely I don't. You mus' be that new housekeeper Holkum talked about."

"I—yes."

"Name's Eli Gillis. I live up the bluff a ways. Jus' tryin' to rummage up some grub is all. Can you help an ole man out?"

Katherine's heart pounded in her chest with such force she expected ripples to appear in the water. Their clothes rested near the rock where the man stood.

He seemed harmless enough, even if his dog was the size of a small horse, but Katherine wasn't about to take any chances, especially not with Jenny. A breeze picked up and prickled her skin where her shoulders edged above the water.

"We have some fish," she said, trying to keep her voice strong and sure. "Down the creek a bit that way." She tilted her head in the direction they had come. "You're welcome to it."

Jenny huffed, obviously not happy with giving up their catch of the day.

"Hush," Katherine whispered.

"Much obliged, ma'am." He hesitated and Katherine held her breath. What more could he want? "Do you think...maybe you could take Rudy for payment?"

"Rudy?"

The dog let out a low pitiful whine. "I hate to do it ma'am, but my dog here...I cain't much look after 'im, but I hate like the dickens to turn him out into the wild. Maybe the sheriff could use 'im, what with two pretty ladies at home and him in town so much. Rudy'd make a great watchdog. Keep you safe, take care of lil' Jenny there." The man nodded in the direction where Jenny had been before Katherine hauled her behind her.

"I can't rightly say if the sheriff will be keen on the idea or not." She eyed the dog. The thing was huge. And dirty. Behind her she could feel Jenny nodding and poking her back.

"Well, I'll jus' leave 'im here, if'n you don't mind. If the sheriff don't want 'im, he can just send 'im back. Rudy'll find his way."

"Mr. Gillis, I don't think—"

"Rudy, you stay here." The man bent and gave the dog's head a rough pat.

"Mr. Gillis, we don't need—Jenny quit poking me!" Katherine tried to brush Jenny's hand from her ribs. When she looked back, the old mountain man had already reached the bend in the creek. "Mr. Gillis!"

Jenny swam around her and started for shore. Katherine grabbed for her drawers but the little girl was too quick. She was up and out of the water by the time Katherine had waded to her knees. "Jenny you get away from that dog right now. He's filthy and—"

Jenny came to an abrupt halt two feet from the dog and her face twisted into a comical expression as her hands waved the air around her. As Katherine drew nearer, she understood why.

"Oh dear Lord, that thing smells positively vile."

Rudy barked in response and Katherine would have sworn the dog actually smiled. She couldn't quite say for certain. She was too dazzled by another.

Jenny stood at the dog's side, her face beaming as she looked up at Katherine, hope stamped all over her features.

Katherine knew she should protest. She had tried Connor's patience enough without bringing this smelly beast home. But she couldn't tell Jenny no. She didn't have the heart to quash the joy lighting up her face.

"I guess we're keeping the dog."

Jenny's smile widened.

～

Leather creaked as Connor swung himself out of the saddle and surveyed the scene before him. He'd come to the spot where he and Grant had whiled away hours of their youth. It had been their special spot, a place they could go and escape the drudgery of chores or schoolwork.

Connor had come here to read the letters Oliver had given

him. Instead, he found the remnants of a picnic scattered around him. Fishing poles crisscrossed each other in the grass and two pairs of shoes littered the clearing. He recognized the ugly, scuffed boots that belonged to Kate resting near the creek's edge.

Connor swallowed the fear congealing in his guts. It left an acrid taste in his mouth. "Where are they?"

Old Man Gillis spun at the growled question. The basket of fish fell from his hands and landed with a splash. A trout plopped out and made a hasty escape back to the creek before Gillis slammed a hand down on the top.

"W-who?"

Just above Gillis, laid over the boulder, a pair of stockings caught the breeze. Unease prickled the hair on the back of his neck.

Don't panic. Don't panic. They were fine. Probably just gone for a walk.

Without their shoes. And stockings.

His fingers skimmed the holstered gun at his hip. "Where are Kate and Jenny?"

"I left 'em down the creek a bit, sheriff. I didn't hurt 'em, I jus' wanted some—"

Connor didn't wait to hear the rest of it. He took off at a run.

Chapter Thirteen

Connor didn't bother remounting his horse. He knew he could maneuver around the thick trees and roots much quicker on foot.

"Kate! Jenny!"

Fear spurred him on until he wasn't even sure his feet touched the ground. He tore past trees and shrubs, ripped through wildflowers and sent a posse of squirrels darting in three different directions. Nothing slowed him down. He rounded the bend. Water splashed in several directions. Connor reached for his gun belt and wrenched the buckle, dropping it to the ground. He didn't stop to think. Didn't stop to consider why Kate and Jenny were even in the water. It didn't matter.

But before he could reach the creek his foot landed in a thick patch of muck and flew out from beneath him. As he hit the ground, three things registered in his mind: a huge gray beast of a dog stood nearly chest high in the creek covered with suds. Kate barely had a stitch of clothing on, and what she did have clung to her wet skin revealing far more of her than he'd seen the previous night. And Jenny.

Jenny was smiling.

The air whooshed out of his lungs as he hit the ground. His feet landed in the creek, sending water and mud flying in several directions.

Connor blinked and swiped at the water dripping from his brow. If he hadn't already been on the ground, her smile would have knocked him flat. The wonder of it turned his heart over. He forgot the hard landing he'd just taken, and the dampness soaking through his denims.

His gaze flew to Kate. She gave a brief squeal and plopped down into the water, her arms flying to cover her breasts. He thought to tell her she was a little too late on that account—he'd already had an eyeful—but he couldn't get the words past the constriction in his throat.

The dog shook, ignorant of the mayhem surrounding him. Suds and water sprayed every which way. Jenny laughed and Connor's heart filled with joy until he thought it would overflow and flood the embankment.

Laughter.

Amazed, his glance flew to Kate again, then quickly skidded in the other direction.

Dammit. Her soaked underclothes afforded her little coverage.

Jenny giggled and pushed the dog toward the center of the creek. He went easily and swam around her in a circle, leaving a trail of soap suds in his wake. Jenny followed the animal and they made their way back to shore. The dog walked up and sniffed him, then shook once more. Too late, Connor fell onto his side and covered his head, the right side of his shirt soaked.

"Jenny?"

His niece stopped squeezing water from the bottom of her shift and looked over at him.

"What is *that?*" Connor pointed at the large gray beast.

Jenny smiled but didn't answer. It hardly mattered. Her

grin was like magic, dusting his heart with hope. He couldn't help but smile back.

It was Kate who answered. "*That* is Rudy. Mr. Gillis asked us to keep him."

Eli. Connor shook his head. He should have known.

He ventured another look at Kate. She remained submerged in the water. Her hair hung in torrents of wet curls. The ends floated around her, reminding him of a water nymph. A very beautiful, delectable water nymph.

"And you said yes?"

As the soap dissipated and the water stilled around her, Connor could see the hint of skin and drawers. His groin hardened and his hand clenched at the earth. He had yet to pull himself out of the puddle of muck. He wasn't sure he could manage it with any sense of coordinated dignity. Having Kate all but naked just ten feet away left his limbs strangely disengaged from his brain.

Her chin jutted out at a stubborn angle. "It was payment."

"For what?"

"He wanted our fish."

Connor struggled into a sitting position. Eli had been pilfering their fish when he'd found him. He hadn't waited around for an explanation, just took off, fearing the worst. He should have known better. Eli had never harmed a fly for the entire time he'd lived on the mountain.

Tearing his eyes away from Kate, Connor watched Jenny and the dog play tug of war with a stick further up the bank. "And I suppose you told him we would keep it?"

"I was hardly in a position to argue." A shiver wracked her body. She tried to hide it by hugging her arms tighter against her chest but it was too late.

Connor pushed to his feet. "You need to get out of there before you catch a chill."

A pretty pink hue tinged the apples of her cheeks. "I'm not getting out with you there. I'm—I'm..."

"Naked," he supplied helpfully, trying his damnedest not to smile. It was a dismal failure.

"No!"

"You might as well be. I can see straight through those flimsy underthings."

She crouched down a little deeper until the water caressed her lower lip.

He shook his head. "Little late to be gettin' all modest now." He'd already had a bit more than a peek of that delicious little body and he had some swollen body parts of his own to prove it. Connor scooped up a dry towel from the ground and held it open. "C'mere, before you catch your death."

"I am not getting out with you standing there." She glanced at Jenny. "It's indecent."

"Well I'm not going anywhere until I know you're safely out of the water. The last thing I need is you slipping on the rocks and knocking yourself unconscious."

"Thank you for your concern, but I assure you—"

"Nothing about concern," he said, cutting her off. "I'm just real hungry, is all." He grinned at the flash of anger in her pretty green eyes just before he closed his own and jiggled the flannel towel in his hands. "Come on. I won't peek. Promise."

She hesitated. "Swear?"

"Cross my heart." He'd already seen enough to fuel his dreams for a long time to come.

The slosh of water told him she'd acquiesced. Seconds later her hands brushed his as she reached for the towel. "Give it to me."

He should have listened to her. He should have handed over the towel and made a hasty retreat. That would have been the sane thing to do. But sanity, he learned, was a tenuous thing. Especially where this woman was concerned.

Connor enfolded her in his arms, wrapping the towel around her shapely frame. She turned to escape, but he held her firm, the soft curve of her bottom pressed lightly into his groin. The scent of creek water and lavender soap teased his senses and his arms tightened in response.

"What are you doing?" Her voice shook, though whether it was from the effects of the cool water or something else, he didn't know.

He kept his eyes closed. He'd promised, after all. "Warming you up. Wouldn't want you to catch a fever or anything." One raged through him right now but he wasn't entirely certain it was contagious.

"I wouldn't catch a fever, I would catch a chill. And either way, I'm fine," she said through chattering teeth.

"Are you?" He wasn't. Not even a little. His insides were a jumbled mess. His outsides weren't faring all that well either.

"Yes," she answered, but the stiffness in her body had eased.

He continued to hold her, letting his arms gently rub hers to warm her up.

"Jenny's—"

"Jenny's fine. She's playing with the dog," he said. "She laughed. I can't believe she laughed." He couldn't help the wonder that filled his voice, or the heat that burned through him when Kate leaned her weight more fully against him. He stopped rubbing her arms and wrapped his around her.

"I know." He could hear the smile in her voice. "It was the dog that did it. We have to keep him."

He wasn't sure the dog deserved all the credit. The changes had started well before that. They had started with Kate. She'd changed things. She was changing him. He could feel it. How else could he explain how quickly he had come to rely on her?

160

How, despite his best efforts, he looked forward to coming home knowing she was there. It had all happened too swiftly for him to stop it.

Connor thought of the letters he'd shoved into his back pocket—the discrepancies between what Kate had told him and what he'd learned from Oliver—and a sharp jab of suspicion broke past his building desire.

"Kate?" Her body molded perfectly to his. He wanted to uncurl his arms and let his hands roam down the length of her. He wanted to turn her around, unwrap the towel and pull her flush against him with no barriers. He had to stop this, but he didn't think he had the strength. It'd been so long since he'd felt the softness of a woman and this one tempted every last one of his senses and pushed him beyond reason.

"What?"

He turned his head slightly. His nose brushed against the soft shell of her ear. God, this woman smelled good.

"Connor?"

Even his name sounded better when she said it. He squeezed his eyes shut tighter. Heaven help him, he was losing it.

Somewhere behind him, the dog barked, reminding him they weren't alone. He grappled for what remained of his self-control.

With great reluctance, he loosened his hold on her and allowed her to step outside the circle of his arms. A cool breeze touched his body where hers had been. He bit down and willed his eyes to stay shut.

"Get dressed," he said, gruffer than he meant.

The grass swished as she picked up her clothes and dressed. "We'll meet you back home," she said as she passed. Her arm brushed his and sent ripples of need washing over him. He stood at the edge of the creek for several long moments, drinking in great gulps of air.

It didn't help.

"Dammit," he muttered.

His fingers fumbled with the buttons on his denims as he stripped down. The cold water bit into his skin as he dove into the creek, letting it cool the traitorous emotions Kate stirred within him.

~

Connor suffered through supper, trying not to look at Kate or be aware of every movement she made as she served up succulent slices of beef smothered in gravy, biscuits, buttered beans and baked potatoes. He tried not to take part in the one-sided conversation she had with Jenny about their day, or answer with more than a grunt when she posed a question to him. He counted the minutes until he could escape. Once Jenny was tucked in for the night, he bolted from the house and made a beeline for the stables, the godforsaken dog trotting at his heels. He had spread the letters on a bale of hay to dry, his fall in the muck having left the pink stationery the worse for wear.

The scent of fresh hay and horseflesh helped ease the mottled emotions spinning inside him like a twister. He had hoped the familiar rhythm of his chores would erase the feelings completely, but even with the stalls cleaned and the horses tended to he couldn't push aside the feeling holding Kate had elicited.

He should have kept his hands to himself. But he hadn't. And now it was impossible to think of anything else but putting them on her again, exploring the gentle curve of her hips, the dip that led to her small waist, the rounded bottom she'd pressed into him.

Connor groaned and dropped his weight next to where

the letters were drying. Beside him the dog whined. He glanced down. "Are you mocking me?"

Rudy stared back with innocent, doleful eyes.

"I know, I'm a fool," he said, reaching for the letters. Water stains blotched the feminine scrawl, blurring the ink and in some areas erasing it completely. The color had leached from the stationery. Connor flipped through the pages. Some were worse than others, but all bore the evidence of his fall.

Stretching an arm over his head, Connor lifted the oil lamp from its hook next to the stall. He brushed away the straw strewn about the floor with his feet and set the lamp next to him.

The first letter, dated the previous November, was ruined, save for the date and salutation. The second hadn't fared much better. The lower half was nearly obliterated, but the top portion spoke of her family, most of which Oliver had already relayed, some he had not, and none of which matched what Kate had told him.

She went on to describe her dream of starting a new life away from the painful memories and loneliness of her current one.

For a brief moment, hope surged within him. This was the Kate he knew. The sense of hope and fear mingled together as she tried to start over. Perhaps he had simply misunderstood or—

He flipped to the last letter and stopped. The crease in the middle had torn the paper nearly in two. The top half was indecipherable, the bottom half-smudged and unreadable, save for a few words near the end.

But it was enough.

Kate had lied to him. Flat out lied. Anger mixed with betrayal and disbelief.

Hannah Stockdale's burns had not healed as Kate had led him to believe.

Connor fought against the words scrolled across the page in neat, even strokes. He didn't want to believe it. It had happened again. And he'd let it. He let her inch her way into his heart with her warm smile and gentle nature only to discover it had all been a lie.

How many times could one man play the fool? Had his experience with Emily taught him nothing? Women, if given the chance, would rip your heart out and stomp it flat with their boot heel.

The muscles in his shoulders tightened and he pulled his spine erect, staring into the shadows where the lamplight didn't reach. Who was this woman, this stranger, who had slipped with such ease past his carefully constructed defenses?

He didn't know.

But one thing he could say for certain—she sure as shootin' wasn't Hannah Elizabeth Stockdale.

Chapter Fourteen

K atherine had drifted off, the skirt she planned to hem for the autumn social this Saturday left untouched in her lap. Somewhere in the misty realm between wakefulness and sleep, Connor's image drifted in. He tempted her with his smile, embraced her with his warmth, made her feel safe and wanted. She had no idea how long she sat there, slouched on the sofa dreaming, when a noise pulled her away from it. She jolted up and found the object of her torment standing in the empty doorway that separated the kitchen from the main room.

"You startled me." Flustered, Katherine reached for the cup of tea she'd poured herself earlier and took a sip to cover her nervousness. Cool liquid slid down her throat.

Connor didn't move.

"You're staring," she pointed out, in case he wasn't aware. She was. All too aware, in fact. She could feel the burn on her skin where his gaze landed. It grew and spread like a wildfire caught in the wind.

"Am I?" Connor leaned a shoulder against the doorframe and crossed his arms over his chest, his manner a study in calm, and yet...yet there was something else. A tension that changed the line of his body. She could feel it vibrate in the space separating them.

He pushed away from the doorframe and came toward her, moving with the litheness of a cat stalking its prey.

"Did you get your chores done?" She grasped for something, anything to cut through the apprehension building inside of her.

"I did."

"Oh." Her grip on the cup and saucer tightened.

Connor stopped when he reached the overstuffed armchair next to the sofa and slid his hands into the back pockets of his denims.

He nudged his chin toward the skirt. "Is that one of Emily's?"

"Oh...yes. I thought...I thought maybe for the social on Saturday. If you wanted to go, that is. You hadn't really said." She was blabbering, the words tumbling out of her mouth in a voice that sounded foreign to her. "I just thought...in case."

Connor shrugged and walked around the low table in front of the sofa and sat down next to her. The cushion dipped beneath his weight. He leaned forward, resting his forearms on his knees, his fingers laced together. The banded muscles of his forearms flexed where he'd rolled up his shirt-sleeves.

Katherine glanced up only to be caught in his penetrating stare. He searched her face, looking for something. What, she didn't know, but the fear he would see the secrets buried deep inside made her turn away. Her fingers ran along the rim of the teacup, discovering a small chip in the china. Spidery cracks crept out and scarred the delicate rose design.

"Did you have a good day?"

His question took her off guard. "Yes. Jenny and I had a

great day." Right up until he'd sent her emotions into a tailspin at the creek.

He nodded and leaned back, forcing her to turn slightly to keep him in her sight. "She's doing better since you arrived."

The cadence of his voice settled over her like a warm blanket. "I'm sure she would have done just as well without—"

"Sure would hate to see that ruined," he said, cutting her off.

Ruined? "I would too."

His gaze shifted to his thumb as he ran it along the calloused edge of his gun hand. Mesmerized, Katherine watched the movement. She couldn't stop herself from wondering what those hands would feel like running over her smooth skin. An odd tickle tripped along her nerves and the teacup rattled against the saucer.

Connor reached over and wordlessly took the dishes from her. Their fingers touched, a small intimate stroke that sent a shiver up her arm.

Heat scalded her cheeks. She dropped her hands away and picked at the hem of the muslin skirt she'd been mending. She could hear her mama's voice whispering in her ear, drowning out the pounding of her heart.

Don't let yourself love a man, Katy. It'll be the ruin of you for sure. He'll leave and break your heart and won't nothing ever be right with you again. You'll just be a bunch of broken pieces swept out the door.

It made her think of the teacup, cracked and scarred.

Katherine gave herself a mental shake. Love had nothing to do with this. For heaven's sake, she had known the man only a few weeks. It was just some strange, unexplained reaction brought on by close quarters and circumstances. And if life had taught her anything, it was that circumstances could change in a heartbeat.

"Jenny's been through a lot," he continued. "She's seen more hurt in her short life than any little girl should have to."

"You mean her father dying?" The words carved into her heart, sharp and painful. "I expect she must miss him a lot."

He nodded then whispered, "We both do." The unreadable mask slipped for a brief second and Katherine saw the ravages of loss and regret engraved deep into the pale blue of his eyes. It robbed her of breath. Without thinking, she put her hand over his to comfort him.

Connor brushed the curve of her hand with his thumb. Short bursts of sensation spiraled up her arm and spread throughout her body like a lightning flash. Not once did he take his eyes off her. Her skin warmed wherever his gaze landed. She wanted to lean closer, bask in the sensation.

"The thing about Grant was," he said, "I trusted him. More than anyone else. Never had any reason not to. Or so I thought. But he pulled the wool over my eyes. Real good. And it was easy, because I never once figured he'd do such a thing. I let my good opinion of him blind me to what was really there."

Tell Con...I'm sorry.

What had Grant done?

"You see, that's the thing about people. They make you believe one thing, and because that's what you want to see, you go along with it. You get pulled in by the need to believe. But it's never really the way things are."

Katherine shook her head, confused. He was talking in riddles, riddles that made her heart pound at a scary pace while her mind worked frantically to unravel them. "I don't understand."

"Look at yourself," he said, flipping a finger at her in a casual manner that belied the rigid tension coiling his muscles.

"Me?"

"You're a bit of a mystery."

"I am?" She pulled her hand away and curled it into a fist to press against the roiling in her belly.

"You draw a man in with your smile, your warmth. You make him think you'd do anything to help. You lead him to believe you won't be any trouble at all. That you can make a difference, make things better."

"I do?" Why didn't that sound like a good thing?

He nodded. "But you never reveal much about yourself. Take your brother for instance."

Her racing heart careened to a sudden stop, slamming into her ribs. She forced words past the band choking her throat. They came out in a stuttered mess. "M-my brother?"

"Yes." Something in his eyes had changed. Hardened. "What was his name again?"

"Oh. His name?" She busied her hands with folding the skirt, shoving it into the wicker basket at her feet. She needed time to think. A near impossible task when he continued to stare at her with those eyes and ask questions she had no answers to.

"You remember your brother's name, don't you?" His voice held an unexpected edge.

She laughed. A high-pitched trill that made her cringe. "Of course I do!" She stood, hugging the sewing basket to her, as if it could shield her from what was happening.

Connor smiled, but it wasn't like before. This one didn't crinkle the corner of his eyes, didn't make them dance or sparkle. "Then what is it?"

Trepidation trampled like a thousand little footprints. Katherine turned on wooden legs and walked to the table at the back of the room, setting the basket down. Through the bay window in front of her, she could see the shadowed outline of the bluff beneath a blanket of stars. She closed her eyes and made a hasty wish on one of them to give her an answer. But the stars weren't granting wishes that night.

"Kate?"

She straightened and turned. Connor had moved behind her while she wasted time on wishes. Mere inches separated them. His nearness rang through her, teasing her senses to life. The scent of leather and outdoors clung to his skin, his clothing. This close, she could see the first hints of stubble shadowing his chin.

His body blocked hers, kept her rooted to the spot.

She gripped the table. "Why are you asking me all these questions? What does it matter about my brother?"

Connor's eyes bored into hers until she thought she would lose her mind and her will. Roughened fingertips grazed the line of her jaw. Blood rushed to her ears, pounded inside her skull. She knew she should stop him, but the idea of letting go of the table seemed foolhardy. It was the only thing holding her up.

"What's your brother's name?"

She closed her eyes and pulled out the first name she could think of. "Patrick."

"Gerald."

Breathing became difficult. "What?"

"Your brother's name is Gerald."

Katherine swallowed. Helpless, lost. "It is?"

Connor nodded and dropped his gaze to her mouth. The pad of his thumb brushed along her lower lip, making her ache for more.

"And your mother." One golden eyebrow arched slowly upward. "Guess what her name is?"

A chill swept over her at the same time heat pooled in her belly. "I—I—"

"Maureen," he supplied when she didn't answer. "Why don't you tell me your full name?"

God help her. "H-Hannah Kathleen Stock—"

A curt shake of his head cut her off. "Elizabeth. Hannah *Elizabeth.*"

His words, his controlled anger, were an icy deluge crashing against her. She couldn't stop the trembling of her hands. Her fingers dug into the table and she squeezed with all her might.

Connor's gaze probed hers, demanding answers. "Who are you?"

She swallowed and his hand slid down to rest against her neck. She couldn't speak; she could only stand there, held captive by eyes that peered into her, through her, searching for answers she couldn't give.

Finally, she broke their hold and looked away. When she answered, the words rang hollow in her ears. "I told you who I am."

His knuckles brushed against the soft skin of her throat, building the ache deep inside of her. Oh, how she longed to lean into him, rest her cheek against his chest and let him shoulder her burden for even just a few moments. How could the one man who held the key to her destruction make her feel so safe?

"I know what you told me." He lowered his voice, let it wrap around her, cocooning them from the outside world. "Now why don't you tell me the truth?"

"I...I..." The words died on her tongue. She couldn't tell him. Better he believe her a liar than know she was a Slade.

"I know you're not Hannah Elizabeth Stockdale. Do you know how I know that?"

She shook her head. She hadn't even begun to consider where he'd come into the information. It hardly mattered. Her lies had caught up with her.

His hand dropped away and he lifted her arm, working the button at the cuff. He pushed the sleeve up to her elbow, ignoring her sputtered protests. His fingers seared a path where they slid over the tender skin of her wrist, making her pulse throb.

"I know that because Hannah Stockdale has scars covering her arms."

"I told you," she said, tugging at her arm with little success. "They healed."

He shook his head. "And on her legs." He grabbed her waist without warning and hoisted her onto the table. "Shall we check to see if those ones have healed too?"

"No!"

He didn't listen. He grabbed the edge of her skirt. Katherine swatted at his hands and tried to push the skirt and petticoats back down. She kicked out at him, anything to pry his grip loose. His swift intake of breath hissed in her ear when her boot connected with his knee. But her victory was short-lived. He grasped her wrists, insinuating himself between her knees. She struggled. The skirt rode up of its own accord, her legs left dangling helplessly over the edge of the table.

"Leave me alone! You've no right! Please...please don't do this."

Her words reached him where her struggles had not. He stopped and pressed his forehead against hers. Her wrists were pressed tightly against his chest where he still held them.

A muscle jumped beneath his ear. "Tell me who you are."

Her heart broke into jagged fragments and pierced her chest. "My name is Kate," she whispered.

"What's your last name?"

She scraped her teeth over her bottom lip. "Does it matter? Will it change anything?" But she knew it would. It would change everything.

He lifted his head. Confusion clouded his eyes, darkening them.

She forged ahead before he could answer. "I'm still the same person I was yesterday. Can't you just let me be Kate

Stockdale? My past is...I just..." She tried to find the right words but they didn't exist. "Please, Connor, just let it be. I'm not hurting anyone. Let me stay and help Jenny. Just until I can repay the Hewitts. Then I'll leave and you'll never see me again."

For a moment, he looked lost, torn. Katherine held her breath.

"Dammit, Kate." The curse tore through her. "Damn everything that brought you here and made me think—"

"Think what?"

He shook his head. "That I could believe in you. That I could—" He stopped but the unspoken words lingered in the air, hers for the taking. She ignored them. She didn't deserve them.

"I'm sorry," she whispered.

"No. Don't."

He stared at her, long and hard. The air between them grew tense and in that moment Katherine saw everything she could have, everything that might have been hers if her life had turned out different.

And then he showed her even more.

Connor's mouth descended on hers. There was a sense of urgency in his kiss, as if he hated that he was doing it, but couldn't stop himself. And she was of no help in that quarter as his hands cupped her face, gentle where the kiss wasn't. Did he think he could draw the truth out of her? Her knees grew weak. She wanted to resist, pull away. Instead her fingers wound into the soft fabric of his shirt to pull him closer.

One arm slid around her back and pulled her off the table, tight against him. Hard thighs pressed against hers, inflaming the desire that had kindled to a slow burn since the first day she laid eyes on him. She gave in to the sensation, pushed aside the warnings going off in her head. When his tongue plundered her mouth, she met him thrust for thrust. Passion overwhelmed her, crashing against her like a cresting wave and dragging her beneath its undertow. She couldn't get enough, not of his taste, his hands, his body melded to hers.

Connor broke the kiss and staggered back. Anger bled across his features and he pinned her with a fierce glare.

"I can't do this. I can't let you in."

His words bruised her heart.

"You and I—" He shook his head. She waited for him to finish but whatever he had been about to say was shoved behind an impenetrable mask. "I need some air," he said.

Seconds later, the kitchen door shut with a bang. Finally, Katherine gave in and sank to the floor. What had she done?

Chapter Fifteen

Bart stuck a cheroot between his teeth and propped his feet on the front of Connor's desk. "Seems to me you oughta just leave it alone."

Connor gave the fire in the pot-bellied stove another jab. "Leave it alone?"

Warmth began to permeate the office, beating back the early October chill. The unpredictable heat of early autumn had come to an abrupt end.

"That's what I said." A match struck behind him and the acrid smell of smoke filled the small space around them. "What difference does it make what her name is, who her brother was, or what she calls her mama? You got yerself a good woman there. She takes care of Jenny right and proper. Hell, you said so yourself that lil' Jenny smiled and laughed yesterday."

Connor touched a hand to the dented coffee pot and pulled it away quickly, the heat singeing his skin.

"Ouch!" He winced and shook his hand, glaring at the offending pot before answering Bart. "Yeah, but—"

"Ain't no buts to be had, son. She's a good woman. She's

good to you and she's good to Jenny. Stop looking for things to be wrong. You cain't go judging every single female by Emily's behavior. Kate ain't Emily."

"It's got nothing to do with that," Connor said. But he knew it wasn't true. He had been looking for cracks in Kate's personality since the minute she staggered into his arms at the train depot. He'd tried to push her away, find a reason not to trust her, keep her at arm's length. He'd been doing that to everyone for the past eight years. It had been easy enough to accomplish. Until now.

But none of that changed the truth. He hadn't fabricated what he'd read in the letters. Sure he may have gone looking for lies, but Kate was the one that told them. He didn't know what hurt worse, that he had been right or that he wished to hell he wasn't.

He'd intended to pry the truth out of her last night, but dammit if he hadn't messed it up but good. When she tried to evade his questions, he'd followed her, cornered her against the table so she couldn't escape. That had been his first mistake, standing in such close proximity. Her soft skin begged to be touched. Long strawberry curls dangled down her back, tied loosely by a scrap of ribbon. The fresh scent of lavender filled the air around her. That close, he could count the freckles that dotted the bridge of her nose. God, even now he could still taste her sweetness, feel the imprint her body left on his.

Connor gripped the handle of the coffee pot and tried to regain control over his wayward thoughts. He emptied the contents of the pot into his cup before returning to his chair behind the desk.

"I don't know who she is." Connor pulled the letters out of his shirt pocket and set the wrinkled pink envelopes onto the desk between them.

Bart dropped his feet to the floor and scuttled closer to the desk. The sound of the chair scraping and his boots shuffling caused Beesom's snore to halt. The prisoner shifted position and flipped over onto his side, the moth-eaten wool blanket twisting around his long legs. Connor waited until the snoring resumed before he spoke again, lowering his voice.

"Nothing in these letters matches what she told me." He jabbed the short pile with his forefinger and pinned them to the desk.

Bart slipped one of the letters out from beneath Connor's finger and held it up. "And she writes it on pink paper. Well, ain't that the thing." He put the letter up to his nose and sniffed. "Smells like roses...and mud."

"And she doesn't."

Bart lifted a bushy eyebrow. "Beg pardon?"

Connor pointed at the letter in his deputy's hand. "She doesn't smell like roses. She smells like lavender. Sometimes vanilla if she's been cooking, but definitely not—"

Bart raised the other eyebrow, a knowing expression enlivening his features. Connor clamped his mouth shut and tried to ignore the sudden heat rising up his neck.

"You seem pretty knowledgeable 'bout what the young lady smells like, Con." Beneath the beard, Connor could see the older man's lips twitching.

"I'm just saying," he mumbled, snatching the letter back. "She's lying through her teeth and I can't get her to tell me the truth."

Bart shrugged. "Maybe she was lookin' to start a new life, with a new name. Put all her past behind her. A whole lotta people come west, hopin' to do just that."

"Then why not just tell me that?" he asked, taking a gulp of coffee. The mug hit the desk with a loud bang as he gagged. With nowhere to spit the foul liquid out, he forced it down. "How long has that been sitting there?"

Bart chuckled. "Oh, since about the time young Crofter took over last night."

"And you couldn't have told me that before I drank it?"

"Could have," Bart said, taking another drag of the cheroot. "But you been right ornery since you walked through that door this morning, so's I figured you'd just bark at me if I tried to stop you."

"I am not ornery." Connor shoved the coffee aside and scowled.

"The hell you ain't. You've got your britches all in a twist over this girl. My guess is you haven't been able to think about much else since she arrived in town."

Connor glowered at Bart. He hated being so transparent. "I don't need any more complications in my life. I just want things to go back to the way they were before."

"Cain't change time, Connor. It don't know how to march backward. Best you can do is just accept that and try to keep up. Now I'm guessin' you gave that poor woman a real hard time over this—" he waved a hand at the letters, "—and she's sittin' back home worryin' whether or not she still has a job."

Guilt forced Connor's gaze to drop to his desk. If Bart only knew just what he'd done to Kate the night before, he'd probably hog-tie him to the back of his horse and drag him through town.

Bart squinted and shifted the cheroot over to the other side of his mouth with a flick of his tongue. "I think maybe you oughta apologize."

"Apologize?" Connor straightened in his chair. He'd done nothing wrong, for crying out loud.

"Yeah, apologize. You need her, or had you forgotten that little tidbit of information while you were busy digging up the rest of it."

He had forgotten it. Not because he worried she might quit on him, he realized, but because he had stopped thinking of her as an employee. Dammit, when had that happened?

Bart stood and stretched his reed-thin body, making small grunting noises. "Now, I'm gonna take these old bones down the street and see if I cain't convince that woman of mine to rustle us up some real coffee and a plateful of grits."

Bart sauntered across the room, lifting his hat off the wall peg. He settled the dusty felt hat onto his head and opened the door. Ed Devers stood on the other side, a wide grin splitting his face in half. He held up a pair of iron shackles and gave them a shake. "Mornin', Bart. I'm here to take a man to his hangin'."

"Well, son, you came to the right place." Bart stepped back inside and made a sweeping gesture with his arm. "Seems we got a man just ripe for a noose."

Ed sauntered into the room, his spurs jangling. "Get up, Beesom!" His deep voice ricocheted off the walls. Connor suspected anyone still sleeping within a one mile radius had just been knocked out of their beds.

Beesom kicked the blanket off and glared from his prone position on the cot. "Rather you just git some pretty girl to whisper sweet in my ear, Devers."

"Ain't taking last requests today. Put your arms out, and don't try anything stupid. My guess is the sheriff here is just lookin' for a reason to shoot you between the eyes and save the nice folks in Bakers the spectacle of a hangin'."

Beesom scowled and rose from the cot. "You can threaten me all you want, bounty hunter. I ain't dyin' in Bakers."

Ed clamped a thick cuff around Beesom's wrist and grinned at the condemned man. "Everybody dies eventually, Beesom. But I'm still bettin' my money that your time is comin' sooner rather than later. Ain't that right, Con?"

A cynical smile pushed at the corners of Connor's mouth. He eyed the outlaw with bitter frustration. Whatever the man knew about Rogan Slade would die with him. And there wasn't a damn thing Connor could do about it. He'd tried, but Beesom had kept mum.

Connor pushed away from his desk and crossed the room, sticking the key in the lock and giving it a hard twist. He stepped back, letting the door swing open. Ed led Beesom out, tugging at the shackles to keep the man off balance.

Beesom smirked at Connor. "You take care of that pretty lil' housekeeper now, Sheriff. Maybe I'll come back one of these days and pay her a visit."

The man's laughter was cut short by a swift cuff to the head courtesy of Ed. He shoved the prisoner out the door toward the awaiting horses.

"Say good riddance to the bad garbage, Con."

Connor didn't bother issuing a good-bye. He'd save his energy for praying the man didn't escape yet again before his hanging came due.

Katherine kneaded the dough for biscuits, then pinched off sections and placed them into a greased skillet. She spread the remaining bacon grease on top of the biscuits before placing them in the stove to bake. Moving to the pantry, she retrieved several large potatoes out of the wooden storage box. Her supper preparations had already become second nature to her. She didn't spare them a thought.

She wished they did occupy her mind. Then, at least, it wouldn't be filled with the events of the previous evening, the feel of Connor's mouth on hers, gentle hands cupping her face, the desire that rushed through at the mere remembrance of his touch.

The kiss had been a mistake. He didn't trust her. And why should he? She'd avoided him this morning, busying herself in the garden while he ate breakfast. His voice filtered through the open kitchen window as he spoke with Jenny, but when he left to retrieve his horse, he didn't spare her more than a passing glance.

She wouldn't be surprised if he asked her to pack her things and leave when he returned at the end of the day.

As if her thoughts had conjured him up, Connor's voice filtered through the open door.

"How's my girl?"

Startled, the potato she held dropped from her hand and rolled lazily across the counter. Katherine grabbed it just before it fell off the edge and plunked it back into the bowl. She peeked out through the window. Connor crouched next to Jenny. She had spent most of the afternoon outside running around with Rudy until the big dog rolled over onto the grass in defeat, too tuckered to do anything but pant. After that, Jenny contented herself with picking wildflowers. Half were put in a vase and sat atop the kitchen table; the other half were braided together and looped around the dog's neck.

Katherine leaned away from the window and brushed her cheeks with the back of her hands, swiping at the dusting of flour she felt on her skin. She patted her hair and tried to poke a few stray strands back into the knot at her nape before she realized what she was doing.

"Don't be so foolish," she chastised herself, dropping her hands. The man didn't want her. Likely had returned home early to demand she leave.

Determined to ignore the burning sensation welling within her, she set her mind to preparing dinner. Dipping her hand into the pot, she retrieved the half-peeled potato and slashed at it with a fury.

"Something smells good."

Katherine's nerves jumped, nearly sending the peeling knife out of her hand. She dropped the last potato into the pot and moved to the stove.

"Thank you." She hadn't been expecting such an innocuous greeting, not after what had transpired the last time they were together. She wasn't sure what to make of it. Mustering her courage, she turned around. His expression gave nothing away.

Nervous hands flitted to the apron tied around her middle. "I made apple cobbler for dessert." Her fingers twisted into the white cotton. "I hope that's okay?"

Connor stepped further into the kitchen, taking off his hat and hooking it onto a peg by the door. His fingers ruffled through thick golden waves.

"Cobbler sounds fine."

Should she say something? Bring up the kiss? Pretend it never happened? Flustered, she occupied her hands and mind. Dishes clanged against each other as she piled the dirty crockery next to the basin.

Connor walked over and leaned against the counter, his nearness doing nothing to squelch her growing nervousness. "I was talkin' to Bart about last night—"

Her hand flew to her mouth on a gasp. Words tumbled between her fingers. "You told him about the kiss?"

"No!" A crimson stain flushed across Connor's cheekbones making him appear younger than his thirty years. He shifted and crossed his arms over his chest. "I told him about the letters."

Katherine shook her head, confused. "What letters?"

"The ones Oliver gave me that Hannah Stockdale had written. That's how I knew about your brother—her brother—and the rest of it."

"Oh." All day she had wondered how he'd come by the information. Of course, Mr. Hewitt would have known. Why hadn't she thought of that in the beginning? Her shoulders slumped. Her ineptitude at deception was reaching epic proportions.

"Bart thinks I should just leave things be."

Hope burst in her heart. "He does? And what do you think?"

Connor gazed at her silently. "I disagreed."

"Oh." The burgeoning hope fizzled in her belly.

Connor sighed and pushed away from the counter, turning toward her. Fine lines fanned out from the corners of his eyes, a testament to years spent outdoors in the elements. It only added to his rugged appeal.

"You lied to me, plain and simple. Even now you keep your secrets to yourself."

"What do you want from me?"

"Something. Anything. A small piece of your past that isn't wrapped in a lie."

Katherine looked up at him. Her heart cracked. The desperate longing to give a part of herself, to put his mind at ease, tore through her. She wanted so badly to give in, to give him what he wanted. What he needed.

"After Pa died, Mama and I fell on hard times," she said, picking her way through her past, finding pieces she could give him. "Mama did what she needed to get by. Most people judged her harsh for it. Of course none of those judging ever held out a hand to help." She couldn't stop the resentment that turned her tone bitter.

"What did she do?"

Katherine felt the old shame rise like bile in her throat. She didn't blame her mother, but she hated what she'd done all the same. "She took in laundry at the mining camp. And..." She couldn't get the words out.

"And men," Connor finished, but she didn't hear any condemnation in his voice.

Katherine nodded.

"Where's your mother now?"

"Dead."

"I'm sorry."

She stared down at her hands. She couldn't keep the sadness from threading the edges of her voice. "I think she was glad of it. She never quite got over Pa dying. She loved him something fierce, but part of her always blamed him for dying and leaving her alone."

"How old were you when your mother passed?"

"Sixteen."

He took another step, the brief separation between them shrinking further. "What did you do?"

"I married a man I barely knew."

For a moment, Connor said nothing, then, "Where is he now?"

Katherine shook her head. "I don't know."

Seconds ticked past and the silence dragged between them. "Are you still married?"

"Yes," she whispered, unable to look at him.

"Is he who you're hiding from? Why you pretended to be someone you're not?"

She nodded.

Connor lifted a hand to her cheek. Katherine inhaled sharply. For a brief second he paused then touched a stray curl where it dangled near her ear.

"Why didn't you tell me this before?"

Before what? Before she fell for him? Before he touched her? "I was afraid you wouldn't hire me if you knew my situation."

He nodded. She could see his mind working, turning over what he had just learned, deciding whether to believe her or not. She wasn't sure what she had said that made the difference, but the hardness in his gaze eased and she felt him relent. "You're safe here. You know that, don't you? He can't hurt you now."

She swallowed. She knew he meant well. She knew he

believed what he said. But the plain and simple truth was if Rogan ever tracked her here, no one would be safe. He'd kill anyone that got in his way. What happened on the stagecoach drove that point home.

Connor moved closer, his fingers brushing her cheek, her jaw. The heat of his body closed in around her, pulling her back to the present.

"What are you doing?"

His brows knit together. "I don't know. I don't know anything where you're concerned. You're like a fever in my blood I can't get rid of."

He cupped her face with both hands, his thumbs gently pressing the underside of her chin, tilting her face toward him. She couldn't breathe. His mouth was so close. His gaze locked on hers and drove into her with such force it pinned her in place, making it impossible to move.

The air between them became charged and nothing else in the world existed. Connor lowered his head until his lips hovered just above her own.

A deep yearning cleaved through her. "Are you going to kiss me again?"

"Yes," he said with a small nod, resignation etched into his features. "I'm afraid I am."

Chapter Sixteen

Connor's lips touched hers, a gentle brush, skin against skin. The breath Katherine held escaped. He lifted his head to take it in. Then the pressure on her mouth returned, firmer this time, yet oh so tender. So different from the previous night's kiss, but no less intoxicating.

Katherine's body tingled, the sensation waking parts of her she hadn't given much consideration to in a very long time. She had never been kissed like this. Like it was going to consume her entire being until nothing remained but a whimpering mass of want and need.

Connor nibbled at her bottom lip, kissed the corner of her mouth, nuzzled his nose against hers. His thumbs brushed the underside of her chin, and his fingers teased the back of her neck. She rested her hands against his hard chest, reveling at the strong beat of his heart beneath her touch. The heat from his body soaked through the soft fabric of his shirt and warmed her palms. She gave into the longing to explore. Her hands slid down the hard ridges of his belly then wound around his back, marveling at the muscles shifting beneath her palms.

Connor's touch was both gentle and demanding, and she wondered how the two could coincide together so beautifully. Did a more wondrous feeling than this exist?

She pressed herself against the length of him, wishing she could melt into his body and stay there forever. A low groan rumbled in his chest and his arms slid around her shoulders and crushed her to him. He deepened the kiss, wanting, demanding. Katherine found herself only too happy to comply, lost in the heady madness his touch had conjured.

A flurry of barking riddled the air, breaking the spell that had wrapped itself around them as if someone had doused them with a bucket of ice water from the creek.

Connor's gaze seared and she could see in his eyes all the things that would have happened had they not been inter- rupted. A shiver rushed through her veins. Would she have stopped him?

No, she realized. She didn't think she possessed that kind of strength.

A voice grew closer and spoke to Jenny, the tone friendly. Connor shot her one last, inscrutable look before moving away from her to the door.

"It's Reverend Sangster."

~

"Old Mrs. Greevy, despite her son's worry to the contrary, still has some kick left in her," Reverend Sangster said, scooping a spoonful of creamy mashed potatoes onto his plate. "Three times this week her son has traveled to town to say his mother had taken a turn for the worse and was asking about me. And three times I arrived at their cabin to find her fit as a fiddle. What do you make of that? A miracle?" He smiled and handed the bowl to Kate.

Warmth radiated from Kate's return smile. She dished out

a helping for Jenny and then herself. A pang of unexpected jealously jabbed at Connor. He wanted her smiles directed at him and him alone, not at the handsome young Reverend with the charming manner that filled a church every Sunday and had the whole congregation singing his praises.

Connor shoved a forkful of garden peas drizzled with butter into his mouth and swallowed the irrational emotion. Will was happily married to Bart's daughter. He wasn't about to steal Kate away. And even if he wanted to, Kate didn't belong to him. She was married.

Married.

Whatever truth he'd been expecting, that hadn't even been on the map. And not just married, but married to a man who scared her enough she had changed her identity to hide should he come looking for her. What had that man done to her? A sick sensation twisted in his guts. He wasn't sure he wanted to know.

"Perhaps Mrs. Greevy likes your company, Reverend," Kate offered, interrupting Connor's thoughts.

"Perhaps so. She certainly makes a point of showing up for service each and every Sunday." He turned his pointed gaze on Connor. "Unlike some other people I know."

Connor squirmed in his chair and stabbed at the seasoned beef steak on his plate. He grunted noncommittally, hoping Will would let it go.

Kate cut in. "I'm afraid it was my fault we missed last Sunday." Color bloomed in her cheeks. Lord, but she was pretty all flushed like that. "I didn't bring much with me to Fatal Bluff and I didn't have anything proper to wear to town. But Connor graciously allowed me to borrow some of Jenny's mother's clothes—"

"Emily's?"

Connor watched from the corner of his eye as Will's attention swung back to him.

"Leave it alone, Will," Connor warned. He had no intention of hashing out his past in front of Kate and reliving the hurt and humiliation all over again.

Kate leaned forward. "Leave what alone?" A spark of curiosity turned her eyes a lovely sage green. A man could get lost in those eyes. A man *had* gotten lost in those eyes. Connor bit down into his beef steak and tried to forget just how lost he'd been. Tried to forget how close he'd come to taking her right there in the kitchen with Jenny on the other side of the door.

When no one answered her, Kate piped up again. "Leave what alone, Reverend?"

"It's just...well I..." Will cleared his throat and straightened the cutlery around his plate. "You know, perhaps now that you've something suitable to wear, Kate, you might convince Connor to bring you and Jenny to the social on Saturday."

Connor dropped his fork onto his plate and leaned back in his chair. That was the last thing he needed. Will smiled and Connor could see the laughter behind his friend's eyes as he pushed his chair back. "Well, I best be going before Beth starts to wonder where I've wandered off to. Thank you for the dessert, Kate. Tastiest cobbler I've ever had. Next to my wife's, of course." He grinned and winked at Kate, who blushed beneath the compliment.

Will gathered his black coat and Connor stood, glad to get the man out of his house before he ran off at the mouth and Connor's entire past was laid bare for Kate to pick over. "I'll walk you out."

Will waited until they were outside before he spoke again. "She doesn't know?"

Connor didn't have to ask what Will referred to. It seemed to be all the townspeople wanted to talk about since he came back. That and getting him married off.

"No." He unwound the reins from the hitching post near

the chicken coop and led the sable-colored horse out of Kate's earshot, forcing Will to follow. "And I prefer to keep it that way, too."

"She's bound to find out eventually, Con. You know how people in this town like to talk. Maybe it's best you tell her yourself?"

Connor shifted his weight uncomfortably from one foot to the other and crossed his arms over his chest. He couldn't look Will in the eye. "No reason she needs to know."

"Isn't there?" His horse snorted impatiently and Connor wished the man would take the hint and head on out. He didn't want to think about all the reasons he should tell Kate. Besides, if she was content to keep her own secrets, shouldn't he be allowed a few of his own?

"I didn't come back to Fatal Bluff to relive the past."

Will patted his horse's neck to settle it down. "If I recall, you didn't want to come back here at all."

Connor couldn't argue with that point. Coming back to Fatal Bluff had been the last thing he wanted. But he'd done it anyway. He'd picked up the threads of a life he'd run away from eight years earlier, only to find its landscape had changed dramatically.

Grant was dead. Emily too. In their place stood a little girl who bore only a faint resemblance to either of them. He began to wonder if he had changed too from the hotheaded young man who had charged out of town, hurt and betrayed, swearing never to return. In the time he'd been gone, the scope of his life had altered, widened. He'd ridden through it, not caring about the passing of days, thinking he had all the time in the world to go back and fix things.

Grant's death brought that assumption to an abrupt halt. In an instant, he'd lost forever the chance to make amends, to put their relationship right. He should have come back when he'd heard of Emily's death, but pride and hurt kept him away.

It took an outlaw's bullet to bring him home, and by then, it was too late.

"Well, I'm here now."

Will nodded and stuck a foot in the stirrup, swinging himself up into the saddle. "Yes, you are. And you have a chance to start over. Kate's a good woman. It's not right the way you have her living here without the benefit of marriage. It won't be long before talk starts and people wonder what's going on—"

"Nothing's going on," Connor shot out.

Will fixed him with a look that said he might as well try to convince him his horse was about to sprout wings and fly home.

"Lying to a man of God, Con?" He clucked his tongue. "You look at her like you're a man dropped in the middle of the desert and she's the oasis."

Connor swallowed. Hell.

"Make things right, Con. And tell her the truth before she hears it from someone else."

But he couldn't make things right. She wasn't free to let that happen. And he wasn't sure he trusted his heart enough to take that step even if she were.

Will reached down and took the reins from Connor. "I'll see you this Saturday."

"I'm not going to the damn social."

Will gave him a knowing smile. "Yes you are," he said, and Connor knew it for the truth. Just last night Kate had been busily hemming a dress in the hopes of attending, and he couldn't find it in himself to dash that hope.

Connor stepped back as Will rode off. He waited until horse and rider grew to a speck on the horizon before he turned back to the house. He stopped halfway and looked through the door.

Kate reached across the table for his plate, piling the silverware on top, chatting away to Jenny. The blue paisley shirt-waist melded to her body, outlining the shape of her breasts and drawing downward to her small waist. One of Emily's, he assumed.

He tried to imagine Emily in it, but couldn't picture her face with any detail or clarity. She remained a fuzzy image in his mind's eye, receding into the blackness.

The realization struck him unexpectedly and squeezed the air from his lungs. There had been a time when he thought her image would be burned into his memory forever. It surprised him he could barely remember the details, or the sound of her voice. Now when he closed his eyes, the image that haunted him had strawberry blond curls, sea-green eyes and a body that fit so perfectly against his he found it difficult to imagine she could be made for anyone else.

Connor changed direction and headed for the barn with swift strides. He couldn't go back inside. Couldn't face Kate after that kiss and not pick up where he'd left off. He needed some time and distance to wrap his head around his raging emotions...and stuff them back down to the dark corner where he'd kept them for the past eight years.

Chapter Seventeen

"We have a traitor in our midst, Sheriff!"

Connor stopped his ascent up the staircase to Amelia's boardinghouse and turned, staring down at Oliver Hewitt. Sunlight glinted off the man's bald head. "Beg your pardon, Hewitt?"

"A traitor, Sheriff."

Connor glanced at the pink envelope in Oliver's hand. The faint trace of rose wafted up in the still air to tickle his senses. He recognized it immediately. It was a letter from Hannah Stockdale.

The *real* Hannah Stockdale. His heart plummeted to his boots.

Connor held out his hand and Oliver stuffed the letter into it. "She says she has changed her mind about our business venture and sends her deepest regrets. It appears she will not be traveling to Fatal Bluff to marry Walter Figg. Do you know what that means, Sheriff?"

Connor swallowed. He knew exactly what that meant. The only problem was, so did Oliver Hewitt. And now the question was, how did he keep the nosy little man's mouth from wagging all about town with the news that Kate was not who she said she was? If she was hiding from an abusive husband—and Connor could only assume that was the case, given that she was rather sketchy on the details—then outing her as a liar in front of the whole town would likely only cause her to run. And he couldn't afford that.

For Jenny's sake.

Connor chose his words carefully. "I know she isn't the real Hannah Stockdale."

Oliver's eyes bulged. "You do? Then why isn't she in jail?"

Connor released a hard breath and stepped down off the staircase into the quiet street. Shops had closed early this evening to allow people to prepare for the social. "She isn't in jail because no crime has been committed."

"Fraud, Sheriff! She has committed fraud! She bilked us out of the train fare and a night's lodgings and she—"

"And if I lock her up you won't be getting one cent of that back," Connor reminded him. That was enough to shut Oliver up. "Listen, the lady has had some difficulties in the past and just wants to start a new life. I say we let her. You'll get your money repaid, I get myself a housekeeper to care for Jenny, and everyone's happy."

"But—"

"But nothing, Oliver," Connor said. He leaned in close and fixed the man with a hard stare. "I don't want you mucking this up. She's not hurting anyone. Now, I'm going to hang onto this letter and I don't want one word of this being breathed to anyone until Kate decides she's ready to tell. Do I make myself clear? Because if I hear you haven't kept your mouth shut, I'm going to be pretty mad, Oliver. And I guarantee you do not want to be on the business end of that. Do we understand each other?"

Oliver's chins quivered as he hastily nodded his head. "Yes, of course, Sheriff. I—I would be more than pleased to keep your confidence. After all, I'm a business man. I know the meaning of discretion, I do."

Connor straightened and folded the letter, shoving it into his shirt pocket. "Good. Now, if you'll excuse me." He turned his back on Oliver and headed up the stairs. He hadn't intended on seeing Kate tonight, but he guessed he'd best warn her that Oliver knew the truth.

Or at least as much of it as anyone did.

T he idea of spending an evening in town at the autumn social made the butterflies flitter about in Katherine's stomach until she could barely concentrate on pinning her unruly curls in place. The only dark shadow cast on her excitement was Connor's firm refusal to attend. Instead, he drove her and Jenny into Fatal Bluff and dropped them at Amelia's boardinghouse, where they would spend the night. She wouldn't see Connor again until the next day when he arrived to bring them home after church services ended.

Disappointment flooded her veins, but Katherine knew it was for the best. She didn't need to be building silly daydreams where Connor was concerned. Besides, if he asked her to dance she'd just trample his toes and make a fool of herself. She'd never been to a dance or social before. Her life had never allowed for such things.

A knock on the guest room door made her jump. "Kate?"

She slid the last pin through the curls piled high on her head, took one final look in the vanity mirror and crossed the room to open the door. Connor stood on the other side, his hat in his hands.

He took a step back, his mouth opened, but no words came out. His gaze traveled up from her toes, stopping briefly at her cinched waist, and again at the ruffled neckline that scooped downward and revealed a rather dazzling display of cleavage she'd forgotten she had. It had been a long time since she'd fit herself into a proper corset.

Katherine looked down at the silk dress with its dark green-and-brown stripes and gathered hem. Beth Sangster had been kind enough to lend her a pair of proper shoes that fit and Amelia had insisted she wear a cameo necklace of hers that dangled just above the swell of her breasts. She'd never worn anything so fine. Part of her worried she would do something to ruin it.

Nerves worked her over and she glanced up into Connor's startled expression. "Maybe I shouldn't go."

He nodded then shook his head.

Confused, Katherine tried to decipher which he meant. "I shouldn't go?"

"No...uh...I mean..." He cleared his throat.

"I should go?"

"You...um..." He winced and the skin across his cheek-bones tightened. "You look real pretty," he said finally, but the words seemed to cost him.

"Oh." Katherine swallowed at the unexpected compliment and smoothed the skirt of her dress with a shaky hand. "Thank you." One rebellious curl escaped its moorings and dangled against her cheek. "Oh drat."

She reached up to fix it but Connor's hand stayed her own. "No, leave it." He touched the buoyant lock, letting it slip between his fingers. Katherine couldn't move, couldn't do anything but stare at the intent expression on his face.

He stared at the curl as if it contained answers to the mysteries of the universe. "When you fell asleep that first day after arriving at the house, I checked in on you."

"You did?" Her lungs constricted.

He nodded then smiled. "I was hungry."

She couldn't help the small laugh that escaped.

"Your hair was loose and had fallen over the pillow. It reminded me of autumn, all red and gold."

"It did?" Lord, how she wanted to close the distance between them. He hadn't touched her since their last kiss and not a minute had passed that she didn't ache for more.

As if her thoughts had set off a warning, Connor dropped the curl and took a step back, the desire she'd seen rising in his gaze quickly smothered. "I just had a talk with Oliver Hewitt."

Katherine froze. The Hewitts had caused nothing but grief for her since she arrived in Fatal Bluff. Mention of their name set her already taxed nerves on edge. "Oh?"

Connor nodded. "Seems he got another letter from Hannah Stockdale telling him she'd changed her mind and wouldn't be making the trip to Fatal Bluff."

Relief over knowing the real Hannah Stockdale was not going to show up was eradicated by the fact her letter had done the damage anyway. Her ruse had been discovered.

Somewhere in the corner of Katherine's eyes blackness threatened. She felt the world tilt slightly as if it were trying to shake her free and leave her tumbling into the void. "He knows."

"He knows you're not Hannah Stockdale, nothing more. He's promised to keep his mouth shut. But I thought you ought to know."

Katherine rested a hand against her stomach, unable to feel it through the boning of the corset. She couldn't breathe, though the lacing was not drawn too tight and up until that moment had been perfectly comfortable. Now it felt as if it was crushing her.

"You alright?"

She shook her head. She was a far cry from being all right. Oliver Hewitt knew she was not Hannah Stockdale. And while he may have promised to hold his tongue, Katherine didn't fool herself into believing that would last. The idyllic picture she had created in her mind, one filled with happiness and laughter and Connor and Jenny, deteriorated. It had been a foolish dream anyhow, but that didn't make its destruction any less painful.

"Kate?"

She pursed her lips and drew in a shaky breath. There was nothing left to do. At month's end, Connor would give her the wages she'd earned. She would pay off the Hewitts and quietly slip away.

"I'm fine. I'm..." There were no words. None she could find that truly encompassed everything she was feeling in that moment. "Thank you for telling me. And for ensuring Mr. Hewitt kept it to himself. I appreciate it."

Connor nodded. "Amelia said they're ready to go. I should get you downstairs."

Absently, Katherine slid her arm through his and let him lead the way, each step taking her closer to leaving, to her heart breaking, and to the knowledge that a life on the run was the only kind of life she would ever have.

When they reached the parlor, all eyes turned. Beth and the Reverend, Amelia and Bart stopped mid conversation. Connor's arm dropped away and Katherine missed the support until she felt the light touch of his hand at the small of her back, his fingertips burning through the layers of silk and boning.

"Well my, my," Amelia said, stepping forward. "Don't you look pretty as a picture."

Katherine fidgeted under the scrutiny until Jenny pushed her way through the adults. Her small hands covered her mouth though not enough to hide the sweet smile beneath.

"Pretty."

Katherine blinked. Every nerve in her body jumped to attention. She stared at Jenny in disbelief. Her voice was raw and rough, barely more than a whisper from months of disuse, but the effect couldn't have been less if she'd shouted it from the rooftop. Behind her, she heard Connor's swift intake of breath. No one moved. They all stared at Jenny in stunned silence.

As if sensing the change in the room, Jenny looked around at the adults. A trickle of apprehension smothered the spark in her eye.

Katherine found her own voice and forced her limbs to move. She knelt before Jenny and smiled, joy beginning to bubble up inside of her, overriding her initial surprise.

"Do you think so, Jenny? I wasn't sure the dress would suit."

Jenny nodded and smiled once again.

"Thank you, sweetie." Katherine gathered the little girl in her arms and hugged her, unable to stop the sting of tears that burned her eyes. "It means a lot to me that you think so. You look very pretty too."

Jenny's arms wound around Katherine's neck and squeezed back. A quiet giggle tickled her ear. When they separated, Katherine took Jenny's hand in hers. "Shall we go then?"

Katherine turned and stopped short, nearly knocking into Connor. He stood, his eyes fixed on her, myriad emotions racing across his expression one on top of the other until she couldn't identify any of them. But she could imagine. All the same emotions raged through her.

Jenny had spoken.

She'd broken the dark silence she'd sunken into and uttered her first word since her father's death. Katherine wanted to shout, cry, jump and cartwheel through the room. But Jenny had been unnerved by the sudden attention, and Katherine realized the best thing to do was to treat it as if she had never stopped speaking in the first place.

"Say good-night to your uncle, Jenny."

She waved a small hand. "'Night."

Connor scooped his niece into his arms and held her against his broad chest. "You know," his voice came out in a croak, his shock and relief barely contained. "I think maybe I'll go after all."

～

Connor didn't set Jenny down until they reached the town hall. He was reluctant to let her go, still amazed at what had happened. He thought if he could hold her forever he could keep her safe, keep her from crawling back into the protective silence she'd wrapped herself in for the past seven months. But by the time they arrived at the doors, Jenny squirmed her way down to chase after Beth's children and disappeared inside. The others followed, Bart with his fiddle in hand. Connor held the door, letting everyone file past.

"Wait!" Kate stopped him when he tried to usher her inside. The stricken look he'd seen at the boardinghouse when he knocked on her door had returned. Connor lifted an eyebrow, easing the door shut. Music filtered out through the thick oak door. He recognized Jeb Gatling's vigorous fiddle playing and knew it was just a matter of minutes before Bart joined in.

"What's wrong?"

Nervousness etched tiny lines into the outer edges of her eyes. Her hands pressed against the silky material. "Was Jenny right? Do I look okay?"

Connor stepped back from the door, careful not to bang his head on the lamp hanging from a hook overhead. Another couple passed by them, and he tipped his hat at Bill and Mandy Cuthbert. The interruption gave him a moment to collect his thoughts, though once he turned to look at Kate they scattered once again.

"You look fine." In truth, she looked nothing short of stunning. Though the dress had belonged to Emily, Kate had made some alterations, bringing it in through the waist and drawing up the hem to keep from tripping over it.

"You think so? I won't be unfashionable? Or stick out? Or—"

Connor shook his head, cutting her off. He didn't know one lick about women's fashions, but even a blind man could tell she'd be the most beautiful woman at the dance. In town, even. Hell, probably the whole country. The promises he'd made to keep his hands to himself faded like smoke caught in the wind.

"You look just fine," he answered. The words came out strangled, and he didn't recognize his own voice.

Kate smiled, relief easing the tension from her features. A tinge of pink colored her cheeks and the smattering of freckles across the bridge of her nose danced in the lamplight. "Thank you. And you're sure Mr. Hewitt won't tell anyone about the letter?"

He nodded. "I'm sure." Not if he knew what was good for him.

"Okay." She nodded. "I'm ready."

She squared her shoulders and faced the door. She looked as though she was facing down a battalion of soldiers and not a hall filled with dancing couples.

Connor opened the door for her and swept an arm toward it. "After you."

If Kate had been concerned about her appearance, she needn't have worried. Based on the amount of attention she received the moment she walked through that door, she would likely never question her appeal again. They had no sooner entered the festively decorated room with its swirling bodies and hum of conversation than she was descended upon by every unattached male in town. Suddenly Connor wished he'd worn his guns; then he could shoot each one of them in the foot every time they came within arm's reach of her. He didn't think anything could cut through the joy of hearing Jenny's voice for the first time, but watching a bevy of bachelors jockeying for position while Kate smiled warmly at each one of them came damn close. Telling himself she was married and in no position to encourage any of them did not make him feel any better.

Connor turned his attention away from the fawning and preening and sought out Jenny, finding her in a group of children near the edge of the refreshment table.

She had spoken. Only two glorious words, but it was a start. If Kate hadn't taken control of the moment, Connor felt certain he'd still be standing in Amelia's parlor, his chin on the floor, staring in disbelief. But Kate had taken control, instinctively knowing what Jenny needed while the rest of them just watched in rapt fascination.

Slowly, the fear that Jenny would never crawl out of her silent shell began to dissipate, and for the first time in a long time, Connor had the courage to hope. To believe he hadn't failed. He knew better than to take the credit. His only part in this was to bring Kate to their home. She had done the rest, providing a soft, steady presence. She'd filled the house with her warmth and made it a home.

Bringing Kate into their lives had been the best thing he could have done for Jenny. And the worst thing for himself.

He wasn't sure how or when it had happened, but somehow, Kate Stockdale—or whatever the hell her last name was —had managed to burrow under his skin until he couldn't think straight anymore. She had wrapped herself so tightly in his mind all thoughts led back to her.

Delbert Mackie's voice rose above the others requesting a dance. Connor couldn't stand it any longer. He shouldered his way through the crowd before Kate could answer.

"Sorry, gentlemen. This dance is promised to me."

K atherine smiled, grateful for the rescue. She'd never had so much attention focused on her at one time before and while it was flattering, she didn't want any of it. The only man she wanted to notice her stood off to the side, ignoring her completely. At least until Mr. Mackie voiced a desire to dance, a request that speared her with dread.

"I can't dance," she admitted, letting Connor lead her out onto the dance floor amidst the crush of bodies. His arm slid easily around her waist and pulled her close, until the space between them shrunk to mere inches.

"Can't? At all?"

"No. I never learned. No one ever asked me before."

"I find that hard to believe."

He pulled her closer, his fingers splayed across her lower back, holding her firmly against him. She stumbled, her foot stepping on his.

"Told you so," she muttered, embarrassed by her lack of grace.

"Well what do you know, you can tell the truth." She heard the smile in his voice, felt his warm breath touch her cheek like a soft caress. Her hand gripped his shoulder as the strength in her legs began to wane and her limbs grew heavy and languid.

"Where is Jenny?" she asked, valiantly trying to turn her thoughts in another, safer, direction.

"Watching from the refreshment table with Beth's girls." Connor spun her around so she faced in the direction of the table. He slowed then, allowing her a chance to watch the three children before he had to spin them once again to avoid colliding with other couples.

His agility on the dance floor surprised her. "You seem to know what you're doing. Do you do this a lot?"

He shook his head, the movement slow, barely perceptible. "Not for a long time."

She breathed in the soapy scent of him, filling her lungs with it. "I'm glad," she whispered, the admission slipping out before she could stop it. The pressure of his hand increased just enough to let her know the desire curling in her belly extended beyond herself.

The music faded away until she barely heard it and the couples around them became nothing more than a swirl of blurred color cocooning the two of them into a world of their own. She could feel the rise and fall of his chest against her, tantalizing, building a slow ache that traveled downward to pool low in her belly. Katherine wished the music would play on forever, never changing. She wanted to rest in the safety of Connor's arms for the next hundred years.

But time refused to stop, and the mournful sounds of the waltz came to an end and a more lively jig began.

"I beg you, please don't make me try to keep up with this one."

She felt Connor's smile against her temple and the pressure of his hand on her back eased. "I think you've trampled my toes enough for now."

She giggled. A strange, gurgling sensation bubbled up from somewhere inside of her. From a place where happiness grew and lies never touched.

Oh, if she could only bottle this night and live it over and over again. Katherine pushed the wistful wish away as Connor led her from the dance floor. She would not waste time on wishes. Tonight she would live, she would revel in what she had and not think about all she would lose now that Jenny was healing and her time to leave had arrived.

The night wore on. Each time a gentleman asked her to

dance she found one excuse or another to decline. The thought of being held in anyone else's arms seemed too wrong. But Connor steered clear. After he'd brought her back to the refreshment table and fortified her with mulled cider, he excused himself and disappeared. Now and again, she'd see his golden head in the crowd, talking to one group of men or another. But he didn't ask her to dance a second time.

Without Connor to distract her, her thoughts began to drift back to Jenny. The fact that she had spoken thrilled Katherine. But her joy was tempered, selfishly so. With Jenny doing better there was nothing keeping her here. She'd kept her promise to Grant. All that remained now was to deliver the letter to Connor, pay off the Hewitts and leave town.

The truth of that tore through her with a ferocity she had been unprepared for. She had always known she could not stay, but she had never imagined the pain leaving would bring. She loved Jenny. She loved this town and the way it looked after its own. She loved Bart and Amelia and Con—

Katherine blinked. No. She did not love Connor...Did she?

Her eyes searched for him in the crowd and found him, his broad shoulders filling her vision. Though most of the men present wore their Sunday best, Connor hadn't changed out of his denims and worn blue chambray shirt. She'd sewn new buttons on that shirt just the other day. Who would do that now? Who would make him his favorite apple cobbler, or cheese biscuits, or the gravy he liked so much? Who would keep his house clean, look after Jenny, or make sure he let Rudy in each night?

Worst of all, who would make him smile so his eyes crinkled at the corners, or trample his toes when they danced, or kiss his lips with more passion than a body had a right to feel?

Who would warm his bed at night and wake to see his

handsome face each morning for the rest of her life? Who would that be?

She only knew it would not be her.

The knowledge clawed at her heart, cutting it to ribbons. She did love him. Sadness smothered her and tears burned her eyes. She loved him and she had to leave. Fate's final retribution for all she had done wrong.

Katherine stumbled from the hall, needing air to fill the sudden emptiness inside of her. The cool October night greeted her and she wished she'd thought to grab her shawl, but she couldn't go back. The need to move, to outrun the pain, propelled her up the tiny rise to the church where Reverend Sangster preached his Sunday services. She bypassed the white clapboard building with its steeple that reached up toward the stars. Following the line of the statuesque elms, she reached a white picket fence. Within its borders, stone and wooden markers dotted the well-tended grass. Scattered amongst the graves, a few brave wildflowers refused to succumb to the frost and dotted the ground with bursts of color that turned blue and silver in the eerie glow of moonlight.

"Kate?"

Katherine did a half turn at the sound of Amelia's voice approaching from behind. "Oh...Hello." She swallowed, not sure if she had it in her to cover up her misery in the face of company. She ducked her chin to avoid the other woman's sharp gaze.

Amelia stopped next to her and handed Katherine her shawl. "Thought you might need this."

As if to punctuate the offer, a stiff breeze buffeted their skirts and made her shiver. Katherine wrapped the wool fabric tight around her shoulders, grateful for its warmth, and for Amelia's thoughtfulness. "Thank you."

"Rather pretty for a final resting place, isn't it?"

Katherine answered with a nod.

"Con's parents are buried right over there," Amelia said, pointing to the far corner of the fenced-in yard. Two narrow slabs jutted from the earth, side by side, tilting toward each other.

"Was their passing recent?" Katherine asked, thankful for the diversion from her mottled emotions.

Amelia shook her head. "Oh no. It was a long time ago now. Con was fourteen, Grant just three years his senior. Their mother had been unwell for quite some time. When she died, their father wasn't far behind. Broken heart, I think, though I'm sure Doc Bolger would come up with some other diagnosis."

"Did you and Bart take them in?"

"No. We would have, gladly. But Grant was determined to do it on his own. He took a job as deputy while Sheriff Moseby was still alive, and set about raising Con up right." Amelia chuckled then. "Though once he realized just how headstrong his younger brother was, I expect he wished he could have changed his mind." She lifted a finger to point near the center of the graveyard. Her voice softened, and Katherine could hear the sadness in her tone. "He's buried right there near the middle, next to his wife."

"Grant?" She could barely force the man's name past the thickness in her throat. She had thought he would have been buried where he died. She never considered his body had been brought home. For that, she was thankful. He deserved to be laid to rest amongst his kin.

Amelia nodded. "He was a good man. Took over after a fashion when Sheriff Moseby retired. Seemed to enjoy it, though it was hard to tell. Grant was always the more serious of the two. Quieter."

"Like Jenny?"

Amelia laughed, a rich, husky sound full of mirth. "Oh heavens, no! Jenny inherited her uncle's easy temperament."

Katherine smiled. When she'd first met Connor she thought him remote, but even then, she sensed the essence beneath the distant façade. Warmth and laughter danced behind those vivid blue eyes, and no matter how hard he tried to hide it, it kept sneaking out.

Katherine turned around and looked at the church, its white steeple stark against the starry night sky, and a question prodded her curiosity. "Why doesn't Connor go to church? Reverend Sangster keeps trying to get him there, but Connor won't budge."

"I suppose that's to be expected." Amelia let her gaze drift down the hill. Some people had congregated outside and Katherine realized things were winding down. She could see Connor standing a little taller than most, his hair windswept by the breeze.

"Expected why?" She let Amelia take her arm and lead her back down the hill.

"Ever since the wedding, he's refused to step foot in the church."

"Th—the wedding?" The words stammered out of her.

"Emily and Connor's wedding."

Katherine tripped over a thick tuft of grass, too shocked to lift her feet to step over it. "Emily and Connor? Don't you mean Grant?"

Amelia stopped before they reached the growing crowd. Her brow puckered in confusion. "No. I mean Connor..." Her voice faded. "He didn't tell you?"

Katherine shook her head, unable to form the words. No, he hadn't told her. He'd asked her plenty of questions, but answers to his own past had been in short supply. Beyond the fact that he'd left town eight years ago and returned after his brother's death, she knew very little about his past. Certainly not that he'd married his brother's wife! How was that even possible?

"Ask him," Amelia said, resting a hand on Katherine's arm. "He's bottled it up inside for far too long. He won't talk to any of us. Bart and I have tried. But I think maybe he'll talk to you."

"Why would he?" With all her lies, she'd be the last person he trusted with the truth.

Amelia smiled. She lifted one hand and pressed its warmth against Katherine's cheek. "I've seen the way he looks at you, the way he watches you when you're not looking. You've managed to wiggle your way past those walls he's spent eight years building. I expect that probably scares the pants off him and he's not sure what to do about it. But you might as well take advantage and get that boy to face up to his past."

"His past?" What could he have done that was so awful, that needed facing up to?

Amelia's eyes softened. "He has a good heart. He's just afraid to listen to it anymore. Thinks because it was wrong once it can't ever be right again. Maybe you can change his mind on that."

But she couldn't. She didn't have that right. She was a married woman, the wife of an outlaw. She was the last person on earth Connor should trust.

And they both knew it.

Amelia gave her arm a final squeeze and left to find Bart. Katherine stood alone for a moment before Connor sought her out.

"You okay?" His voice brushed over her, scrambling her senses and making her nerves sing.

She nodded, unable to speak just yet. Too many unanswered questions whirled in her brain. She feared that if she opened her mouth, they would all tumble out at once.

"Beth asked to take Jenny home with her tonight. You said

being around other children would be good for her, so I thought especially now…" His voice trailed off and he looked at her expectantly until Katherine realized he sought her agreement.

She bobbed her head. "Yes…yes, I think that's good."

Connor rolled the brim of his hat in his fingers and stared at the ground. After a silent moment, he glanced up at the stars. "I can take you home if you'd like. Bring you back to town in the morning to pick up Jenny." He shrugged. "Or you can stay here if you'd prefer."

Katherine shook her head. Her days here were numbered. She could feel the end coming and knew there was nothing she could do to stop it. She wanted to spend what time she had left at the one place where she felt safe and needed.

However illusory that feeling was.

"Take me home."

Chapter Eighteen

"*T*ake me home."

Kate's words echoed in Connor's mind long after the ride home. He'd dropped her off at the house and continued on to the barn to unhitch the buggy. She'd been quiet the whole way, barely saying a word. Perhaps not terribly unusual, but she'd been so happy at the dance, he couldn't imagine what had changed. Hewitt had steered clear of her, Connor's warning apparently doing its job. And near as he could tell no one said anything untoward about their living arrangements. That left only one thing.

He'd seen her at Grant's graveside with Amelia.

Had Amelia said something to her? And if so, what?

Connor closed the door to Belle's stall and let his weight sag against it. Being with Kate stirred up a quagmire of emotions he didn't want to deal with. For eight years he'd ignored them, heaped anger on top of them and buried the hurt well beneath it.

He discovered early on it was easier to be angry than hurt. Anger fueled him, kept him moving, pushed him on. Hurt... well, that just stopped a body cold in its tracks. Took your breath away until you fell to your knees gasping for air. Anger didn't break your heart the way hurt did. It kept you busy, so you didn't have to think about how your insides were shattered into pieces so small they no longer fit back together the way they used to.

And for the longest time it hadn't mattered that he was broken. Hell, after a while he stopped caring. Until he came home. Until he hired Kate and suddenly all the feelings he thought were dead and gone came raging back. No matter how hard he tried to stuff them down, they kept popping back up. Day after day, her smile and her warmth wormed their way in. Little by little, her presence sewed the broken pieces back together. He hadn't even noticed it because it felt so damn natural just being around her. Like she belonged there.

Like she belonged with him.

But she didn't, he reminded himself. She was another man's wife.

A man who scared her so intensely she was willing to assume another woman's identity to hide away from him. A man he wanted to protect her from. Save her from.

Dammit.

Had he felt that way with Emily? Connor shook his head. He could barely recall. For years, the only thing about Emily he allowed himself to remember was her betrayal. His memory of her paled after that final day. One thing he did know—and the truth of it did little to quell the confusion welling inside of him—but even on her best day, Emily wasn't half the woman Kate was.

Kate was strong and sweet and genuine. Despite the lies she'd told, the past she still kept hidden, his instincts told him he could trust her. And his heart stood firm in its agreement.

He loved her.

The realization slammed into him and squeezed the air from his lungs.

Dear God, it couldn't be true. Not so soon. Not this fast.

But there it was. Truer than anything he had ever known.

He loved her.

He loved a woman he didn't know. A woman who refused to trust him with her truth. A woman whose touch filled him with all the dreams he thought he'd left behind eight years ago.

Maybe Will had the right of it. Maybe it was time he fessed up to her before someone else filled her in on the truth. Maybe then she'd feel free to confess her past to him and they could find a way to free her from her husband.

And she could be his.

He returned to the house and found Kate standing by the kitchen table, her arms methodically kneading a shapeless lump of dough. Flour dusted her forearms and sprinkled the front of her dress. She had changed back into her yellow calico. The soft glow from the lamp brought out streaks of gold that wound through her curls.

"You're baking bread?"

She glanced at him briefly before returning to work. "We need some for the morning. And I wasn't that tired, so..." Her words drifted off.

"Kate?"

"Hmm?" She pressed her hands into the dough one last time before shaping it into an oval and dropping it into the waiting pan.

"I saw you at the graveyard with Amelia."

Kate nodded and covered the bread with a tea towel, returning it to the counter to rise. "Yes. She showed me where your brother's grave was."

"Did she say anything else?"

Kate shrugged, keeping her back to him. "Just that he raised you after your parents died." She stopped for a moment, then added, "And that you and Emily were married."

"She said what?"

213

Kate turned. "But I don't understand. How could you marry her when she was already married to your brother?"

Connor didn't know where to start, other than to blurt out the whole sordid mess. "Emily was my fiancée."

"But Amelia said—"

"You must have misunderstood. I courted Emily for over a year. I was twenty-two. Reckless. Headstrong. Thought I owned the world. I had all these lofty ideas about heading north, maybe getting a spread of my own, raise some cattle. Didn't have one sweet clue how I planned to accomplish such a feat with barely a nickel to my name, but I was going to do it, and I was going to take Emily with me. I thought it would be a great adventure."

Kate shook her head. "What happened?"

His past reassembled itself in his mind, pulling together pieces he had refused to think about for years, resurrecting the pain, dulled by time yet honed by regret. "The day Emily and I were to be married, Grant and I stood waiting at the front of the church. The whole town had stuffed themselves into the pews to watch us say our vows. But an hour passed, and Emily didn't show."

"Where was she?"

Connor tensed, remembering the humiliation of having to go search for his bride while the town clucked their tongues in pity. "Grant and I found her back at her pa's place, sitting in the kitchen, wearing her wedding dress."

Kate rested her hand lightly on his forearm. Warmth seeped through his shirtsleeve into his skin and he closed his eyes, soaking it in. That small bit of encouragement made it easier to go on.

"I asked her why she wasn't at the church. She said—" he stumbled over the memory, "—she said she couldn't marry me. Said I was too wild. She couldn't count on me to provide a good home or be a good husband and father. She said she wanted a man like my brother. Not someone like me."

"Did Grant...did he know how she felt?"

Connor shrugged. The pain of his brother's duplicity still stung even after all this time. Emily's betrayal he could take, it had been Grant's that had hurt the most. "Guess so. They married less than a month later."

"What did he say when you confronted him about it?"

Connor laughed, the sound bitter and mirthless. "I didn't. I was too angry. I stormed out of the house, packed a bag and rode straight out of town as fast as I could." He let out a long, pent-up sigh. "I never saw or spoke to my brother again. Bart sent word they had married, and shortly thereafter when Jenny was born. Then a few years later to tell me Emily had taken ill and died."

"How did Bart know where to find you?"

"I didn't want them to worry about me, so I kept in touch, just in case..."

He let his words trail off. In case what? He hadn't believed anything could ever happen to Grant. He was strong, steady and dependable. Connor never considered for a moment any misfortune would ever befall his older brother. But it had.

"Why didn't you come home after Emily died?"

Connor took Kate's hand and pulled her closer. He needed her touch, needed the comfort of having her close. Resurrecting his past had left him raw and exposed. "Pride, I guess."

"I'm sorry you were hurt."

Her words slid past his barriers to a dark corner and shone a warm light where he kept his pain hidden. Funny how she did that, lit up the places no one else could reach.

"I wish I understood why he betrayed me like that," he said. The question had worn a deep path through his heart, but he'd never found a satisfactory answer. And he'd had too much of that damned pride to ask Bart and Amelia.

"Sometimes people make mistakes, big ones. They rush in thinking they're doing the right thing and then find out they were wrong. But by then it's too late, and the damage is done."

Connor looked at her, into her. Was she talking about Grant or herself? There was something buried in her expression, struggling to the surface. "Is that what happened to you?"

Regret blazed in her eyes. She took a step back, her withdrawal hitting him like a bitter gust of wind.

"Everyone makes mistakes, Connor. And sometimes we can't go back and fix them."

He reached for her, pulling her back to him. She didn't resist, didn't pull away when he cupped the side of her face. "Whatever mistake you made, you're safe now. Here with me. I won't let anything happen to you."

An unexpected tear trickled down her cheek. He swept it away with his thumb and lowered his head, hesitating for one final second, before brushing his lips over the trail of moisture left behind.

"Connor..." His name on her breath fueled him. His lips sought hers, a shudder coursing through him as they met. Soft at first, gentle. He wanted to comfort her. To take away their pasts and make them not matter. The tension in her body eased and she leaned in, pressing her lithe curves against the length of him. It proved his undoing.

He devoured her, breathed her in. Warm flour and lavender clung to her like a tantalizing mist, teasing his senses into madness. God help him, he couldn't get enough of this woman—this stranger who had invaded his mind, his heart, his very soul. One touch would never be enough. He knew that now. He had to have her, to make her his.

A small whimper escaped her and he drew it in, gentling

his kiss until his lips barely moved over hers. Just a light whisper of skin touching skin, breath mingling with breath. His fingertips slid slowly down over the curve of her neck. Connor thought he might lose what was left of his mind. He wasn't at all sure he'd miss it. It took every ounce of his will not to crush her to him, to pick her up and carry her off to the bedroom. Peel away every item of clothing piece by piece until she lay naked beneath him.

"We shouldn't," she whispered. It sounded more like a question than a statement.

"No, we shouldn't." There were probably a hundred reasons why she was right. The biggest one being the husband who lurked in the background. But he could take care of that. They could divorce. It wouldn't be easy, but they'd figure it out. Then they could be together. A family. The two of them and Jenny. Kids of their own—

"I'm leaving." Her words cut straight into his heart.

He lifted his head. "What?"

"You owe me my wages. It's been a month. I'm going to pay off the Hewitts and move on." Her words had the sickening ring of finality to them.

"And go where?"

"It doesn't matter." She closed her eyes and rested her forehead against his cheek. "Please don't kiss me again. I can't stand it. Promise you won't."

"I can't promise you that," he whispered.

Her eyes opened, filled with surprise. "Why not?"

"I'd never be able to keep it."

Chapter Nineteen

onnor didn't give Kate the chance to argue. Proving his point, he kissed her again. Fully, completely, taking possession of her mouth. He swept his tongue over her lips, which parted with a gasp of surprise. She let her weight press against him, her hands sliding up over his chest.

Liquid heat raced through his veins. His tongue slid past the barrier of her teeth and boldly she met him with her own. He nibbled and played, sunk both hands into her hair and freed the glorious mane from the haphazard bun struggling to contain it. Pins clattered against the hardwood floor.

His breathing came in rapid gasps and need raged through his body, demanding release. Her fingers twisted into his shirt. She trembled in his arms and a low moan shivered through her, proving to him she was not immune, that whatever existed between them had infected her as well.

God help him, if he didn't stop now, he would take her right here in the middle of the kitchen. She deserved better than that. She deserved to know this meant something to him. Everything. That he intended on her being a permanent fixture in his life.

He had to convince her not to leave.

Connor dug deep for the tiny shred of decency he had left and broke the kiss. He lifted his head and tried to restore reason—an almost impossible task with her still so close, her breasts heaving against his chest with each ragged breath.

"You can't keep doing that," she said, her voice small and breathless.

He wasn't entirely sure why. The reason escaped him at the moment. Perhaps it would come back to him when he picked up the scattered remnants of his mind and pieced it back together. But for now—for now he couldn't think of anything he wanted more than to feel her next to him.

"You have to let me go."

He shook his head. Why did she keep saying that? Why couldn't she see this was meant to be? Unless...did she not feel it too? "Is that what you want?"

"No. Yes." Katherine couldn't think of a reasonable argument to counter him. The instant his lips touched hers, every particle of her being stopped functioning properly and focused solely on the feel of his mouth, the way it moved against hers, the unsettling exhilaration that tore through her. She wanted him to touch her, to kiss her, to desire her. She'd tried to deny it, but the attempt had been flimsy at best and destined for failure.

She grasped onto the only thing she could to push him away. "I'm married."

"I know."

"But you don't know all of it."

"Then tell me the rest."

Her mind reeled. Tell him the rest? Tell him he had just kissed a Slade? That the woman he held in his arms was responsible for his brother's death? A chill crept into her bones. This had gone too far. She had let herself feel too much and pulled Connor into her heart when she should have pushed him away. She flattened her hands against his chest and pushed now, taking a step back on shaky legs.

Her insides trembled. She had waded into dangerous territory. She couldn't stay here. Couldn't risk his finding out the truth. He had been betrayed once, horribly. She couldn't be the one to hurt him again. This thing between them, whatever it was, could destroy them both.

But oh Lord, what a sweet destruction it would be.

"I should never have let things get this far."

His face hardened, as if bracing for the hurt.

"I'm a married woman," she repeated.

He took a step toward her, a dangerous glint illuminating the black flecks in his eyes. "You've left your husband and I'm guessing you have no intention of going back."

"In the eyes of the law—"

"Don't quote the law to me, Kate."

Connor took another step. She retreated and threw her hand up between them. "Don't."

"Don't what?" He stopped. "Don't touch you? Don't kiss you again? Don't make you sigh with pleasure like you did before?"

She swallowed. Sweet heaven, make him stop talking. "All of it."

"Because you still love your husband?"

"No!" Revulsion shook her. "He's a cruel man. But I married him and I can't change that."

"You can divorce him."

She shook her head. It would never be that easy. "He would never let me go." And he would never let anyone else have her. He'd kill whoever got in his way. Hadn't attacking the stagecoach proven that? Innocent people had died. Good people. Connor's people. "You don't understand."

"Then make me understand."

"I can't."

His penetrating gaze rocked her. "You won't."

She pressed her lips together. Her heart beat painfully in her chest, each pulse sending shards of hurt shooting through every inch of her. If he so much as touched her, she would splinter into a million tiny pieces. "Please, just leave me be. I don't want you. Not in that way."

For a moment, she thought he would ignore her request. She knew if he did the last vestiges of her resilience would crumble to dust. But just when she thought her battle lost, Connor spun on his heel and stalked toward the door without another word. It slammed behind him with a forceful finality.

Katherine's body sagged. She closed her eyes and pressed a shaking hand against her forehead. What had she done? She'd sent away the only man she'd ever cared about, made him think she didn't love him. But she did. She loved him so much her heart ached from the force of it.

The door shuddered against the frame and her gaze shot up just in time to see Connor descending upon her with all the determination of an avenging angel.

"Dammit, Kate, that was the biggest load of crap I've ever heard!"

She didn't have time to mount a protest. Connor's body slammed into hers, propelling her back against the wall. His mouth possessed her. His tongue plundered. Explored, tasted, coaxed. The last of Katherine's defenses disintegrated and she returned his kiss with all the pent-up desire she'd tried so hard to overcome. She couldn't help herself. She wanted him with a ferocity that terrified her.

His fingers inched her skirt up. She hadn't bothered with stockings when she'd changed and his hands on her bare skin drove her mad with longing. She wanted his hands everywhere, on the most intimate parts of her. She lifted her leg to brush against his. He cupped the underside of her knee, tugging her closer, until not even a wisp of air could fit between their bodies. His hardness pressed into her.

Katherine lost all sense of time, of right and wrong, of promises and fear and the fact nothing could ever come of this. Everything fell away until all that remained was this moment, this man, and the feelings erupting through her body and bursting from her heart.

When she thought she would drown in the madness of it all, Connor lifted his mouth from hers. A gentle hand caressed the ridge of her cheekbone, as if she were made of glass so delicate it would shatter at the smallest touch.

"Tell me again you don't want this." Desperation and desire colored his voice. "Tell me you don't want me."

One last opportunity dangled in front of her. She could say the word and he would let her go, walk away. She knew he would. One more lie and she could save herself. Save them both.

She closed her eyes and shook her head. "I can't."

Connor wrapped her in his arms and lifted her off the floor. His mouth never left hers as he blindly made his way from the kitchen. Her feet didn't touch down until they reached the bedroom.

"Once I shut this door, there's no turning back. If you don't want this—if you've any doubts—tell me now."

Her chest rose and fell. She should stop this. She knew she should. It didn't change anything. She would still leave, there was no helping that. But God help her, she wanted just one perfect moment before she did. She needed to know what it was like to be held in arms that loved instead of destroyed, by hands that gave instead of took, by a heart that touched her own.

"I want this." More than she had ever wanted anything. More than her next breath.

Connor reached behind him and with a quick flick of his wrist cut off her last chance to do the right thing and just walk away.

Their breaths mingled and for a moment neither of them moved. Tension crackled in the air between them. Katherine reached up and cupped the side of his face, the bristles of his evening beard rough against her palm. His brilliant blue gaze pierced her through the moonlight that filtered into the room.

Connor lowered his head slowly. His body trembled with restraint. She knew he wanted to toss her back onto the bed and find his release deep within her. She wanted it too, with a desperate, pulsing ache she was powerless to ignore.

His lips touched hers, tentative at first. She opened her mouth to his, let the tip of her tongue gently sweep across his bottom lip. He inhaled sharply and gathered her to him, crushing their bodies together. The kiss deepened as he eased her back onto the mattress.

No words were exchanged. His hands explored her body, peeling away each layer of their clothing piece by piece until no barriers existed between them but her chemise and drawers. Time and again, his hands and his mouth brought her to the brink, then shied away, until she thought she would scream from the exquisite agony of the sensations pulsing through her body.

Her breath caught as his tongue flicked over her nipple, moistening the thin cotton still covering it. As he took the hardened bud in his mouth and suckled it, she thought she would go mad. Perhaps she already had. Every inch of her demanded his touch.

His questing fingers brushed against her ribcage.

She jumped, startled by the sensation and the bubble of laughter that welled inside of her.

Connor lifted his head from her breast, one golden eyebrow raised. He flashed a grin, roguish and unguarded. The strain and stress of his life peeled away, giving her a glimpse of the boy beneath the man. It robbed her of breath.

"Why, Kate," he said, his husky voice dancing over her nerves. "Are you ticklish?"

"It appears I am," she whispered, though she hadn't realized until just this moment. No one had ever tickled her before, even inadvertently. Her heart fluttered like a hummingbird's wings, beating against her chest.

His eyes softened and he lowered his mouth to hers. "Mmm, I'll be sure to keep that in mind."

She could feel the smile playing on his lips. The idea that she was responsible for it filled her with a strange protectiveness, a need to keep it there, to keep the harshness of the world from stealing it away again. She wanted to give him ease and comfort. She wanted to give him herself, join herself to him. It made no sense, they had no future. But she couldn't stop herself.

Katherine struggled for sanity, but with each touch, each caress, her tenuous grip on reason grew weaker. She was drowning in him, and it both frightened and consumed her.

Connor inched his body downward. His mouth burned a line of kisses from her breast to her navel until the tip of his tongue trailed along the edge of her drawers. She drank in a greedy gulp of air. Her stomach tightened against the assault.

His hand glided past her hip and took a slow, deliberate path over her thigh and shin, scalding every inch of her sensitive skin as it brushed along the back of her leg. Then he reached beneath her and cupped her bottom.

He held her to him, his fingers playing with the edge of her drawers. They teased the small of her back as his tongue darted against her belly.

Was there a sweeter torment than this? She couldn't think of one. She couldn't think much at all beyond the havoc he was wreaking upon her senses. She craved more. She had never experienced such exhilaration. A primal need surged from somewhere deep inside of her and threatened to erupt. She shifted slightly, coaxing him to settle between her legs, the need to feel him within more potent than ever.

Connor lifted his head, the dainty pink tie to her drawers held between his teeth. He reached up far enough so the bow undid itself. The material around her waist loosened and he let the ribbon go. It fell against her skin, followed by his lips as he placed a soft kiss against her stomach. He glanced up at her through dark lashes. The moonlight caught his blue eyes, turning them silver. There was a question in them, and Katherine realized he was waiting for her permission before he went any further.

With a shaky breath she realized this was it. The point of no return.

She lifted her hips, a silent answer to his unspoken question. The hint of a smile played about the corners of his mouth. He inched his body downward, taking her drawers with him as he went. His knuckles grazed her backside, sending rivulets of pleasure spiraling outward. He leaned forward and placed a gentle kiss against the cotton still covering the curls at the juncture of her thighs.

"Connor!" His name rasped out of her as she bucked against him. He yanked her drawers further down and she kicked them free, reaching for him. But he had lifted himself onto his elbows, just out of her reach. He lingered above her thighs, his tantalizing mouth too close to her most sensitive spot for her to even think clearly.

"God, you're even more beautiful than I imagined."

He had imagined her like this? The notion made her tingle, part pride, part embarrassment as he lay there looking at her as if he wanted to devour her. She wished he would.

"Come here," she pleaded, needing him closer.

He crawled over her, holding his weight in his forearms,

his gaze steady on hers. Slowly he lowered himself down, and she savored the moment, that delicious instant when their bodies met without any barriers between them. Skin touched skin, inflaming her inch by inch. His arms enfolded her, his need pressed hard against her thigh.

She thought she would die from the want of him.

He kissed her eyelids closed, then pressed his mouth against her temple, her cheek, her ear.

"Kate..."

He brushed his thumb over her bottom lip. Impatience flooded through her. Her legs tightened about his waist and she rocked against him, urging him on. Her hands grasped at his back. Nails dug into his flesh, reaching for something only he could provide.

"Please," she whispered against his mouth.

Connor raised his head and peered into her eyes. Two narrow lines etched deeply between his brows. "Kate—"

She understood what he was about to tell her before he spoke the words. His feelings were carved into every line of his face. But she couldn't risk hearing the words. Couldn't risk what they would do to her.

She lifted a hand and pressed it against his lips. "Don't. Don't say it."

He gently grabbed her wrist and pulled it away. Determination set his mouth in a tight line. "I love you."

The words cut into her and robbed her of breath. "No you don't," she whispered, shaking her head. "You can't."

"I can, and I do."

Her heart became a battleground, joy and pain wielding their weapons of desire and truth. She couldn't speak, could only lie there beneath him and watch eager anticipation light his eyes from the inside.

His smile faltered slightly. "This would be a good time for you to say you love me, too."

Her soul lurched, reaching for him. She pushed it back and swallowed the words before they jumped out of their own volition. "I can't."

His face tightened for an instant. Then, as if he came to his own conclusion on the matter, he relaxed, the hint of a smile softening his gaze. "Yes, you do."

She closed her eyes to hide the truth. He was right. She did. She loved him with an intensity that scared her and filled her and made her shake. But she couldn't tell him, couldn't say the words and then walk away. He deserved better than that.

She pulled her lips in and pursed them tightly, managing a small shake of her head. "No."

C onnor smiled. She really was a horrible liar.
His hand slid down the length of her body until he found the soft mound of curls between her thighs. He cupped his hand over her warmth.

She grasped his wrist. "What are you doing?"

He placed a gentle kiss against her mouth, then murmured his answer against her lips. "Loving you."

"Stop it."

One finger slipped inside her hot, slick center.

"O-oh."

He smiled and slowly withdrew, nibbling at her ear. His fingertips played lightly at her opening, touching then retreating, teasing her until her breath came in short gasps.

"Connor..."

"Do you want me to keep going?"

She arched her hips against his hand. "Oh, yes...please."

He pressed his mouth against her ear. "Then say the words."

She writhed beneath the torment, seeking the release his touch promised. "I said please."

He chuckled low in his throat and slipped his fingers inside her once again. She shivered in response. "Not quite the ones I was looking for."

"Connor...I can't...please." Her breathing grew more labored and he withdrew once again.

"Yes, you can."

She opened her eyes and sent him a silent plea. He could almost hear her begging him to let it alone. His resistance faltered. He wouldn't force the words out of her. If she wouldn't give them willingly, he would content himself with the knowledge they existed in silence.

He lowered his mouth to hers and shifted his weight to rest where his hand had been. She was ready for him. His erection throbbed hard and urgent, desperate to feel her soft, tight walls close around him.

He entered her slowly, watching her as he probed the warmth between her legs. He pushed just beyond it and stopped, fascinated by the play of emotion that flashed across her face.

"Oh..." Her eyelids fluttered closed. She bit down, her teeth scraping against her bottom lip and she thrust against him, bringing him further into her. Connor let out an expletive as her legs tightened around him. A shiver vibrated through her body and into his.

He leaned down and kissed her, hot, teasing. "More?"

She arched against him. "More. All."

Inch by glorious inch he pushed inside of her, filling her until she surrounded him. She became all there was. The beginning, the ending, the in between. Connor could no longer discern where he left off and she began. Nor did he care.

He moved within her and she met his thrusts. Their

bodies moved as one, timeless, endless. Tension built inside of him like a coiled spring. She tightened around him, a soft exclamation expelling with her next breath. He quickened his pace, driving harder.

She moved her hips, undulating against him, burying him deeper, driving him to the brink and threatening to push him over. He held on for her sake, fighting for control, wanting to give her pleasure before he lost himself in his own.

Tension built inside of him like a coiled spring. She tightened around him, her hands urging him on. Tremors shook her body and she called out his name in passionate abandon.

He shattered, from the inside out, torn apart mind and soul and then put back together, different than he had been before.

Piece by piece he came back to earth, became aware of the things around him. Their uneven breathing. Their sweat-slicked bodies and tangled limbs.

He gathered her in his arms and rolled to his back, taking her with him.

"I do, you know," she whispered against his neck.

He trailed a hand down the ridge of her spine. "I know."

"I just can't say it."

"Okay." His arms tightened around her. Connor closed his eyes tightly and held on for dear life, lost, and not sure if he wanted to be found.

Katherine awoke cuddled in the warm alcove of Connor's body, relishing the feel of his arm wrapped protectively around her, holding her close. She pressed her face more fully into his chest and stretched. Stiff muscles resisted then gave way to the movement. A satisfied moan inadvertently escaped from her lips. They had dozed, then awoken, then made love again, a cycle that continued until exhaustion claimed them and they succumbed to sleep.

A small itch tickled her nose and she rubbed it against Connor's warm skin. He smelled of sleep and male, an intoxicating blend that made her crave him all over again.

She looked up to find him staring down at her, an amused expression lighting his face. The early hint of morning sunlight seeped through the window and slashed across the bed, intensifying the blue of his eyes.

"Hi," he whispered. A tender smile spread across his face and touched a soft place deep inside of her.

She stretched again, relishing the friction of her bare skin against his, and placed a gentle kiss against his lips.

"Hi," she answered, murmuring the words against his mouth—a mouth that had given her endless pleasures through the night and well into the morning.

Connor growled and rolled her back onto the mattress, half covering her body with his. Sleep and their lovemaking had mussed his golden hair. Emboldened, she reached up and ran a hand through it, then pulled him down for another searing kiss.

"You keep that up," he said, finally coming up for air, "and I may never let you out of this bed."

She laughed and curled into his body, letting his warmth seep into her. "Now there's an interesting proposition."

His mouth rested near her ear, sending little shivers down her body. "No regrets, then?"

"No," she murmured into his neck. "No regrets." She ignored the sharp jab of her conscience. She would save any regrets for later. She didn't want to ruin this moment or taint its memory when it fed her in the years to come. Later, regret would visit her in abundance, swallow her whole. But for now...for now she wanted the moment of happiness to last as long as possible.

"I want you to stay."

Her heart stuttered and the moment came to a shattering end. She pulled away, just enough to peer up at him. The wall Connor had built to protect himself, the armor he wore around his heart, had been stripped away. She could see it in his eyes, in the softness of his gaze. Guilt stabbed her in the chest and buried the blade deep. She had done that. And for what? To break it again? To give herself a memory to stave off the loneliness she deserved? The truth dealt a stinging blow, awakening her to reality.

"What?"

"Stay," he repeated, tucking a stray curl behind her ear.

She blinked. Perhaps she had misunderstood. "Here? With you?"

A hint of impatience darkened his expression. "No, out in the barn with the horses. Yes, here with me. And Jenny. I want us to be a family."

Daggers of pain sliced through her, shredding her heart. She rolled off the bed, gathering the twisted sheet around her. She kept her back to Connor, unable to look at him. It was too easy to believe everything would be okay when she peered into his eyes.

"You know I can't." Her desperate whisper resonated through the quiet room.

The ropes beneath the mattress creaked as Connor moved closer. "I love you, Kate. And I know you feel the same way, even if you won't say it. I want us to be a family."

Anger burst in her chest. How dare he dangle the only thing she'd ever wished for in front of her, expecting her to grasp it with both hands. Why couldn't he just leave it alone? He knew she wouldn't do it. Why couldn't he just let her have this one night?

"I thought you didn't want to get married," she reminded him. "You've been harping on that since I arrived here."

"I didn't. Now I do. Isn't a man entitled to change his mind if the right woman comes along?"

"I am not free to marry you."

"You can be." His hand slipped beneath the mane of hair trailing down her back. One finger traced a line along her spine. Tingles followed the path and Katherine had to close her eyes and fight to retain her composure. "I know it won't be easy, Kate, but we can do it." He sounded so sure, so convinced.

He had no idea.

"No," she answered, her voice cracking. She struggled to control it. "I can't."

It was a nice dream, but it wasn't hers. It belonged to someone else. To someone who hadn't made all the wrong choices. To someone who didn't have blood on her hands and lies propping up her conscience.

His touch stilled. The onslaught against her skin halted. "You're serious?" His hand fell away and the mattress shifted.

"You don't understand. My husband—"

"—will never hurt you again. I'd kill him first."

"No!" She had seen how that could end. Grant had been a good man, a strong one. He'd even killed Rogan's brother. But he'd been no match for her husband's ruthlessness. The man would stop at nothing to get her back. She would not stand by and let Connor be his next victim.

"Dammit, Kate!" Connor pushed himself up on one elbow. "Are you telling me, after last night, you can just walk away? That it meant nothing?"

Her heart split in two at his words. She opened her eyes and gazed down into his, pained by the confusion warring with frustration she saw in them.

"It meant everything," she whispered.

"Then stay. We'll figure this out."

She shook her head.

Connor got out of bed and slid into his denims before walking to the window, staring out in silence. Her gaze greedily devoured the sight of him, shirtless, his back muscles shifting beneath the smooth skin as he ran his fingers through his hair. God, she still wanted him. How long before that torment would leave her? Weeks? Months? Longer? Would she live out the rest of her days remembering his touch? His kiss?

"Then at least tell me why. I deserve that much, don't I?"

She couldn't take her eyes off him, strong and hurt and prideful. He loved her. In spite of all her lies, he saw through to who she really was beneath all the bad choices and guilt and regret.

She knew then he would never let her go. He would stand his ground and fight to the bitter end. And it would be bitter indeed, because eventually Rogan would figure out where she was. He always did. And she would have more blood on her hands. Only this time the stain would never wash away, never fade.

She needed him to release her. And there was only one way she knew of to make that happen.

She took a deep breath and let the truth out. "My name is Katherine Slade. My husband is Rogan Slade."

Chapter Twenty

Connor shook his head, as if by doing so the words would rearrange themselves and become something else. They didn't.

"You're a Slade?" But no, not just any Slade. She was the wife of the man who had murdered his brother. Suddenly it all made sense. The secrets, the evasiveness. All of her lies culminated in one horrible truth.

She was a Slade.

And then it dawned on him, slowly, sinking through the miasma of pain that wracked his body. She was the woman. The one on the stagecoach. The one they were looking for. She'd been under his nose the entire time.

He crossed the room and grabbed her by the arms, hauling her against him. Tears filled her eyes, spilling over, seeping into his heart and stinging its tattered edges. "Why did you come here?" It was no accident. Not even Fate was that cruel a mistress.

Her face paled and she swallowed. When she spoke her voice was barely more than a whisper. "Your brother sent me here."

"My brother is dead!"

"I know!" The words came out in broken sobs. "He died in my arms."

"What?" His grip loosened, but she continued to lean into him.

"He tried to save me, but he was wounded. I couldn't help him. I tried, but he wouldn't stop bleeding. He asked me... he..." She hiccupped, unable to catch her breath.

He pushed her away, her words scalding his skin, and stumbled back toward the door. He shook his head and squeezed his eyes shut as if he could block it out. It couldn't be true. This couldn't be happening. *Oh God, please don't make this true.*

But it was. The look on her face said it all.

"You're one of them," he whispered, defeated. The words tasted like bile in his mouth.

"I'm sorry. Oh God, I am so sorry..." Her hand clenched at the sheet still draped loosely about her naked body. Part of him wanted to go to her, comfort her. She seemed so broken, so lost. He quashed the feeling. "Please, Connor..."

Please what? Forgive her?

"All this time, living here, you—" He stopped, choking on the images of holding her in his arms, the feel of her moving beneath him, the rightness of it. "And last night? Was that just another lie?"

She shook her head. Fiery gold curls bounced around the frame of her tear-stained face. "No! It wasn't like that at all."

"Then how the hell was it?" he shouted, desperate, enraged.

"I had to come here. I had to make sure you were—"

He cut her off. "What? Broken? Destroyed? Well, congratulations! Because we were—me and Jenny both."

The mention of Jenny's name broke her. She sank to the floor and curled in on herself. A small moan filled the room.

He closed his eyes. The sight of her like that slashed through him with such force he wondered a man could survive that much pain.

He had to get away. He made for the bedroom door and stumbled outside of the house into the cold October sunrise. The wind whistled through the center of his bare chest. He felt empty now, ripped apart. He fell to his knees, unable to go any further.

She reappeared, a minute later, an hour, he didn't know. Her hair was still tangled from their lovemaking; the ravages of truth scarred her face, still beautiful even in its treachery. She'd pulled on the yellow calico, but it gaped in the front where she hadn't finished with the buttons. She'd gathered her composure, but even he could see through his own pain enough to know it hung by a thin thread.

"Let me explain. Please." She knelt on the ground in front of him and reached out, his shirt dangling from her fingertips. "There's a letter—"

He batted her hand away. "Don't. Don't touch me. Don't say another damn word. I've heard enough." What was left? She was a Slade. And fool that he was he'd let her into his heart. Let himself fall in love with her.

And she'd betrayed him.

Everything they'd shared, everything he believed in, was gone in an instant, leaving him empty and raw inside.

He didn't need to know anything else.

"I want you out of here. Today."

The horses picked their way carefully through the path marred by undergrowth and still slick from the morning frost. Thin shards of sunlight struggled through the thick trees to cast a weak light over the moss and lichen.

Katherine inhaled and let it out slowly. Warm breath merged with the colder air, creating a white cloud. Ice dripped through her veins. She was numb from the inside out.

It had taken only minutes for her to pack. She was carrying nothing more than what she brought with her. Emily's clothes went back into the trunk that had held them for the past five years. Along with all her hopes and dreams for a normal life.

She should have known better.

People like her didn't get happy endings.

"Can we stop by the church?" she asked, calling ahead to Connor. He didn't answer. "I want to say good-bye to Jenny before I leave." Connor had paid her what he owed, money that now felt dirty and tainted. But she had taken it just the same. She would use it to pay the Hewitts, and whatever was left to take the next train out of town. She didn't care where it was going. It hardly mattered.

Connor glared over his shoulder at her when she spoke Jenny's name, silence his only answer. She touched her pocket where Grant's letter rested. She would give it to him just before she left, along with the message that went with it. Her last act of contrition—but it would never be enough. The damage the truth had done was irreparable. Pain rifled through her. She wished she could accept her fate with grace and dignity. It was all she could do not to beg Connor to forgive her. But she didn't deserve it.

She was a Slade.

In Connor's mind she might as well have pulled the trigger that killed his brother.

They rode through the thick canopy of trees, crows cawing overhead. Their relentless squawks punctuated the silence, echoing around them in the empty air.

As they reached town, Katherine watched the large crowd in front of the church. Throngs of cheerful parishioners in their Sunday best milled near the front steps. Their chatter mixed with laughter. Children raced about, weaving around the clustered adults, their squeals carrying on the breeze. Neighbors called out greetings to each other as buggies pulled alongside the pathway and unloaded their passengers. Jenny would already be there with the Holkums. Would she wonder where her father and Kate were? Church bells pealed through the air, reverberating in her chest.

Connor reined in his horse outside of his office, not bothering to look at her. "You want to say good-bye to Jenny, go on ahead."

His dismissal cut through her like a jagged blade. She had been successful. He wanted nothing more to do with her. It was a hollow victory.

Katherine left her bag tied to the back of her mare and dismounted, walking down Main Street to the church at the far end. By now, the front yard was deserted. The parishioners had filed in and taken their seats in the pews. For a moment, she hesitated, not wanting to disturb the sanctity of the church. But she couldn't help herself. She had a few precious moments left to spend with Jenny, and her selfish heart wanted to use every last one of them.

She walked up the steps to the church. Reverend Sangster's resonating tone stopped mid-sentence. Katherine opened her mouth to apologize for the interruption when cold steel pressed against the soft hollow beneath her ear.

"Hey there, Katy-girl. Miss me?"

Chapter Twenty-One

"**E**d!" Connor bolted out of his chair as Ed Devers burst into the sheriff's office, supporting the weight of a larger man.

"Give me a hand, Con."

Connor opened the door to the empty cell and helped Ed drag the injured man onto the bed. Blood saturated the top half of his jacket. There was no way of telling whether he was more dead or alive.

"What the hell is going on?"

"It's Slade." Ed's words gripped the dagger Kate had driven into his heart and twisted it hard. "I got word Beesom escaped from Bakers. Nate and I tracked him down just outside of town," he said, motioning to the man on the cot. "But he'd already gotten to Slade. By the time we caught up to him, the whole damn gang was riding hard to get here. We tried to stop 'em, but there were too many. Nate took a bullet. Figured it was best to try and outrun them to give you fair warning."

"He's come for Kate," Connor said, leaving the cell and grabbing his gun belt, strapping it around his waist. She said he would. That he'd never let her go. Guess that was one thing she hadn't lied about.

Ed followed him out. "Kate? Your housekeeper?"

"Slade's wife." Connor held up a hand before Ed could ask. "It's a long story and we've got no time. I sent Kate to church to say good-bye to Jenny. We best get her somewhere safe."

Regardless of what she'd done, Slade would have to kill him dead before he let him lay a hand on her.

"Get the doc and meet me at the church."

"What's the matter, Katy? Cat got your tongue?" Rogan pushed her further up the aisle separating the rows of pews.

Katherine's brain churned and raced. Her gaze swept the crowded church. There were too many people here. Too many innocent lives. She spied Jenny near the front with Bart and Amelia. Her heart picked up speed.

Will stepped forward. "Can we help you, stranger?" Katherine closed her eyes and prayed he would not try to be a hero. "You're more than welcome to join our services this morning, but we don't allow guns in the church."

Rogan chuckled, cold and harsh. "That a fact?"

"What do you want," Katherine whispered, forcing the words past the fear in her throat.

He pressed his mouth against her ear. "You and me, we got a little unfinished business." From the corner of her eye she could see Rogan's finger trace the ugly scar that cut down his temple and stopped near the edge of his cheekbone. The skin around it puckered and pulled. Three months ago he'd nearly caught her, but she'd hit him with a hot poker, leaving him sprawled on the floor of her hotel room.

What she wouldn't give to have that poker in her hands now.

Katherine shook her head. "I'm not leaving with you."

"Oh, I think you are, Katy. I didn't come all the way into town to fetch you just to leave empty handed."

Near the front of the church, Bart stood up.

Rogan waved the gun at him. "I'll shoot you where you stand, old man, you even think of gettin' heroic on me. And I'm warnin' you now. Once I get started shootin', I'm not going to be overly inclined to stop."

She looked over at the deputy. "Please Bart, he means it."

All around her Katherine could hear the muffled cries and quieted rumbles of outrage of the parishioners. Katherine tried not to think of poor Jenny, bearing witness to this. She prayed once again for some type of divine intervention that would allow her to get this man out of the church and away from the townspeople. Away from Jenny.

Rogan grinned, an action that should have made him handsome, but instead just made him terrifying. "These people know who you are, Katy-girl? Do they know you're my wife? Or are they still under the misguided belief you're this —" he raised an eyebrow, "—mail-order bride, was it?"

The congregation grew silent. Frank Beesom. Damn his miserable hide. He'd broken free and made it back to Rogan. Had he told him about Connor? Her heart squeezed. Grant had killed Rogan's younger brother. Rogan would not leave town until he had his revenge. Unless she gave him reason to.

"Leave these people be, Rogan. They have nothing to do with this."

"Don't much matter to me whether they do or not."

Fear clamped down on her heart. This couldn't be happening. But it was. It was every one of her nightmares unfurling before her. Only her nightmares had never included more innocent lives being taken.

"Tell me Katy-girl, did your precious sheriff know who you really were while you were out there playin' house with him? Or did you crawl into his bed without him bein' any the wiser? Did he know he was plantin' his seed in a Slade?"

She jerked against him. "You're a disgusting pig. Connor never—"

Rogan's arm held her tight. His gun taunted the parishioners, pointing it at one then another, watching them flinch.

"You're mine, Katy-girl. It's about time you settled yourself to that fact. Now we're gonna leave here, all well behaved like, and not cause a fuss. Is that clear?"

"You can't take her!"

Jenny's voice, torn raw with fear, rose above the quiet sobs of the women and children.

"Well, well, well. And who might you be?"

Sharp talons of fear clawed into Katherine's gut and dug deep. "Leave her alone."

Rogan ignored her. "What's your name, little one?"

Amelia's urgent murmurs reached Katherine's ears though the exact words were lost, drowned out by the hammering of her heart.

"J-Jenny. Jenny Langston."

"Well ain't that the thing." Rogan laughed and cocked his head to one side to gaze at Katherine. "Pretty chummy with a dead man's kin, ain't ya, Katy? You think you could just ride into town and make things all better? Make up for the fact you got blood on your hands?"

"I didn't kill him, you bastard."

Rogan shrugged. "Makes no never mind either way. People die, Katy. That's just the way of it."

Katherine struggled against him. "He didn't die, he was murdered!"

Rogan smiled. The distinction meant little to him. To her dying day, she would never understand how he could kill a man then walk away as if he'd done nothing more than swill a shot of cheap whiskey.

"Maybe we should take her with us."

"Over my dead body," Bart said, taking a step forward.

"That can be easily arranged, old man. Just one more step and they'll be plantin' you outside in the bone orchard."

"Bart, don't," Katherine pleaded. Tension saturated the room. She had to act. She turned her head to look up at Rogan. "Leave them alone. I'll go with you without a fight, if you'll just leave them alone. I'll give you whatever you want." The words tasted like bile on her tongue.

Rogan smiled, and for a brief moment something flared in his eyes, some emotion Katherine couldn't quite grasp. "Sure you will, Katy. But you won't like it, will you?" His voice dropped to a whisper. The knuckles of his gun hand lifted to stroke the side of her face, almost tender. His eyes watched the motion of his hand where it touched her skin, but she sensed he didn't really see it. His brow furrowed. "Why is that? Why do you always turn away from me like I'm nothin' better than the dirt beneath your feet?"

Katherine swallowed. "You're a murderer."

Rogan's smile withered and a strange emptiness filled his dark gaze. "Everybody's gotta make a livin', Katy. I just chose mine by the gun."

His hand dropped away and he gazed at the congregation, then to the door behind them, debating his options.

"You got a horse?"

She shook her head, not wanting him anywhere near Connor's office. "No."

"You try anythin' stupid, Katy, and I'll kill you right dead. Then I'll come back for the rest of them. You got that?"

She nodded once, swallowing past the fear. She could do this. If it saved Jenny, if it kept everyone safe, she could do this.

"Good girl," Rogan said, the words sliding over her like a

thick ooze. He turned to the others. "Now here's the way it is. I see just one of you so much as peek your face out this door, I'll put a bullet in her head faster than you can spit."

Rogan no sooner had the pronouncement out when the sound of gunfire volleyed in the distance. Several of the parishioners jumped. A few screamed. Rogan chuckled, an ugly rumbling sound Katherine had come to hate. "Looks like my boys have found your sheriff, Katy."

Her eyes widened. "No..."

He lifted a brow. "Didn't think I came here all on my own, did ya? Let's go."

⌘

C onnor never made it past the front door of his office.

"Get down," he shouted, pushing Ed to the floor and crouching low behind the desk. Another gunshot pierced the still morning. A chill settled over Connor that had nothing to do with the cool October air.

"Slade," Ed said through gritted teeth. He kept low and threw himself behind the desk with Connor. Together, they inched their way toward the window.

The street was clear, but movement on the roof across the street caught Connor's eye. He lined up his shot and squeezed the trigger. A man grunted and toppled from the roof, landing with a thud on the road below.

"How many men is Slade running with?"

"There were three others, near as we could tell," Ed said. "Guess two now. Down there." Ed motioned with his chin to the corner alley. Connor watched as Frank Beesom ran out and dove behind a rain barrel. Ed fired off two shots but both missed. "C'mon out, Beesom. Ain't nowhere for you to go. We got you surrounded."

"Think I'll take my chances. Ain't no way in hell, I'm—

ungh!" Ed grinned as his shot found its mark, but it turned to a scowl when he heard Beesom's curse. "Son of a bitch!"

"Bastard can't even do the decent thing and die proper," Ed grumbled. "What you want to do, Con?"

He wanted to find Slade. But wherever the man hiding, he was well out of sight.

"You best come on out, Sheriff," Beesom taunted. "If'n you don't, I'm guessin' you're going to have a church full of dead people afore the service is even halfway over."

The blood in Connor's veins turned to ice. "What are you talking about?"

"I ain't come back here because I like the hospitality, Sheriff. We come back here to get that lil' housekeeper you been hiding. Why, Rogan's at the church collecting her now. Who knows, maybe they'll renew their vows while they're there."

"Christ!" Jenny was in that church. And Kate. Connor bolted for the door, Ed's shout falling on deaf ears.

He was beyond listening.

Chapter Twenty-Two

Connor ducked into the alley next to The Last Chance Saloon. From his vantage point, he could see Rogan had Kate on the opposite side of the street. Her yellow calico stood out against the dusty road. They were arguing as he hauled her along by the arm, but even as the two drew nearer, their words were pulled away on the breeze. Jenny was nowhere in sight. For that, at least, Connor was thankful.

"Dammit, Con, least you could do was wait." Ed moved to crouch beside him.

Connor motioned to the street. "He's got Kate."

"That ain't good. Gives him leverage."

Connor nodded. "I know."

"Might be we have to forget about that. Put it out of our minds so we can do what needs doin'. You start worryin' about the consequences and there's sure to be some. Gotta put your head first on this one, Con. Leave your heart back in this here alleyway. It's just gonna get you and Kate killed if you don't."

The truth had an ugly ring to it. But Connor didn't know how to separate his fear for Kate's safety from the worry that one wrong move on his part could spell her end. But they had to do something, and fast. He couldn't let Rogan get away. As long as the man was free, he was a threat to Kate.

"Hello, boys."

Ed jumped. "Jesus, old man! Don't be sneaking up on someone like that. You're liable to get shot."

Bart grinned. "Ain't seen you outdraw me yet, Devers."

Ed muttered under his breath and turned back to watch Slade, then pointed toward the church. "Where's he going?"

"I think he's planning on paying you a visit, Con."

Connor started. "What's he want with me?"

"Seems he doesn't like the idea of you and his *wife*," Bart said, lifting an eyebrow. Connor realized he would have some explaining to do when this was all said and done.

"Not to mention your brother killed his brother," Ed added. "Could be he's lookin' for some payback."

"Shit." This was going from bad to worse fast.

Bart rested a hand on Connor's shoulder. "I told everyone else to stay put inside the church. Will and Amelia are doin' their best to keep everyone calm. Figure there's little chance of Slade doublin' back there. But just in case, we'd best get some fire power over there anyway."

Will was adamant that no guns ever pass through the door of his church, but Connor was willing to bet he'd make an exception today.

"How's Jenny?"

"Madder than a hornet. Doesn't understand why we let the bad man take Kate."

Connor glared over his shoulder. A whole church half-filled with men had him wondering the same thing himself. "How exactly did that happen?"

"Kate offered herself up as the sacrificial lamb if he promised to leave the church without killin' anyone. Wasn't anything we could do about it without having him start shootin' just outta spite."

Ed let out a low whistle. "One brave housekeeper you got yourself, Con. Any woman married to Slade is gonna know he don't take well to bein' walked out on. Hell, he dropped a man in Reno just for gettin' up from the table before his meal was done."

Connor gave Ed a hard look. "Thank you. Good to know."

"I'm just sayin', man's got a hair-trigger temper."

"You two gonna sit here jawin' on it all day or you gonna do something about it?" Bart asked.

Slade and Kate had made it halfway down Main Street. She had started dragging her feet, slowing them down, but she was no match for Slade's strength.

Connor's office was on the corner. The building had only one door in. If they made it there, the two would be pinned down and trapped inside. There was no telling what Slade would do under those circumstances, but Connor doubted it would be good.

"Bart, wake Bentley up." Connor said, jerking his head toward the saloon. "Have him take some of his men and go back to the church. Barricade yourselves in there and keep everyone away from the windows. Get the kids hidden under the pews. Ed and I will deal with Slade."

"What about his men?" Bart asked. "You sure you don't need any extra guns out here?"

Connor shook his head. "Beesom's injured. One man's dead. That leaves Slade and one other. We can deal with them. I'd rather you make sure the townspeople are safe." And that the man who had been like a father to him was well out of harm's way. If the worst came to pass, Connor needed to know Jenny would still have a home to go to.

Connor waited until Bart disappeared inside the saloon.

"We can't let him reach your office, Con. Nate's in there helpless as a babe. If Slade sees him, we might as well start diggin' his grave right now."

Connor didn't have time to agree. A shot broke through the eerie quiet.

"Shit!" His attention snapped to the commotion in the saloon. He heard Bart's shout.

"What the hell you doin', Bentley?"

Garrett Bentley stood in the doorway of The Last Chance, rifle drawn on Slade.

Slade pulled Kate against him and fired a shot in Garrett's direction, forcing him back inside. The saloonkeeper took refuge behind the swinging doors and fired a return volley that fell short of the mark.

"Stop shooting, you imbecile!" Connor yelled. "You'll kill her!"

Slade fired another shot, this one closer to the alley. Connor and Ed had been spotted. A flurry of curses carried from across the street as Slade shouldered his way with force through the door of Milo's Haberdashery. Within seconds, a small pane of glass broke and shards tinkled against the board-walk like chimes in the wind.

They'd succeeded in keeping him from reaching the sher-iff's office, but at what cost?

Ed scowled. "There goes the element of surprise. Looks like he's settling in for a fight."

Only the need to see Kate safe overrode Connor's desire to throttle Garrett Bentley. "Get down to the church now! I see that damn gun pointing anywhere near Slade and I'll shoot you myself." The last thing he needed was some idiot who spent his morning breathing cheap whiskey fumes shooting up a storm and getting them all killed.

Ed surveyed the street. "We gotta rush the place. No other way."

Connor considered. He hated it, but it was their only option. The longer they left Kate with a desperate Rogan, the less probability she'd have of getting out alive. He studied the distance between the alleyway and the haberdashery. "If we loop around behind the saloon to the other side, that'll take us down the street a bit." He waved his gun to his right. "We can come up on him, get to the front door. He doesn't have a wide firing range through the small break in that window, but he'll try either way."

Ed nodded. "We'll be movin'. Less chance he'll be able to hit us."

Connor didn't like their odds—there was no telling just where Rogan's remaining man was stationed—but those were the only odds they had to play at the moment.

"Ready?"

Ed nodded and bolted down the alley. Connor followed on his heels. Once they reached the street, bullets rained from two different directions, slamming into the ground. Puffs of dried dirt kicked up close to their feet as they made a mad dash toward the store, zigzagging back and forth to make themselves less of a target.

They reached the side of the store. Connor pressed himself flat against the wall. Ed dropped to a crouch, aimed toward the roof of the bakery across the street, and fired. A rifle clattered to the street below, discharging on impact.

"Three down," Connor said.

"Yup." Ed pulled his hat off and swiped at his forehead before jamming it back on. "And Beesom's injured, which means he's probably crawled off somewhere to safety. He ain't big on dying. That leaves just Slade. Guess you'll be goin' in there?"

Connor nodded. There was no other way. If Slade remained in there for too long he'd grow more desperate by the minute. He bunched his muscles, ready to spring. "Distract him."

Ed fired a shot into the sidewalk near the window. Rogan's gun barrel jerked back inside. Connor lunged for the door, driving his shoulder into it. The door gave way with a sickening crack and slammed against the back wall. Slade fired as Connor somersaulted through the opening, but the shelves that ran down the middle of the store kept him protected as bullets split the wood around him.

"Connor!"

Katherine's heart stopped. She watched Connor roll behind the waist-high counter at the front of the store. It provided refuge from Rogan's direct line of sight. She held her breath, waiting, praying none of Rogan's bullets had found their mark.

"It's all over, Slade. Let the woman go."

Katherine gasped air in relief. Thank God, he was unhurt.

"It ain't over by half," Rogan shot back. "I got the girl. So unless you want her blood spilt, you'll be lettin' me walk outta here."

Katherine didn't doubt Rogan would do it. She'd left him. In his mind, that was a killing offense. If it came down to a choice between her life and his freedom, she had no illusions which one he would choose.

The barrel of Rogan's gun pressed against her temple. She tried to draw back from its heat, but there was nowhere to go.

"Hear that, Katy? You be a good girl, or you'll be a dead one. Now I'm guessing that door leads to an office," he said, pointing his gun to a curtained doorway along the side wall. "And that office most likely has a door to the outside. Am I right?"

"I don't know." She'd only been in the store once. He

pressed the barrel tighter against her flesh. Katherine bit back the pain. "I swear I don't know!"

"Then you best persuade that sheriff of yours that he needs to step down and let us out of here."

The thought of leaving with Rogan, of what would happen to her when she did, roiled in Katherine's gut until she thought she'd be sick. But the idea of anything happening to Connor was even worse.

"Let us go, Connor. Please. It's okay. I—I want to go. He's my husband." The words echoed in the still air, hollow and unconvincing.

"Never gonna happen, Kate."

She closed her eyes. Damn the man for being so stubborn. "If you love me, you'll give me the chance to get out of here, Connor. Please. The law will see me as an accomplice. If they catch me, I'll hang!"

"Better listen to the lil' lady, Sheriff. Sure would hate to see this pretty neck stretched, wouldn't you?"

"Can't say I care one way or the other if she gets her neck stretched. She's a Slade. Far as I can tell, that's reason enough to tighten the noose." The cold indifference startled her, and she realized with a sudden clarity that this wasn't about her at all. He didn't want to protect her, or even see her safe. He just wanted his revenge for the death of his brother. The truth of it lodged itself in her throat. She guessed she had earned his derision, but that didn't take the pain of it away.

"I'll kill her, Sheriff. You don't let me ride outta here, I'll shoot her where she stands." Desperation filled Rogan's voice.

"That's just one less bullet I have to use, Slade."

The words cut into Katherine with more force than any gunshot.

Rogan cursed and surged to his feet, dragging Katherine with him. Firing shots in Connor's direction, he made a break for the backroom. Katherine waited for Connor's return fire, but nothing came. No shots. No sound. Nothing.

"Connor!"

With a rough yank, Rogan pulled her back against him. "Shut up!"

"Yoo hoo!"

Rogan spun quickly, his gun arm stretched out. He used her body as a shield. Ed Devers stood in the back doorway that led into the alley.

"Goin' somewhere?" The man seemed completely unconcerned with the fact a wanted criminal had a gun trained on him. Then again, he held the same position, his gun pointed just above Katherine's head.

"I'll kill her, you don't let me pass. I already killed your damn sheriff."

"I don't die that easy, Slade."

The voice came from behind. Katherine barely had time to register the surge of joy that swept through her when Rogan turned again. The momentum swung her around and she used it to push away from him, stumbling backward and landing hard against the narrow file cabinet next to the desk. Gunshots echoed loudly, reverberating in the small room. The acrid scent of powder burned her nostrils.

Katherine's gaze flew to Connor, then over to Rogan. A look of surprise froze his features. It was the last expression he would ever wear.

S lade dropped to his knees. Then, like a felled timber, he keeled over.

"Connor!"

Kate flew into his arms. Her weight knocked him back a step, bringing everything back into focus. He wound his arms around her and tried to hold her tight but his left arm wouldn't work properly. His upper body burned as if someone had stabbed him through the shoulder with a hot blade.

Kate stepped back and blinked, her gaze going from his face to his chest and back up again. "Connor?"

Her voice faded into the distance. From the shadowed corner of his eyes he was vaguely aware of Ed approaching, but it was Kate's beautiful face filled with worry and fear that held his attention.

"Connor...you're shot."

He read her lips more than heard her voice. There was a strange rushing in his ears.

"Kinda hurts," he muttered, but he wasn't sure if the words were coherent. Blackness encroached. Arms reached around him and he smelled the sweet scent of lavender mixed with a faint tinny odor. Then he was falling down a deep, dark hole that seemed to have no bottom.

Chapter Twenty-Three

F eeling slowly ebbed back into Connor's body, inch by inch, limb by limb. When it reached his shoulder and head, he quickly reconsidered oblivion. The former burned and the latter throbbed. To add to his list of ailments, his mouth felt as if every last lick of moisture had packed up and moved out.

Somewhere nearby, a bird chirped. The cheerful warbling carried on a soft breeze that lightly touched the skin on his chest. His clothes were gone. Where were his clothes?

A soft rustling came from his other side. He tried to turn his head, to open his eyes, but his body ignored his commands. He remained immobile like a useless lump of flesh.

Was he dead? He didn't think he'd feel this much pain once he passed over. Wasn't that the deal? You got to leave all the agony of life behind? If not, Will Sangster was going to have some explaining to do when he saw him next.

The rustling sounded again and his right side dipped. He was on a bed. He wasn't dead. Surely, they didn't have beds in Heaven, or Hell for that matter. He filled his lungs with relief. The scent of lavender filled his senses.

Kate...

A light touch brushed down the side of his face, prickling the growth of beard that covered his cheek. How long had he been here? He'd shaved just...just...

Connor struggled to sift through his memory for something solid, a tangible recollection of what had happened to put him here, lying in this state of limbo, unable to move or speak or even swallow. But all his mind would serve up were sensations of soft, silky skin and lush curves, the moan of his name on Kate's lips, the blinding satisfaction of burying himself deep inside her.

His groin stiffened. No...definitely not dead, but quite possibly still in Hell.

A cool cloth came to rest against his forehead and steady fingers ran through his hair, brushing it away from his face.

"Connor?"

Her voice whispered like the soft murmur of an angel's wings. He let the sound soak into him. The feather mattress shifted slightly. He felt her lean closer, her scent growing stronger, tantalizing his senses. God, he wished he could move his damn hands, touch her face, pull her to him. But he couldn't even muster the strength to lift his lids.

Her sigh breezed against his lips and his insides shivered.

"I brought Jenny in to see you last night. I told her you were sleeping so she wouldn't worry. I hope that was the right thing...I don't know. It seemed to help. Amelia is trying to keep her occupied, letting her help in the kitchen."

Kitchen? Amelia? Was he at the boardinghouse? He tried to concentrate on the sounds around him. Voices drifted up, muffled and distant, somewhere in the background. What was wrong with him? Why couldn't he move? Why couldn't he—

"Rogan Slade is my husband."

His insides recoiled at the memory. Images and words and everything else came rushing back, swirling through his mind

256

like a twister bent on destruction. Kate, the woman he loved, was a Slade.

"Connor? Connor, are you awake?"

Her hand cupped his face. He tried to answer, tried to get his brain and muscles to work in concert.

"Slade..." His voice sounded foreign to him, scraping his vocal cords raw.

She moved away. Her absence touched him like a frigid wind blowing down from the bluff.

"Yes...Slade." She cleared her throat.

Though his eyes refused to open, he could picture her clearly in his mind, sitting on the edge of the bed, her hands folded primly in her lap, fingers twisting around each other. Her backbone would be ramrod straight and no doubt her chin jutted out at a stubborn angle. But her eyes...those beautiful sea-green eyes that disguised nothing would hold all the pain and misery of what her life had been, of the choices she had made and the consequences they had wrought. Did she regret it? Did she regret him?

When she spoke again, anguish invaded her tone. "I've spoken to Judge Malton. He arrived in town yesterday." He heard her sigh. "They don't hold me responsible for what happened to your brother, but I do. He didn't deserve to die, not like that, and certainly not for me."

She sniffed and a warm wetness splashed against the back of his hand.

"I didn't get a chance to finish telling you why I came to Fatal Bluff, and I don't know if you can hear me now, but I've left Grant's letter on the table next to your bed. That's why I came. He asked me to deliver it, to make sure his girl was okay, and to tell you he was sorry. I thought Con *was* the girl, I didn't..." She drew in a shaky breath. "I didn't know it was two different people until after I'd arrived, and then—" Her voice cracked and she stopped.

A random memory presented itself in his mind's eye. The look of shock when they'd first met, after Walter Figg had thrown her into his arms. Someone had said his name. She'd gasped and stared up at him. He remembered the fear in her eyes. Now he understood why.

The mattress shifted again. She was leaving.

"I've made such a mess of things. I'm sorry. I hated lying to you, but I didn't know what else to do to try and make things right."

He wanted to tell her it wasn't her fault, that he didn't blame her, but he wasn't sure if it was true, and he couldn't get the words out anyway. Maybe she had done the best she could under the circumstances she'd found herself in. Maybe she should have done more. He didn't know anymore.

Part of him still raged, fought against the pull to forgive her. He'd trusted her, and she'd lied. He'd loved her, and she'd betrayed him. Just like Emily. Just like Grant.

Her lips brushed his, briefly, lightly. He tried to steel himself against her touch but it was gone before he could, and in its wake, her words caused far more damage to a heart already tangled with warring emotions.

"I do love you."

Connor struggled against the exhaustion trying to claim him. He wanted to talk to her. To find a way to set things right. To not lose her. But his sense of her, the sounds of the everyday, the chirping birds all began to fade and he had nothing left inside of him to push the darkness away.

The bustle of people conducting their daily business had fallen silent when Connor next regained consciousness. Only a deep rumble from across the room filled the darkness.

His eyes opened this time with little struggle. It took a

moment for them to adjust, but when they did, he made out Bart's wiry frame stretched out in a chair pulled near the bed. His chin rested on his chest, his arms crossed beneath them. The low flame of the kerosene lamp next to his bed flickered, pushing the blackness to the end of the bed. Next to the lantern sat a white envelope.

Connor's gaze searched the room for Kate, but she was gone. He hated how keenly he felt her absence, like a growing ache in the center of his chest that went far deeper than the burning in his shoulder.

The throbbing in his head had eased to a dull ache. Annoying, but no longer debilitating. His eyes went to the letter again. Kate had risked everything to deliver it. It seemed a lot to go through when she could have easily sent it by post and walked away.

Gritting his teeth, he marshaled his strength and reached for the letter. Pain ripped through his shoulder and knocked him back against the pillow, bringing his breath in short gasps.

Dammit.

He lifted his head up far enough to look at his snoring deputy. He considered waking him and then decided against it. There was no telling what was in the letter. He and Grant had not parted on the best of terms.

Memories of his brother stopped that day over eight years ago when Connor had left him in a flurry of anger and accusations. The hurtful words he'd lashed at Grant still resonated in his mind. He'd called him every name he could think of, came up with a few new ones then repeated them all over again. Grant hadn't tried to defend himself, hadn't tried to stop Connor or calm his anger. So Connor had railed until he was spent, and then he walked out, never looking back. It was the last time he'd seen his brother.

He closed his eyes against the flood of remorse. God how

he wished things could be different. That he could take back the past and make it untrue.

Is that how Kate felt? Did she live with the same guilt?

He reached again, this time with more success. His fingers crawled over the envelope and slid it close enough for him to lift. Something caught the lamplight beneath it and glowed a warm gold. A wedding band.

Connor fumbled before managing to slip the band over the tip of his finger. It was small, barely making it over his first knuckle. Emily's, he guessed. Connor maneuvered it onto his pinky. He'd keep it; give it to Jenny when she got older.

He held the envelope up for inspection. Small dark markings marred the worn white exterior. He angled it closer to the lantern. The bloody smudges were fingerprints, too tiny to belong to his brother, but the perfect size for Kate's hand. Her fingerprints, his brother's blood.

"I do love you."

Grief squeezed his heart. How had it all come to this? Tears lumped in his throat and it took several long moments for him to beat back the urge to rail and cry and scream his lungs out at the injustice of it all. For his brother's sake, he wanted to hate her. Didn't Grant deserve that much from him? But for his own sake, he wanted to give in to the urge to forgive her, to forget the past, to start fresh. He wanted to hold on to her and never let her go.

But how could he? Their pasts were too entangled in who she was and what had happened. Could they ever get beyond it?

Connor stared at the ceiling, watching the shadows dance against the stark whiteness. He had no answers.

His fingers moved along the lip of the envelope, tearing it open and pulling out two sheets of paper. He recognized Grant's even strokes.

. . .

*D*ear Connor,
  Too much time has passed since we've spoken, years I've let go by knowing I should do something to make things right. Before you left, you called me a coward for not telling you about Emily. You were right about my being a coward, but not in the way you think.

Emily didn't love me. She simply feared leaving everything and everyone she knew behind to follow you to Montana. I was a safe alternative, nothing more. She loved you, always did. I think she lived with the regret of her choice until the day she died.

We didn't marry for love. We married for necessity. Three weeks after you disappeared, Emily came to me. She was with child. Your child.

Connor's heart slammed painfully against his ribcage and the letter trembled in his hand, making the words swim before him. He closed his eyes and tried to control his reeling emotions. That one reckless night a week before their wedding when she had come to him and he'd let youthful passion override common sense.

His child. His.

He forced himself to read on.

There was no time to find you, so I married Emily to save her and the baby from shame. It was a quick ceremony and no one questioned when the baby was born a little early. They suspected—as you did—that Emily had changed her mind about which brother she wanted.

Grant hadn't betrayed him? He'd been so certain. All these years, carrying the anger of a betrayal that had never happened. What Grant did was done out of loyalty. Shame burned in Connor's gut. If only he'd given Grant the chance to explain. If only he hadn't left town that night.

As the baby's birth grew near, I wanted to tell you. You had a right to know. But I fell in love. Not with Emily, but with Jenny. Emily passed away last year. Fever. It's just me and Jenny now. I wish you could see her, and yet I fear what will happen if you do.

I love this little girl, Connor. She's the one bright thing in my life. Yet every day I watch her and see you in everything she does and the regret near drives me mad. I know you and Jenny both deserve the truth.

But in the end, you were right. I am a coward. Fear of losing her has bought my silence.

Someday I hope I'll find the courage to send this letter, until then I'll carry it with me. I pray that when the time comes you'll forgive me for what I've done.

I love you, brother. At least know that. And I did the best I could by Jenny.

Your brother,

Grant

The thin sheets of paper containing Grant's words slipped from Connor's fingers and fluttered to the bed. He was a father. Jenny's father. Moisture trickled a lazy path down his face.

"You okay?"

Bart's voice startled him. He leaned forward in his chair, his arms resting on his knees. Connor hadn't even noticed the snoring had stopped.

He swiped the back of his hand over his cheek. His mouth moved, but the words that came out were random and nonsensical. He gave up and shook his head. No. He wasn't okay. He was happy and sad and angry and confused. He handed the letter to Bart.

The legs of the chair scuffed the hardwood floor as Bart dragged it closer to the light. It took little time for him to scan the two pages that had changed Connor's world forever. When he finished, a long sigh escaped from deep within him.

"I suspected as much."

"You did?"

Bart shrugged one shoulder. "I watched you grow from the time you was in short pants. When I saw Jenny, it was like watching you all over again. She's just like you, the spittin' image, inside and out."

"Why didn't you ever say anything?"

"Didn't know for sure, and since you weren't around, figured it was best to leave well enough alone. 'Sides, it wasn't my truth to be tellin'."

"She's mine." The words filled him with wonder, and yet confirmed what he suspected a part of him had known from the first moment he saw her. How many times had he looked at her and seen his own reflection? How many times had he searched for Grant in Jenny and come up empty?

Bart nodded. "She's yours."

Connor sank back into the welcoming softness of the plump, feathered pillows. "Do I tell her?"

"I cain't give you that answer. Guess you'll have to figure it out on your own. You'll know what to do when the time comes."

Connor wasn't so sure he shared Bart's optimism or faith in his abilities. He needed Kate. Needed to talk to her, to hear her opinion. To tell her he was a father. To hear her voice remind him that he could do this.

"Where's Kate?"

"Middle of the night, Con. I 'spect she's sleepin' like the rest of the world." Bart stretched his arms over his head and grunted.

"Does everyone know—about Kate, I mean?"

Bart nodded. "Yup. After what happened in the church, word spread pretty fast to anyone that missed it. And Jenny isn't being too quiet about it, tellin' everyone who will listen that Kate's a bonafide hero for saving them in the church."

Connor shook his head. Katherine had to know she was walking to her death, and yet she'd gone willingly for the sake of others. For Jenny. She was braver than most men he knew. Definitely braver than him. He had let one betrayal define his life and instead of dealing with it, he'd run away. But not Kate. She didn't turn tail and run. When his brother asked for her promise, she made it. And kept it.

She was quite simply the most remarkable woman he had ever met.

Bart patted his leg, then stood and set the letter on the nightstand. "Get some sleep. I'll send Amelia up in the mornin'. No doubt she'll want to start fattenin' you up again now that you're awake."

Connor scratched at the whiskers on his chin. "How long have I been here?"

"Oh, 'bout four days now."

"Four days!" He tried to lift himself up but a sharp stab of pain pushed him back into the mattress.

"Fever, son. Had the women plumb scared out of their minds."

"And you?"

Bart chuckled and turned down the lamp, shrouding the room in darkness. "Well, I have the benefit of knowin' you're too damn stubborn to die." Bart smiled, but despite his words, Connor could see the relief in the old man's face. "Get some sleep, son. Things always look better in the morn."

Connor wasn't sure he believed that, but he didn't have enough energy left to argue.

~

"I'm really not that hungry, and I can feed myself," Connor said, twisting his head to avoid the spoon of lumpy oatmeal Amelia attempted to shove into his mouth.

She dropped the spoon back into the bowl and fixed him with her sternest look. "Connor Douglas Langston, do you want to get your strength back and get out of this bed, or not?"

He wanted nothing more. He'd drifted in and out after Bart had left, his sleep peppered with dreams of his brother and Jenny and Kate, all snarled together until one dream meshed into the other and none of them made sense. Much like his waking life.

If he could just see Kate, maybe he could try to set a few things right, but she hadn't been back to his room and no one seemed interested in giving him a straight answer as to where she was.

Amelia lifted the spoon once more. "Open up."

Connor scowled but quickly forgot about Amelia and the oatmeal when the door swung wide. Jenny ran into the room, the large beast of a dog ambling in behind her, his toenails clicking against the hardwood. He opened his mouth to greet his niece—daughter...Lord, that still blew his mind—when Amelia took the opportunity to jam the spoon of oatmeal into his mouth. He shot her a dark look, swallowing the thick, tasteless lump.

"Uncle Con, you're awake!" Jenny hurled her small frame against the bed. The motion jostled his shoulder, making him wince slightly, but the pain was gradually easing and his strength returning. He no longer felt like a mewling kitten unable to fend for itself.

Connor still hadn't reached any conclusions on the right way to tell Jenny the truth. He knew he eventually would. Lies had a way of making things far more difficult than they needed to be. But all in good time. And preferably with Kate at his side so she could stop him from making a total muck of it.

"I'm awake, sweetheart."

"You got dressed too," she said, plucking the soft red flannel of the shirt he'd manage to struggle into earlier.

"Thought I'd make myself presentable for visitors," he told her.

He had refused to touch even a mouthful of breakfast until Amelia helped him clean up. He said it would make him feel more human after four days of bed rest. In truth, his pride just didn't want him looking like he'd been dragged through town tied to the back of a horse should Kate decide to grace his room with her presence again.

She hadn't, though.

He turned to Jenny. "Have you been keeping busy while I've wasted my time lying around in bed?"

"I made bread and Kate let me chop carrots for soup and we had a tea party. Can you get up now? Can we go home?"

Connor chuckled. The rustiness of Jenny's voice had disappeared. Amelia had told him earlier she'd barely stopped talking long enough to take a breath between sentences. It was music to his ears.

"You're ready to head back, huh?" God, she looked like him. Bart had been right. She was the spittin' image. This close he could even see the flecks of black in her blue eyes.

"I'm ready. So's Kate. She packed her things this morning."

"She did?" Connor's gaze met Amelia's over the top of Jenny's blond head. He knew it would be at least a few days yet before Bart or Amelia let him out of sight long enough to return home.

Amelia pointedly avoided his gaze, twirling the spoon in the oatmeal. A trickle of unease crept down the length of his spine.

"I think it might be a couple of days yet, Jenny. Think you can wait that long?"

"Guess so. Should I tell Kate to unpack? She didn't bring

much, Uncle Con. She left all her new dresses behind. And you bled all over her yellow one. They told me you were just sleepin', but I'm not a baby. I know the difference. And it's too bad, because I think she looked right pretty in the yellow one. Don't you?"

Jenny's quick-fire comments made his head whirl but he nodded in agreement. A burlap sack thrown over Kate's head and tied with a strip of rope at the waist probably wouldn't detract from her beauty.

"I do."

"Maybe you can buy her a new one. Are you going to marry her? You should marry her. Everyone says so. The bad man she married is dead so Uncle Will says it's okay. I think Kate's real sad you're hurt. Even her smiles are sad. You should get up so she won't be so sad anymore."

Connor smiled, unable to prevent the chuckle that bubbled up from inside him, squeezing past the worry over Kate's state of mind. "You think my being up and about will make her feel better?"

Jenny nodded and returned his smile. Rich laughter danced in her eyes, so much like his own. Connor couldn't help but wonder if he'd be able to keep it there.

And whether Kate would be there to help him achieve that goal.

Chapter Twenty-Four

Katherine pulled the ribbon from her hair and wrapped it around the stems of late season daisies, kneeling down to place them upon the hard ground. A sharp October wind whipped at her curls. She didn't attempt to restore order. They'd be tangled but good before she left here, yet somehow it didn't seem to matter. Everything inside of her had been twisted into knots—it was only fitting her outsides should match.

She touched the stone marker erected at the head of the grave. Grant Langston's name and the years denoting his birth and death were etched into its surface. The monument must have cost a pretty penny, no doubt bought and paid for by the people in Fatal Bluff, a clear testament to what the town had thought of him. She wished she'd known him better, and yet she wished they'd never met at all.

"Jenny's doing fine," she whispered, picking up a rock and laying it over the stems so the wind didn't whisk the flowers away. "She's talking up a storm. I can barely get a word in edgewise." Not that it mattered. What was left to say?

"I gave Connor the letter, like you asked. Not sure if he

read it yet, but I guess once he's feeling better..." Would he ever feel better? Would there come a time when he would wake up and not feel the bitter sting of her betrayal? She hoped so. She wanted him to forget her, although the thought of that pained her to no end. She would carry his memory in her heart until the day she died. Perhaps that was her penance, the price she paid for all the hurt she'd caused.

A tear slid down her cheek and landed on the ground next to the wildflowers. She used her other hand to swipe the offending moisture off her face. She thought she would have cried herself out by now.

"If it's any consolation, Rogan is dead. I know it's probably wrong of me to feel relief over such a thing, but I do. I can't help it. Though it hardly seems enough."

What would be enough? What would make things right, or better, or less painful? She didn't know. All she knew was her leaving was the best thing all around. She'd packed her bag yesterday. Poor Jenny thought it was to take them all back to the homestead. Katherine would have to explain to her that wasn't how it would be. She just hadn't found the words yet, but she would have to soon. Her train left this evening.

"I'm sorry I made such a mess of things. I tried, I really did, but...I guess deception just isn't my forte." She tried to smile, but the effort died on her lips.

"I can second that."

Katherine's head shot up. "Connor!"

His lips twitched and he inclined his head. "Mornin'."

Despite the pallor of his skin and the empty sleeve of his sheepskin jacket flapping in the wind, she'd never seen a more beautiful sight. She pushed herself to her feet and tried to ignore the unsteady wobble of her knees.

"What are you doing out of bed?"

He shrugged, then winced at the effort. "Seems I got this

lump on my head. It makes me confused and prone to wandering."

Katherine dropped her gaze. "I'm sorry. I tried to catch you, but you were too heavy. You banged your head on the counter when you fell."

"Hmm...I wondered how that happened. Did I land on you?"

His question caught her off guard. "Land on me? No. No, you were kind enough to roll to your side and allow me room to escape."

The twitch of his lips eased into a slow, sexy grin that she felt all the way down to her toes. "Mighty gentlemanly of me, wouldn't you say?"

She nodded, unsure of how to take his banter. The anger of their last conversation seemed all but forgotten, as if it had never happened. But despite his affable manner, she could see the hint of nervousness crease the corners of his eyes and fan down to touch his cheekbone.

"Doc Bolger had to dig quite hard to get the bullet out of your shoulder. Then a fever set in." She didn't know why she was telling him this. No doubt the doctor, or Bart, or someone else had already informed him of his condition and the prognosis of a full recovery.

"Guess that explains why I feel like I've been beaten within an inch of my life." He chuckled, a rich, rumbling sound that seeped beneath the surface of her skin.

"I—I'm leaving," she blurted out.

His smile disappeared and the humor of a moment ago became lost in the furrow of his brow. "I thought you might be considering that."

She pulled the wool shawl she'd borrowed from Amelia tighter around her shoulders. "It's for the best."

"Is it?" Connor slowly rounded his brother's grave, his movements jerky and slow.

"You should sit down." She reached out and took his arm, trying to ignore the thrill that small contact gave her. She led him to a small wooden bench sheltered by an old elm. He shouldn't even be out of bed. What was he doing here?

"How did you find me?"

He lifted his hand to the boardinghouse across the street then let it fall back to his lap. "I saw you from my window."

"Oh." Had he been looking for her?

He shifted and turned his body slightly to face her. "How will you live if you leave?"

She hated his practical questions. "I'll figure something out."

"Seems to me like you'll need a job."

She swallowed. There were too few respectable jobs out there for a woman with no one to recommend her. "I suppose it would be asking too much for you to provide me with a reference?"

Connor shook his head, brushing away some imagined piece of lint from his jacket. The breeze ruffled his hair, giving him a rather boyish appearance that pulled at her heart.

"No," he said, making a clicking sound with his tongue. "You really weren't that good at your job."

"Not good?" Katherine straightened and turned toward him. "What are you talking about? I was a great housekeeper. I had the meals on time, the house was clean, the—"

He held up one hand counting off with his fingers. "You fell asleep your first night there, snooped through my things, broke my favorite bowl—"

"That was not my fault! That rooster has it in for me and you know it," Katherine shot back, pointing her finger at him.

He wrapped his hand around her finger and pulled her hand against his chest. "And you're contrary," Connor said, lowering his voice so that it caressed her like a soft touch. "Did I mention that?"

His touch battered her flagging strength and she fought valiantly to shore up the crumbling walls of her reserve, but there was little left to fight with.

"Come here," he said, moving his hand up her arm and coaxing her closer.

Giving in, she scuttled closer and let her forehead rest against his good shoulder. The solid strength of him felt so good. It was all she ever wanted. It killed her to say good-bye. Katherine turned and pressed her face into the curve of Connor's neck. His skin was warm and he smelled of soap and fresh air, not like a man who had been lying about in a sick bed for the past several days. Katherine inhaled his scent and wished for the millionth time she could change things.

But she couldn't.

She pushed away and stood up, putting some distance between them. "I need to go." She had to get away. She couldn't think clearly when he was around. She started thinking of all the things she wanted, all the dreams she had. Hope flared in her heart like it had some right to be there.

"You said you loved me."

She stopped cold and turned. "You heard that?"

Connor stood with some effort and crossed the space that separated them. His arm slid around her waist and pulled her against him. "I heard."

"I thought you were still feverish."

Connor smiled, leaned in and nuzzled her neck. "Maybe I was. Just not in the way you thought."

Katherine gripped the sides of his sheepskin jacket, careful not to put undue pressure against his injured shoulder. "You need to stop that."

His lips found that sensitive hollow just beneath her ear. "I can't."

"You have to."

"No, I mean I can't. If I let go of you I'm liable to keel over."

The warmth of his body seeped through her clothing and spread through her like a wildfire. "I should get you back to bed."

"Yes...yes, you should." The inflection in his tone left no question as to the train of his thoughts.

"Not like that!" Why did he have to make this so hard?

He chuckled. "Suppose it might be a few days yet before I have that kind of energy."

"Connor, this is ridiculous." Lord, how was she expected to think with him holding her like this, talking like that. Like they had a chance. He must still be delirious from the fever. "I'm leaving town tonight."

"Say it again."

"Say what? That I'm leaving?" Was he so anxious for her to be gone that the very words gave him a thrill?

"No. Say what you did when you thought I was feverish and couldn't hear."

She hesitated. "I can't."

"Sure you can." His warm breath made the skin on her neck tingle.

"Don't make me." She knew he could. Already her resistance was fading. The need to tell him what was in her heart pleaded to get out.

"I haven't a mind to make you do anything you don't want to, Kate. I just can't shake the feeling that you do. So maybe I'll just pester you 'til you admit to it."

The tip of his tongue flicked out and pressed against her pulse, making it jump. "That's not fair."

He lifted his head and grinned at her. The fever had done nothing to dim the sparkle in his eye. "No, but is it effective?"

She pursed her lips. It was more than effective. It was downright sinful. The smallest of touches from him had a way of burning away her good sense to cinder and ash. And when he smiled at her, teased her, the last of her wobbly defenses fell away.

"If I say the words, will you let me go?"

Connor started to nod, his grin spreading across his handsome features until it reached his eyes, making the blue sparkle as if sunlight poured directly into them. "Not on your life."

"You don't love me. You can't."

"I do, and I can. The only thing I can't seem to do is help it."

"You'll stop loving me eventually," she countered. "Look at who I am. What I've done."

His fingertips lightly traced the curve of her cheekbone before he cupped the side of her face. She pressed her cheek into it, desperate for his touch.

"I know exactly who you are. I've thought of little else since you told me and I won't lie to you—I'm not thrilled that you didn't tell me straight out. But you were right. If I had known, I would have tossed you out on your pretty little behind that first night. And if I'd done that, I would have missed out on this."

He kissed her, his lips warm and enticing, coaxing her with such tenderness she couldn't stop the tears that squeezed out of the corner of her eyes.

Connor lifted his head, his gaze roaming over her face. "I'm not going to stop loving you. Not today, not tomorrow, not thirty years from now. I won't promise it will be easy, but life rarely is. And I'm not denying we have a past to contend with, because we do. But I love you. And I don't blame you for my brother's death. Sometimes things just happen and nothing we do, or don't do, can stop them. You did the best you could. And if Grant trusted you enough in the last moments of his life to send you here, well—" he shrugged with his good shoulder, "—then maybe in the grand scheme of things that's just the way it was meant to be."

"But Jenny—"

"Jenny loves you. And I already promised her I'd damn well bring you back, come Hell or high water."

Katherine pulled away just far enough to fix a censuring glare on him. "You didn't use those exact words?"

Confusion marred his handsome features. "Well...yes."

"Connor Langston, you cannot be using that kind of profanity around an impressionable young girl! Especially now that she is talking non-stop."

His smile tightened. "Well, perhaps if I had a wife to remind me of these things I'd do a far better job of remembering that."

Katherine's heart stumbled. "W-wife?"

He sighed. "Yes, wife. Why do you think I dragged my sorry ass out of bed to ask you to stay? I can't countenance a contrary housekeeper, but I guess in a wife it could make things pretty interesting."

The ground tilted beneath her and she looked around, expecting to find the landscape had changed. It hadn't. The sun continued to shine. The wind continued to blow.

"What about the townspeople? What would they think?"

"It appears they all think you're some kind of hero, leading Rogan out of the church the way you did. Besides, these people have been trying to marry me off since I arrived back in town. I'm sure they'll be pleased as all get-out to hear I'm finally getting around to it. Now, will you marry me, or do I have to throw you over my shoulder like Walter Figg and drag you to the church kicking and screaming?"

Something shifted in her then. The fear of losing him, of his not loving her, turned from a solid lump in her stomach to vapors drifting away on the breeze.

Katherine laid her hands on Connor's chest. "What

275

happened to not making me do something I don't want to do?"

"What happened to telling me you love me one more time?"

She smiled and looked up at him. Those three little words hardly seemed adequate enough to encompass the wealth of feeling she had for this man. But they were all she had. The rest she could show him in other ways. Her face warmed with anticipation.

"I love you."

One corner of his mouth twitched. "I know."

She lifted a hand to swat at his arrogance, but his mouth descended on hers and scattered her thoughts. Her hand came to rest gently against the side of his face, the prickly stubble of whiskers rough against her palm.

He broke the kiss and rested his forehead against hers, peering into her eyes. "I was thinking maybe we could find Will and see about changing that last name of yours to Langston."

"Kate Langston," she smiled and brushed her lips against his. "I like the sound of that."

"I'm kind of partial to it myself," Connor said, wrapping his arm around her and holding her tight. "I love you, Kate."

"I love you, too," she said, the words coming easy. "Now let's find Reverend Sangster so you can take me home."

Connor threw his head back and laughed. "And bossy too!"

"You might as well get used to it."

He planted a quick kiss on her mouth. "Might take a lifetime."

"Well, we've got one of those, don't we?"

"We sure do, Mrs. Langston." Connor pressed a kiss against her forehead and held her tight. "We sure do."

Also by Kelly Boyce

THE SINS & SCANDALS SERIES

An Invitation to Scandal

A Scandalous Passion

A Sinful Temptation

The Lady's Sinful Secret

Surrender To Scandal

A Sinner No More

The Sweetest Sin

A Most Scandalous Christmas

A Hint of Scandal

THE SALVATION FALLS SERIES

Salvation in the Rancher's Arms - Coming Soon!

Salvation in the Sheriff's Kiss

The Cowboy of Christmas Past

Christmas in Salvation Falls

Dear Reader

Thank you so much for reading **THE OUTLAW BRIDE**, Book #1 in the *Brides of Fatal Bluff Series*. This was my first published book and holds a special place in my heart. I am so pleased to have regained the rights, so that I can re-release it back out into the world once again. Conner and Katherine, and the host of other characters in the book, have made a return to Fatal Bluff an enjoyable journey for this writer.

If this is your first introduction to my books, I encourage you to check out my Regency Romance series: *The Sins & Scandals Series*; **Book 1: AN INVITATION TO SCANDAL** is currently **FREE** on all digital retailers.

To keep informed on new releases, check out my **website book page (kellyboyce.com)**, and sign up for my **Newsletter** to keep abreast of breaking news and new releases!

I love to connect with my readers through social media and email and you can find all of my relevant links (Facebook Page, Goodreads, Instagram) on my **website**!

Lastly, the first book in my western series, **The Salvation Falls Series**, will soon be re-released as well. Keep an eye out!

Again, thank you for reading **THE OUTLAW BRIDE** and I hope you will consider leaving a review at your favorite online retailer to help others discover my books!

Happy reading!

--Kelly

About the Author

About the Author

Kelly Boyce started writing stories in Grade 2 when her favorite teacher, Mrs. Matheson, showed up with a box filled with plot ideas and she was immediately hooked. But it wasn't until she read Lisa Gregory's *Bitterleaf* that she fell in love with historical romance. She soon discovered Romance Writers of Atlantic Canada and after that, it was full steam ahead.

A life-long Nova Scotian, Kelly lives near the Atlantic Ocean with her incredibly supportive husband and a clownish golden retriever with a stubborn streak a mile wide. She loves writing stories about relationships and creating a sense of community around the hero and heroine filled with secondary characters who take on a life of their own.

Her first release, a western historical, **The Outlaw Bride**, released by Carina Press is now re-released under her own banner, along with the first book in the **Salvation Falls Series, Salvation in the Rancher's Kiss. Salvation in the Sheriff's Arms**, and two Christmas novellas: **The Cowboy of Christmas Past** and **Christmas in Salvation Falls** are still available through Harlequin.

If you enjoy Regency Romances, check out, *THE SINS & SCANDALS SERIES*, where we learn that for some, scandal is just a sin away...

Acknowledgments

As much as writing is a solitary occupation, I've been fortunate to have a group of great people on my side during the journey to publication. I would be remiss if I didn't acknowledge their part in the process.

A huge thank-you to Pam Callow. You were with me every step of the way with this manuscript and not only are you the world's greatest critique partner, but you're an awesome friend as well. A loud shout out to Julianne MacLean for your constant encouragement and critiquing skills—much appreciated. Cathryn Fox for all your help along the way and always making me laugh. Anne MacFarlane, Lilly Cain, and Annette MacPhee—thanks for the regular Saturday morning meetings that kept me on track.

Lisa MacDougall—all those after-school writing sessions finally paid off! Also, I think you'll recognise some of the names of places used in the book.

Romance Writers of Atlantic Canada—you are the most talented group of writers I've ever encountered and I've learned so much from all of you.

ISBN: 9780994867285